"Larsen, if we fail it's up to you. You'll be the only one who can stop him."

Her mouth tightened. "I know. I'll do whatever I have to."

"You'll foresee more deaths. You'll have to stop them, and recruit the unenchantables to help you in this fight."

"I've thought about it, too, Jack. It's all I've thought about since the vision." Emotional tears overflowed her eyes. "What am I going to do if I lose you?" she whispered.

His heart clenched. *"Larsen..."* He rose and reached for her hands, pulling her into his arms.

"I thought you were afraid to touch me."

"I always want to touch you," he said.

"Scary, sexy, and with a truly disturbing villain, *The Dark Gate* is a real page-turner."
—*Locus* bestselling author Laura Anne Gilman

PAMELA PALMER

Pamela Palmer admits to a passion for all things paranormal, fed by years of *Star Trek*, *Buffy the Vampire Slayer* and Tolkien's classic, *The Lord of the Rings*. Though she grew up wanting to be an astronaut (until she realized the space shuttle wasn't likely to get her beyond Earth's orbit), she became an industrial engineer for a major computer maker before surrendering to the romantic, exciting, otherworldly stories that crowded her head, demanding to be told. Her writing has won numerous awards, including a prestigious Golden Heart. Pamela lives in Virginia with her husband and two kids, and she would love to hear from readers through her Web site, www.pamelapalmer.net.

THE DARK GATE

PAMELA PALMER

Silhouette Books

nocturne™

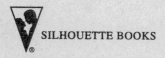

SILHOUETTE BOOKS

ISBN-13: 978-0-373-61760-9
ISBN-10:   0-373-61760-7

THE DARK GATE

This edition published by arrangement with Harlequin Books S.A.

® and TM are trademarks of Harlequin Books S.A., used under license. Trademarks indicated with ® are registered in the United States Patent and Trademark Office, the Canadian Trade Marks Office and in other countries.

www.silhouettenocturne.com

Printed in U.S.A.

Dear Reader,

I've always loved the question, "What if...?" It sends my imagination spinning in a thousand exciting directions. What if an old legend actually had a basis in fact? What if a long-forgotten enemy found his way back into our world? What if we were faced with a danger we no longer believed in?

These are the questions I explore in *The Dark Gate*, the very questions Larsen Vale and Jack Hallihan don't know to ask. I love to throw my characters into impossible situations, then watch them sink... until they learn to trust one another and open themselves to love.

The Dark Gate is my writing debut, the culmination of years of the effort, frustration and joy that come with any attempt to master something entirely different. My love of the story and of romance, in particular, saw me through to my own happy ending and this launch of a brand-new career.

I hope you enjoy Larsen and Jack's adventure as much as I enjoyed writing it. Visit my Web site at www.pamelapalmer.net or drop me a note at pamela@pamelapalmer.net. I'd love to hear from you!

Best wishes,

Pamela Palmer

To my parents, Stew and Pat Palmer,
for believing I could be anything I wished...
and for raising me to believe

Acknowledgments

If I were to list all the people who've helped me get
to this place—the publication of my first book—
the acknowledgments would rival the novel for
sheer number of pages. So, in an effort to save the
pages for the story, I want to thank a few special
people who have made all the difference.
Laurin Wittig, Kathryn Caskie, Denise McInerney,
Elizabeth Holcolme, Ann Shaw Moran and
Sophia Nash for their critiques, advice,
encouragement and unyielding support.
My husband and kids for always being there to
celebrate the joys. The Mom's Book Club, who
cheered me on every step of the way and were
waiting with bottles of champagne when the dream
came true. And last, though never least, my agent,
Helen Breitwieser, and my editors, Ann Leslie Tuttle
and Tara Gavin, for taking a chance and opening
the door to a dream. My heartfelt thanks.

Chapter 1

"Three assaults in five days, more than a dozen bystanders and no one remembers a thing. *How in the hell is he doing it?*"

Metropolitan Police Detective Jack Hallihan paced the aft deck of the small cabin cruiser docked on the Potomac River in downtown Washington, D.C., his steps echoing his frustration. A jet roared overhead, making its final approach into Reagan National, while the summer sun beat down on the back of his neck, sending sweat rolling between his shoulder blades. He was running out of time.

"He's gotta be knocking 'em out, Jack." Duke Robinson, a fellow detective and the wiry dark-skinned owner of the boat, tipped his baseball cap to shield his eyes from the afternoon sun even as his head turned, his gaze following the progress of a pair of young women strolling down the dock in bikini tops and short-shorts. "What's up, ladies?"

The voices in Jack's head surged suddenly, unintelligible voices that filled his head night and day, and had for as long as he could remember. He clenched his teeth and dug his fingers into his dark hair, pressing his fingers to his scalp, trying to quiet the ceaseless chatter, if only a little.

"You okay, man?" Henry Jefferson, Jack's partner of ten years, eyed him with concern from the second deck chair as he rolled a cold Budweiser across a forehead several shades darker than Duke's. Henry was as tall as Jack, but no longer lean. Too many years of his wife, Mei's, fried egg rolls had softened him around the middle. There was nothing soft about the gaze he leveled on Jack. "You need to see someone about those headaches of yours."

Jack snatched his hand from his head. *Hell.* The last thing he needed was to bring attention to his worsening condition. No one knew he suffered from the same madness that destroyed his father. If he had his way, no one ever would.

"It's just the heat," he told his friend. If only. He'd be happy if they were just headaches. Sometimes he felt as though he lived in the middle of a raucous party that never ended, a party where everyone spoke Bulgarian, or Mongolian, or some other language he would never understand. Usually he could tamp down the noise so it didn't overwhelm his mind, like moving the party into the next room. But the past couple of weeks the voices had been all but shouting in his ears. It was starting to scare the shit out of him.

He pulled the discussion back to the problem at hand, a mysterious rapist terrorizing the Dupont Circle neighborhood of D.C. "In each of the three cases, multiple victims were knocked unconscious by some unknown means to awaken simultaneously a short while later—estimated at anywhere from fifteen to thirty minutes. In each case, one young woman among them woke to find her clothing partially removed and blood and semen between her legs. In each case, no one, including the assault victim, remembered anything to help us identify the attacker and solve this case."

"It makes no sense," Duke said. "How is he knocking them out before they ever get a look at him?"

"We need those tox reports," Jack said. "He's got to be using some kind of gas or drug."

The muscle in Henry's jaw visibly tightened. "I want him *now,* before he hurts another girl. The last assault victim was just eighteen years old. Barely more than a kid."

Henry's own daughter, Sabrina, was only a handful of years younger. She and her brother were belowdeck even now. Henry wasn't leaving her home alone. He wasn't taking any chances. Jack didn't blame him a bit.

"And what does the theft at the Smithsonian have to do with all this?" Henry wondered out loud. During the first attack, an ancient stone amulet had been stolen.

"What did you find out about this *Stone of Ezrie?*" he asked his friend. But Duke's gaze was firmly fixed on a well-endowed woman making her way along the dock.

Henry gave Duke's shoulder a hard slug. "Stay in the game, man. We want to know what you learned."

Duke released a frustrated sigh. "It's Sunday. Even cops need a day off."

"Not when girls are being attacked," Henry said.

"Yeah, okay." Duke pulled out his wallet and removed a small paper photo. *"The Stone of Ezrie."*

Jack took the piece of paper and held it for Henry to see. The photo revealed a sky-blue, teardrop-shaped stone hanging from a simple silver chain. Engraved on the surface of the stone was a seven-point star.

"Why would anyone want this thing?" Henry asked, echoing Jack's own thoughts. "What kind of rock is it, anyway?"

Duke shrugged. "Nothing valuable. The Smithsonian dude didn't know why anyone would steal it. There were better things all around. The only thing this rock has going for it is some quack legend. Something about it being the key that opens the gates to Ezrie."

Henry lifted a thick brow. "What's Ezrie?"

"Don't know. It's all bogus, man. Prime bogus. There ain't no way to solve this case or to catch the perp until the son of a bitch screws up and leaves us a witness or clue. We've been over everything a dozen times." Duke reached for another beer. "*I* need a day off, even if you two don't. So no more talk about work. How 'bout them Nationals, huh?"

Jack took a long drink of Coke, letting it fizz on his tongue as impatience boiled under his skin. He didn't have time for talk of baseball. He'd managed to push the voices back, but for how long? How much longer until he couldn't control them at all?

He had to solve this case while he still had the mental strength to do it, before the voices became too much to bear and he ended up like his dad—an alcoholic with a gun in his mouth and his brains decorating the living room wall.

The silken sound of a woman's laughter yanked him out of his dark musings, stealing every thought from his head. His gaze snapped to the houseboat in the next slip as a tall, slender blonde in nice pants and a trim sleeveless sweater emerged from the door of the boat, holding a cell phone to her ear. She was laughing as she stepped outside, her chin-length hair glowing golden in the summer sunshine.

Jack swallowed. "Who's that?"

"Larsen Vale. Bleeding-heart lawyer and Ice Bitch extraordinaire. Forget about her. She don't give it up for no man." Duke's words were too loud for the small distance between the boats, but he didn't seem to care.

The woman glanced up. The laughter drained from her features as though someone had pulled a plug. All emotion fled. Her gaze slid over the men, one after the other, as if they were nothing more than inanimate objects unworthy of her notice…until her gaze slammed into Jack's. His heart bucked in his chest, a physical jolt like he'd been sucker punched. She held his gaze, then dropped it, shattering it as she turned away.

She clicked her cell phone closed and started across the boat's narrow deck with quick, confident strides, a briefcase swinging at her side. Without another glance his way, she hopped lightly onto the dock and strode away.

Jack exhaled. "Wow."

"She's cold, dude," Duke insisted. "Ice cold. Don't waste your time."

"Dad." Henry's ten-year-old son, David, ran up the stairs from below, making enough noise for three kids despite his slight build. "When are we sailing?"

"You don't sail a motorboat, moron." His sister, Sabrina, flounced up the stairs behind him.

"Sorry, you two. We're not taking the boat out," Henry told his kids. "This is a marina party, not a river cruise."

"What party?" David asked. "This is boring."

"David…"

Jack set his half-empty Coke can on the railing. "Who's up for a walk?" He had too much on his mind to make small talk. If he had to take the afternoon off, he'd rather spend his time with the kids, anyway. He sure as hell wouldn't have any of his own. Not after what his dad had put his own family through.

"Me, Uncle Jack, me," David exclaimed, jumping up and down. "Can I get the football out of the car, Dad?"

Henry nodded and Jack turned to Sabrina. "You coming, beautiful?" At fourteen, the girl was already showing signs of the heartbreaker she was destined to become. Unlike her brother, she'd inherited a healthy dose of the exotic from her mother's ancestry. Her skin was a light coffee color, her intelligent eyes slightly tilted and her hair silky black as she flicked it behind her back with a toss of her head.

He held his breath, waiting for her reply, wondering if this would be the time she'd finally grown too cool to have anything to do with her "uncle" Jack. But she flashed him a smile full of braces and youthful exuberance, and he knew today wasn't that day. They found a patch of grass in front of the marina to pass the football.

"You suck," Sabrina shouted as David ran for the ball he'd missed.

"*You* suck," the boy called back, laughing. If there was a natural athlete lurking in the kid somewhere, he had yet to show himself. David grabbed the ball and started running toward them.

Jack held up his hands. "Throw it, pal." But the boy kept running. Jack laughed, happier out here with these two than he'd been in weeks.

"Throw it, David." Sabrina waved her hands in the air.

The boy finally heaved the football, getting a nice spiral on it, at last. Unfortunately his aim was off. Way off. The ball sailed directly at the door of the marina office and the woman exiting through it—the Ice Bitch, Larsen Vale.

Jack cringed as the ball hit her square in the arm, knocking her briefcase out of her hand. The briefcase hit the wall and clattered to the sidewalk, snapping open. Papers spilled everywhere.

Hell. She was going to tear the kid to pieces. As David started toward her in his loping run, Jack headed after him, determined to save him from a tongue-lashing that would make his sister's impatient comments sound like sweet nothings.

"Sorry," David called good-naturedly as he approached the she-devil.

The woman picked up the ball. To Jack's amazement she gave David a rueful smile and cocked her arm as if to throw it.

"Go long," she told him.

David grinned and started running. The woman threw an admirable pass with only a slight wobble, right into the boy's arms.

"Yesss!" David did his own little version of the touchdown shuffle.

Jack looked at Larsen Vale thoughtfully as she knelt to gather up her papers. He'd heard her name before today. He knew she'd earned herself a reputation for ruthlessness in the courtroom, particularly in defense of women abused by their high-profile husbands. Duke wasn't the only one who called her the Ice Bitch. Yet she'd just been exceedingly kind in a situation that would have provoked most people to anger.

Jack joined her. "Let me give you a hand with those." He knelt beside her and began picking up the loose papers. He'd thought her attractive on the boat. This close, she was stunning. Her mouth was wide and lush, perfectly framed by a strong, stubborn jaw. Her eyes had a natural, heavy-lidded appearance that was sexy as hell. And her skin was lightly tanned and flawlessly smooth.

Heat tightened things low in his body. He couldn't

remember the last time he'd been hit with this kind of lust at first sight. Too bad she was ignoring him.

"Thanks for being patient with David. He's a little careless sometimes."

She looked up and gave him the same expressionless look she had on the boat. Her eyes were a clear golden-brown beneath a thin layer of frost.

"Were you afraid I'd shatter him with my ice wand?"

Jack winced. So she'd heard Duke's comment. "You had a right to be angry with him. I appreciate your patience."

She stopped in her gathering and glanced toward the kids. "He was just being a boy."

"Yeah. I apologize for my friend's rudeness back there, too. His comments were out of line." Jack tapped the papers he'd collected on the sidewalk to neaten the stack. "He's a little too cocksure of his success with women." He handed the stack to her and their fingers brushed. A bare slide of flesh on flesh.

Inexplicably the chatter in his head went silent. *Silent.* For the first time in…*forever.*

She jerked, dropping the papers. "Damn."

The voices rushed back as if they'd never left at all. Jack's heart slammed in his chest. Had he imagined it?

She gathered up the last of the papers and put them back in her expensive-looking briefcase. As she started to close the lid, the breeze caught a loose sheet. Jack grabbed for it at the same time she did. Their hands brushed again.

Silence. It was her.

Larsen Vale clicked her briefcase shut and rose. She met his gaze, briefly, as dispassionately as before. "Thanks," she said, and turned away.

Jack stared after her, stunned. *She'd quieted the voices.*

Hope roared through his veins like a flood through a parched gully. *She'd quieted the damn voices.*

She was his salvation. *His cure.*

He hurried after her as she started across the parking lot. "Wait."

She stopped and turned to look at him, a hint of a question in her eyes.

"I'm…Jack." He thrust out his hand, partly from habit, partly from an intense desire to touch her again. "Jack Hallihan."

She glanced at his hand, but made no move to take it. "I know." Then she turned and walked away as if she hadn't just changed his life.

"You're an angel, Ms. Vale."

Larsen Vale cut a wry look at the mother of the bride standing beside her. "I'm afraid a lot of people would disagree with you, Mrs. Ramirez. But thank you. I'm glad I could help Veronica."

Across the crowded, flower-bedecked fellowship hall of the Dupont Circle All Saints Church, her former client, Veronica Hernandez, and her new husband posed for the photographer while one of the bridesmaids artfully arranged the drape of the classic wedding gown.

Veronica's mother, a compact woman in her fifties, smiled, tears in her eyes. "It will be different this time. Juan is not like Nicky. He is a good man. He will treat my daughter well."

Larsen gazed at the newly married couple, at the glowing joy in the bride's face, and remembered the first time she'd seen Veronica. Bruises had lurked beneath her heavy makeup like stones in a still pond, and fear had haunted her eyes. Now adoration lit those same eyes, an adoration mirrored in her new husband's.

The signs were good that this marriage would be a far cry from Veronica's last, but Larsen had long ago quit believing in fairy-tale endings.

"I must see to the cutting of the cake," the older woman said shyly, and slipped away, leaving Larsen standing alone. A place she was all too used to.

Larsen didn't mind her mostly solitary path through life, but there were times, like now, when she remembered other plans, other dreams. A man to love her. A wedding of her own.

But that was before she'd realized she was different—that love and family could never be hers.

She took a sip of the dark, sweet punch and grimaced inwardly, wishing Veronica had splurged on a few bottles of champagne. Nearby, a man eyed her with interest, earning her standard, *back-off* look. The man next to him leaned closer and said something that Larsen was pretty sure ended in *bitch*. The first man stiffened and turned his back on her in a hurry.

The encounter neither amused nor disturbed her. She wasn't the man-hater everyone thought she was, though it was a miracle she wasn't, given her line of work. Day after day she saw the disasters men made of their marriages and the pain they caused those who loved them. No, she didn't hate them. She just didn't let *anyone* get that close.

Unfortunately she'd been cursed with looks that invited nearly continuous male attention. Unwanted attention. So she'd developed a haughty manner that kept even the most determined at bay. She was perfectly happy on her own. No one making demands on her time or asking too many questions. She didn't need anyone. She certainly didn't need a *man*.

Larsen tossed back the rest of the sickly sweet punch.

If only her hormones agreed. She groaned at the memory

of Jack Hallihan watching her from the deck of his friend's boat yesterday, those laser-sharp blue eyes boring into her. An unwelcome rush of heat spiraled deep inside her.

She'd never actually met him before, but she'd known who he was. One of her law clerks had pointed him out in the courthouse last fall. Tall and broad-shouldered, with gorgeous blue eyes and a thatch of dark hair that appeared perpetually mussed, he'd walked with an easy confidence and casual strength that had drawn her attention and refused to let go, especially when he'd flashed a grin that had sent her pulse through the ceiling. She'd found herself watching for him every time she went to court for months afterward. She never again caught a glimpse of him.

Until yesterday, when she'd found him staring at her.

A flush of embarrassment rose into her cheeks as she remembered the way she'd dropped her papers at the touch of his hand, like a schoolgirl with her first crush. He hadn't called her on it. She'd seen no amusement in those blue eyes, no knowing smile that said he knew she'd been affected by the touch. He'd barely reacted at all.

A day later and she was still reacting. Even the memory of their brief meeting had turned the air in her lungs warm and heavy. With a groan of self-disgust she headed for the punch bowl and a cool refill, her heeled sandals clicking on the bare linoleum floor.

She didn't want to be attracted to a man. Attraction led to wanting and to wishing for things that could never be.

The conversation in the room eased as the guests' attention turned toward the cutting of the cake.

As she poured another ladle of the dark red punch into her cup, she heard a soft sound of laughter and glanced up to find a girl standing in the doorway to the kitchen, her pretty, delicate features awash with a poignant wistfulness.

A tiny thing, barely five feet tall, she was far too thin. Larsen guessed she was in her late teens, maybe early twenties. She wore a pair of jeans and a Redskins T-shirt that were both miles too big for her as if she, and not they, had gone through the dryer and shrunk. Her skin was a deep tan in color, her head shiny and bald like a chemo patient's.

Larsen's heart twisted with sympathy and she took a step toward her. "Hi, there. May I bring you a piece of cake?"

The girl started and turned to Larsen with a guilty, wide-eyed gaze. "I…nay, m'lady." The words stumbled out in a charmingly accented rush. "I should not have…*nay.*"

"It's all right," Larsen assured her. "There's a piece for me and I really don't want it. I'd be happy to bring it to you."

The girl cocked her head as if pondering Larsen's offer…or Larsen herself. The girl's eyes, an amazing shade of violet, looked suddenly older than her years.

"My thanks," she said shyly. "But I cannot." Then she turned and fled into the kitchen.

Larsen sighed, sorry she'd chased the girl away. She turned back toward the festivities, but as she took a sip of the too sweet punch, her vision suddenly went black.

Pain shot through her head and she grabbed for the wall, cool punch splashing her bare legs even as her sight returned. Except…*she wasn't seeing with her eyes.*

She could feel the hair on her arms leap upright, her heart beginning to pound with a terrible dread. For the first time in fifteen years she was about to watch someone die.

The scene unfolded in front of her—the same, yet altered. Though still in the fellowship hall, she watched from above now, as if she'd been plastered to the ceiling. Time had lurched forward. The cake was gone, the bride and groom stood near the door, ready to leave. Women gathered around the bride, preparing to catch the bouquet.

Mouths moved, shoulders shook with laughter, but Larsen heard none of it—like watching a silent movie. Then suddenly everyone went still, their expressions sliding off their faces, leaving them looking like mannequins...or wax figures.

No, not everyone. A man, the strangest man she'd ever seen, appeared to be talking. He was dressed like something out of a medieval play. His tunic was a shimmering forest-green, his leggings brown with metallic gold flecks that caught the light. But the strangest things about him were his long, lank hair and his skin—both a matching, startling white.

As she watched, he motioned to one of the bridesmaids. The plump young woman left the throng of women and went to him, her dark ringlets brushing the shoulders of her cobalt gown. When she reached him, she turned her back to him, pulled up her tea-length skirt to her waist, and bent over. The odd-looking man started to untie his leggings.

Shocked realization jolted her. Larsen opened her mouth to yell at him, but nothing came out. As she watched in helpless frustration, two people strode angrily into the premonition—a man in a suit and a woman in the same apple-green sheath dress Larsen wore even now.

It was her! She was watching *herself.*

The albino in the tunic stared at the two of them with surprise, even as he pulled his distended penis from his leggings. He scowled, then flicked his free hand. Like an army of well-dressed zombies, the wedding guests surrounded the pair and attacked. Without hesitation. Without mercy.

With horror, Larsen watched her other self crash to the bare floor and disappear beneath a barrage of kicking, stomping feet, her apple-green dress turning a sickly, purplish blood-stained brown.

The attack ended as suddenly as it began. Like puppets jerked upright by a dozen sets of strings, the guests stood at attention, blank-faced and splattered with gore. At their feet lay Larsen's and the unknown man's mutilated remains.

They'd killed her. The blood roared in her ears.

He'd killed her. The pale, evil puppet master who'd controlled the others.

His thin face wore an expression of fevered satisfaction as he thrust his hips against the bridesmaid, taking her from behind. White hair whipped around his head as if a small whirlwind attacked him alone.

He suddenly looked up at the point from where Larsen watched the premonition, like an actor staring directly into the camera.

With a frown, he looked at her body and then back at her.

He saw her. The hair rose at the back of her neck and she mentally jerked back. *He saw her watching him.* Eyes narrowed with a malevolent light, he leveled his index finger at her menacingly, then shook his head and the vision was gone.

"Miss, are you okay? Miss!"

Larsen blinked, pulse pounding. The room swam back into view, exactly as it had been before, the wedding festivities still in full swing, the guests eating cake. A woman she didn't know was pushing her onto a chair.

"Sit. I'll get you some water."

"No." Terror tore at her lungs. Pain exploded in her head. He'd killed her.

"I— I'm not feeling well." Her stomach rolled and clenched, and she lurched to her feet. She was going to be sick. "I've got to go."

Larsen stumbled from the room and pushed through the outer door to the empty playground at the back of the church. She clutched at the rough brick wall and vomited onto the dirt.

He'd killed her. And she'd seen it. *She'd seen it.*

Dear God, her death visions were back. Larsen sagged against the wall and swiped a trembling hand across her mouth. *Not again.* She squeezed her eyes closed. *Not again.*

She pushed herself away from the wall and started across the parched yard on legs that suddenly felt too long for her body. The curse that haunted her life had lain dormant for more than fifteen years. She'd thought the nightmare was over. Every night she prayed her devil's sight would never return. Now it was back. People were going to die.

She was going to die.

Chapter 2

Jack felt like a lovesick teenager, though he was acting more like a stalker as he sat on a bench under a large oak across the street from the All Saints Church and waited for Larsen Vale to emerge from the wedding reception.

He had to see her again.

He had to know if she'd really quieted the voices or if the gut-kick reaction he'd gotten from touching her had somehow short-circuited his brain so much that he simply hadn't heard them for a moment. And if she really could quiet his head? Then he had to convince her to stay by his side for the rest of his life. That simple. That impossible.

He leaned back against the uneven bench slats and stretched his legs out in front of him as the Monday afternoon traffic passed under a hazy summer sky. On the sidewalk in front of him, tourists walked by with their guidebooks and fanny packs.

Sweat rolled down his scalp as the ever-present voices conspired to further destroy his sanity. As a kid he'd barely noticed the noise, the voices little more than static in the background of his thoughts. Not until he was in high school did the sound escalate and distinguish itself as a mob of individual, though unintelligible, voices. But even that he'd learned to deal with until these past couple of weeks, when they'd begun to grow louder, more numerous, more agitated, by the day. He shoved his hand through his damp hair, pressing his fingers against his scalp.

Shut up. Just shut up.

But, if anything, the horde in his head grew even louder. With an angry flick of his thumb, he pushed up the volume on his iPod in a useless attempt to drown them out, and concentrated on watching for Larsen.

What were the chances she'd believe he just happened to be hanging around Dupont Circle this afternoon? That he just happened to be walking by as she left the wedding reception?

Jack grunted. Nil. Hell, even if she did believe him, her secretary would give him away the moment she told Larsen he'd stopped by her office this morning looking for her. Police business, he'd said.

He was so screwed.

His only chance of success depended on him knocking her off her feet with a single lethal blow of his charm. Yeah, right. The formidable Ms. Vale was probably immune to any man's charm.

Damn, this sucked. He'd never had trouble attracting a woman before. *He* was the one women accidentally ran into, never the other way around. Now here he was, broiling in the summer sun, praying the woman would give him the time of day. She had to. He had to know if her touch was really his salvation.

A movement across the street caught his attention—a woman in a bright green dress walking out from behind the church. Stumbling, more like it. Her hair shone like gold in the sun. Her dress was splattered...red.

Larsen.

He lunged to his feet and dashed across the busy road, weaving between the traffic, heedless of the honk of horns and the squeal of brakes as he completely forgot his pretense of running into her by accident.

In the minute it took him to cross the street, she'd pulled herself together and now walked calmly, almost normally. Except he was a cop and knew better. There was a paleness to her face and a wildness in her eyes that hadn't been there yesterday.

Those eyes were pointed straight at him, but he could swear she didn't see him.

"Larsen."

She visibly started, then stopped abruptly, blinking as if disoriented. As he watched, she pulled herself in and away, snapping a cool facade in place. Once more, she was the remote woman he'd met before.

"What are you doing here?" she asked with only a hint of a wobble to her voice.

"Screw that. What happened to you? You..." He motioned helplessly at the red dotting her dress. His eyes narrowed as he stared at the spots. From a distance, they'd looked like blood.

She glanced down at herself. "I spilled my punch. Once again, what are you doing here?"

Either she was amazingly adept at hiding her emotions, or he'd screwed up. Badly. But he saw something move in her eyes, a glimmer of the fear he was convinced she struggled to hide, and he knew his instincts were dead-on.

Her cool facade crumbled and she cringed and pressed her palm to her forehead.

"What's the matter?" Jack curled his fingers around her forearm to steady her, but the moment his fingers brushed her skin, his head noise went silent. The "Hallelujah Chorus" nearly erupted from his mouth.

It wasn't his imagination. *She quieted the damn voices.*

Slowly she lowered her hand. If she'd been anyone else, he might have thought he saw a sheen of tears in her eyes.

"I don't feel well. I'm going home."

He tightened his grip on her arm. "What happened in there?"

Her response was a moment too long in coming. "Nothing. I have a migraine. I want to get home before I throw up again." She looked pointedly at the hand still gripping her arm, avoiding his gaze.

"Larsen..." His cell rang and he grabbed his phone and checked the Caller I.D. Police business. *Hell.* He stared at her, torn, as the percussion beat of his ring tone continued. He could see the faint tremble of her ripe lips, a tremble echoed in the vibration of her arm beneath his fingers.

Her gaze suddenly snapped to his. "Are you going to get that?"

"Yeah." He gritted his teeth, bracing himself for the rush of noise in his head, and released her.

Without a moment's hesitation, she brushed past him and strode away.

The death visions were back.

Larsen sat on the navy chenille sofa in her little houseboat and shook. Outside, the miserable day had slowly turned to a miserable evening, the sky darkening as if her mood were sucking the very color from the sky.

It didn't happen. It couldn't have happened. Just a dream. A terrible, waking nightmare. She hadn't had a premonition in fifteen years. Fifteen *years*. She'd thought they'd stopped. *Prayed* they'd stopped. How could she go through this again?

Hours had passed since the wedding, yet her stomach still rolled and clenched as her mind forced her to relive the savage attacks. The blood. The rape of that poor girl.

God.

Sick guilt raked her insides with sharp claws. She'd fled. Instead of trying to stop it, instead of trying to save them, she'd fled.

Hot tears burned the backs of her eyes as the weight of too many years, too many deaths, pressed her into the cushions. As a kid, she'd believed she caused them. She'd dream about people dying and they died. Her fault. The evil living inside her.

She was eight when she saw her first premonition, the car accident that killed her mother and older brother, Kevin. She never told anyone, not even her father. How could she when she was afraid she'd somehow caused the accident? The last came when she was thirteen and saw her grandfather's fatal tumble down the stairs.

It never once occurred to her to try to change the outcome of one of her visions. Not until today. Not until she'd run... *and not died.*

Restlessness forced Larsen to her feet and she paced the small houseboat, the court papers she should be reading all but forgotten in her hand. *She was supposed to have died.*

Always before, the cursed devil's sight had shown her the

death of someone she loved. Her mom. Her brother. But this time she'd watched her own death. And that of a stranger. Why? What did it mean?

As she paused at the window, her reflection peered back at her, riddled with a dozen dots of light from nearby apartments as if she'd captured the nightscape and her likeness in a single double exposure.

She couldn't have seen what she thought she'd seen. One man could not control the minds of so many. Veronica had called to tell her about the terrible attack that had occurred at the wedding and to make sure she was okay. Veronica said no one remembered anything. All those who'd been hypnotized, all those who'd killed, had awakened without any memory of what they'd done.

But she hadn't been hypnotized. She would have remembered. As would the man behind her. But she'd fled. And he'd died.

A chunk of ice settled in her stomach. She turned toward the kitchen to pour herself a glass of wine, hoping it would take the sharp edge off her misery. But as she reached for the refrigerator handle, the houseboat bobbed with the telltale lurch that heralded the arrival of an intruder. Larsen tensed. She rarely had visitors, and never uninvited.

"Larsen?" The male voice was followed by the brisk rap of knuckles on the glass door. "Larsen? It's Jack Hallihan."

Cop. Her heart sank even as her pulse leaped with a strange and unwanted rush of pleasure. She swallowed hard. She couldn't very well ignore him. The blinds were still open. He knew she was here. She took a deep breath and started toward the door in her bare feet.

Through the window she could see Jack Hallihan's

imposing form in the light's soft glow. Exhaustion swept over her with the certain knowledge this was no social call. She couldn't deal with his questions tonight. But refusing to talk to him would only make him suspicious.

With a sigh, Larsen opened the door and slipped outside into the steamy night. If she let him inside, she might have more trouble getting rid of him. Closing the door behind her, she met the piercing blue gaze leveled on her. The small light above the door cast the bones of his face in high relief, making him look even more attractive, if such a thing were possible. Heat radiated from his body and twined with the spicy scent of his aftershave, stimulating her senses.

Distance. She needed distance. She tried to move past him, but he reached for her, sliding the rough pads of his fingers down her bare arm, sending awareness dancing over her skin. Larsen looked at him, startled by the unexpected touch. His eyes had widened as if he were as surprised by the touch as she was. Why was he here? To continue his earlier line of questioning her about what she saw at the church? Or was he here for more personal reasons? She wasn't sure. All she knew for certain was that he couldn't succeed at either.

She threw him her stock glare, hoping to cover for the way she'd reacted to his touch, and led him aft, away from the lights, where those eyes of his couldn't see quite so much. At the back rail, Larsen turned to face him, crossing her arms over her chest.

"What can I do for you, Detective?"

He came to stand beside her, leaning a hip against the rail. Too close. She sensed a restlessness in him, a tension, that made her question the wisdom of seeking out the dark.

"I was worried about you." His voice was as deep and rich

as she remembered, a calming voice that nevertheless turned her pulse strangely erratic. She felt his probing gaze like a physical stroke. "How are you feeling?"

"I'm fine." A lie. Tension coiled deep in her stomach. They both knew he wasn't here out of concern for her supposed migraine.

"I assume you heard about the murder."

Even knowing why he was here, she couldn't stop the jerk, the small involuntary movement she prayed he hadn't noticed.

"Yes, I heard." But her voice was no longer steady. Just the mention brought it all rushing back. *The blood.* Somehow she had to convince him her running from the church was innocent, or he'd never leave her alone.

"The best I can figure…" he said, cocking his head and crossing his arms over his chest in a way that warned she had some serious explaining to do. "It happened about twenty minutes after I saw you outside the church."

Her muscles bunched with the need to put distance between them, if not to outright run, but she knew better than to show fear to an adversary.

"Seems my migraine was timely." She pretended not to see his frown. Instead, heart racing, she looked up at the clouds blotting out the night sky, glowing a dull orange with the reflection of the city's lights. She felt him staring at her.

For long moments he watched her, studying her, turning her breath quick and shallow.

"Here's the thing." His tone was almost conversational. "I interviewed dozens of people today. Not one of them saw anything. They were upset, sure. A dead body and blood will do that." He straightened, moving until he blocked her escape, his gaze sharp enough to cut. "But of all the people

I talked to who attended that wedding, only one had eyes with the wildness that comes from witnessing violent crime. One."

He leaned toward her until he was almost in her face. "You."

Larsen struggled to hold her ground even as her throat went dry. "You misread me, Detective. I left the reception early because I was getting a migraine. The only wildness you saw was fear that I was going to vomit on the Metro on the way home. Which I did, by the way."

His expression turned hard and disappointed. "You're going to deny you saw something?"

She uncrossed her arms and moved away, unable to withstand his probing stare a moment longer. He could have stopped her if he'd wanted, but he didn't. "There's nothing to deny. I wasn't there when the murder happened."

"I'm not trying to say you were. But you saw something, or someone, that alarmed you. Something that might help me solve this case."

"The only person who alarmed me was a poor girl who looked like she'd been undergoing chemotherapy. Otherwise, I'm afraid you're mistaken—"

He grabbed her wrist and turned her to face him. "I'm not mistaken. I know the difference between illness, worry and fear, lady. I've seen them all. What I saw in your eyes was raw terror."

"You saw what you wanted to see."

"You're lying to me." He pulled her closer until she could see the deck lights reflected in his eyes like chips of blue ice. "You know something. When I first saw you outside the church, you were running. Don't try to tell me you weren't."

It was as if he could see right through her! Larsen gathered every ounce of coldness she could manufacture and stared pointedly at her bound wrist, then into his eyes, but he ignored her not-so-subtle hint.

"Four women have been assaulted, now a man brutally murdered, and I don't have a single witness." He finally released her and turned away, raking a hand through his hair. "Not a single clue to help me solve this case."

He whirled back to face her. "It'll happen again, *Ms. Vale*. Again and again and again, and I don't know how to stop it."

She didn't want to hear this. Guilt already tore her to shreds, but she couldn't tell him. She could never tell anyone.

"Help me, Larsen." His handsome face implored her to cooperate. "Help me stop him before he does it again."

"I can't. I don't know anything."

He stared at her for long minutes, then released his breath on a slow burst of air. "Tell me about the chemo patient."

Larsen frowned. "Why? She was just a sick kid."

"She caught your eye."

"Well…*yeah*."

"It's all we've got to go on, Larsen. Maybe it's nothing, but the subconscious tends to see more than we realize. Humor me."

So she told him what she remembered about the girl in the too large clothes with the clean-shaven head and startlingly violet eyes.

When she was through, Jack's mouth skewed left. "Doesn't sound like much of a lead, but maybe she saw something. It should be easy enough to track her down. Was there anyone or anything else that caught your attention? Anything at all?"

"No. Nothing." Nothing in real time, anyway. Nothing she could tell him.

His gaze held her captive even as she prayed he'd accept her answers and give up. She sensed rather than saw the predatory tension ease out of him.

"All right. If you think of anything else…"

Larsen had to bite back a nearly audible sigh of relief. "I'll be sure to let you know."

Jack Hallihan pulled out his wallet and handed her his card. As she shoved it into her pocket with one hand, his hand closed around her other. "Larsen…"

As his warm fingers slid over hers, a flash of movement sliced through her peripheral vision. Pain exploded in her shoulder, knocking her back into the rail. *She'd been hit.* With a panicked gasp, she realized the thing was still on her.

An arrow. An arrow was sticking out of her shoulder! Was this some kind of sick joke?

"Get it out of me. Get it out!" She grabbed it, trying to pull it away, but pain seared through her body.

Jack grabbed her wrist. "Don't touch it. You'll do more damage." He swept her into his arms and ran for the door to her houseboat. Every step made the arrow bounce, setting fire searing in her shoulder. She squeezed her eyes closed and clamped her jaw shut to keep from crying out.

"Stay here. I'm going to try to catch the archer."

She felt the soft cushions of the sofa at her back, then Jack released her and ran for the door. Agony radiated from her shoulder outward, as if a shark had clamped onto her and would not let go. *She wanted it out of her.* She squeezed her eyes closed as tears ran down her cheeks.

An eternity later Jack was beside her again, his forehead glistening with sweat.

"Did you…catch him?"

"No." He leaned over her, his blue eyes tight with concern. "Hang on. There's an ambulance on the way."

She could hear sirens. They were growing louder. "Did you see who did it?"

"Yeah." He took her hand, his expression grim. "It was a bald girl, Larsen. A tiny little thing in a Redskins T-shirt."

She stared at him. Her mouth opened then snapped shut on the metallic taste of fear.

Jack's expression turned grave and worried. "I don't know what you've gotten yourself into." He stroked her hair back from her face. "But I think you're in over your head. Sooner or later you're going to have to trust someone."

She blinked, sending more tears sliding down her cheeks. *Trust someone.* The one thing she could never do.

He had to win her trust.

Jack glanced into the rearview mirror of the police-issue sedan. Tucked into the corner of the seat behind him, hidden behind tinted windows, was Larsen Vale. The answer to his prayers.

Tension tightened his grip on the steering wheel as he maneuvered the roads clogged with morning work traffic. He didn't remember the last time he'd been this nervous over an assignment. Over *anything.* But never had anything mattered so much.

She quieted the voices. If he could just figure out how. Hell, he didn't care how. All that mattered was keeping her close enough to touch.

And the only way to do that was to make her fall for him. To win her as his own. A girlfriend would stay by his side. A wife. He had to make her love him if he wanted to save his sanity. Crazy, yeah, but it was all he could think of.

Unfortunately he also had to get to the bottom of her involvement in this case, but pushing her to tell him what she knew would only earn her anger, if not her hatred. He squeezed the steering wheel until he feared it would snap off in his hands. How could he possibly win both the woman and her secrets?

He had to win her trust. Get her to volunteer the information. Yeah, right. He'd just wine and dine her for…what? Twenty minutes? *He didn't have time.* Every day he didn't catch the rapist was another day a young woman might lose her innocence…or her life. Someone had died, now. Things were escalating.

The only thing in his favor was the bizarre twist of fate that had dropped the pretty attorney right into his hands. He had one chance to charm her. Once chance to win her over. But he had to move fast. And he had no clue how to go about charming a man-hater.

"This is kidnapping," she muttered, her words slurred from the heavy sedative they'd given her before they'd dug the arrow out of her shoulder in the emergency room.

He glanced at her again. Her head was back, her eyes closed, a scowl marring the beauty of her face.

"Yeah. So sue me for not taking you back to your houseboat where the little archer could take another shot at you."

"I want you to take me to a motel."

"For the time being, you're stuck with me."

"I don't want to be stuck with you. I don't want to be stuck with anyone."

Jack sighed. He'd known this wouldn't be easy. "Your life's been threatened by a murder suspect, Larsen. You're under police protection until the captain decides otherwise."

"I need to go back to my houseboat. I need some things."

"You can borrow one of my T-shirts and a toothbrush. My partner's wife can loan you whatever else you need. Try to think of this as a short vacation."

Her frown deepened. "At *your* house."

"Only the finest for D.C.'s most formidable prosecutor."

"You're mocking me."

"You? No. My house? Maybe."

She didn't reply. He glanced into the rearview mirror to find her expression had evened out. The pain medication was kicking in.

She'd been lucky. The arrowhead was small and had gone cleanly through her shoulder, doing minimal damage. A few inches and the arrow would have gone through her heart. His own heart lurched at the thought of how easily he might have lost her—his salvation gone in the blink of an eye.

By an arrow. What in the hell was going on?

Somehow, Larsen Vale held the key to this case. How, he couldn't begin to guess, but he'd stake his life and his reputation on the fact that she'd seen something in that church yesterday. She'd witnessed something that had sent her running from the scene. And someone knew it. All he could do now was protect her—and get her to confide in him before she was permanently silenced.

By the time he arrived at his modest row house apartment, the focus of his thoughts was fast asleep. He carried her inside and back to his bedroom, laying her on his bed. The morning sun shone through the blinds, casting thin rows of bright sunlight across both the woman and the unmade bed.

He pulled the cord, adjusting the blinds, then stared down at his very own sleeping beauty.

"What am I going to do with you?" He slid a thick lock of silky golden hair between his thumb and forefinger, feeling a shaft of desire spear through him. Damn. His own lust was a complication he could do without. But she was beautiful. There was no denying it.

His gaze traveled over her features as he drank his fill, at last. He brushed the pad of his thumb over the softness of her cheek, a fine possessiveness rising inside him. She was made for him, the cure to his madness, the escape from his own private hell.

Determination bordering on desperation fired his blood. He wouldn't lose her. He *couldn't*. He couldn't return to the building insanity in his head knowing...*knowing*...the cure was lost to him. If he ran Larsen off now, how would he stay sane when the noise grew beyond bearing? How would he stand it when he knew a single touch of her hand would silence the chaos?

Stay by my side. Silence my madness.

"Trust me, Larsen," he whispered into the stillness of the room. "When you wake up, tell me what you know. Help me catch these guys before they hurt you again."

His gaze slid from her face to her shoulder. The sight of the bandaged wound made his gut clench. He'd whispered the words for her benefit, in the hope she'd remember them subconsciously, but he meant them, he realized. He didn't want her hurt again. There was something about her, something fierce and proud, that drew him. Something within her he recognized in himself.

Secrets.

Chapter 3

Larsen opened heavy eyelids. Where was she? *Why wasn't her boat rocking?* Her sleepy gaze caught the slow spin of a fan on the ceiling above and she felt the breeze waft over her. The musical score from *Les Miserables* drifted in from another room, accompanied by a deep masculine voice.

Jack Hallihan's.

Memory slammed into her, stealing her breath. She was in his house. *In his bed.* Thanks to the little bald girl.

She'd tried to kill her.

A surge of fear jolted her awake.

Why would the girl have attacked her? She'd seemed so sweet. So shy. It didn't make sense. But then, not much in her life ever had. All she knew for certain was that death seemed to have his eyes on *her* this time.

Heaven help her.

She was suddenly glad for her cop bodyguard. *Jack.* If only he would stop asking questions.

Larsen levered herself to a sitting position, her shoulder throbbing beneath the heavy bandage. Her gaze drifted, taking in the Spartan masculinity of the room. The dresser was made from the same sturdy oak as the bed. In the corner, a single chair, barely visible beneath a mound of discarded clothes, appeared to serve as the hamper.

The light filtering through the blinds had a late-afternoon feel to it. A glance at the bedside clock told her it was almost seven. She'd slept the entire day. The entire Tuesday.

Damn. She'd had two meetings with clients and a court appearance on her calendar for today. First thing in the morning she'd have to make some phone calls to apologize.

Larsen pushed back the sheet and swung her legs over the side of the bed, then stilled at the waft of air across her privates. *What in the…?* Her startled gaze dropped to her lap. The oversize T-shirt was bunched at her hips, but there was no hiding the fact she no longer wore anything beneath.

Jack.

Her heart lurched in her chest. What had he done? Just how badly had she misjudged him?

As she grabbed the sheet and yanked it over her lower half, her gaze snagged on something familiar lying across the bunched-up bedspread at her feet. Two somethings. Her shorts and panties, looking freshly washed.

She stared at them, her heart rate slowing. He'd washed them. Jack Hallihan had washed her bloodstained clothes… after undressing her.

Her breath caught in her throat. The thought should have outraged her. Instead heat pooled deep in her abdomen and throbbed between her legs. A fine time for her hormones to decide to do the cha-cha. Not that they hadn't been practicing that little step for months now, since the first time she'd seen the handsome cop.

She reached for the clothes and managed to get the panties on one-handed with maximum struggle. Exhausted, shoulder throbbing, she sat on the edge of the bed and stared at the shorts with their neat little zipper and button. No way.

"Need help?" Jack stood in the doorway looking impossibly handsome, one muscled shoulder propped against the doorframe. He was casually dressed in khaki shorts and a navy T-shirt with MPD emblazoned across the chest in bold white letters. His short dark hair was appealingly tousled.

He watched her with that blue intensity she was becoming used to, but this time it was warmed by sympathy...and something more. Something that made her increasingly aware she wore nothing beneath the oversize tee but a thin pair of panties.

She tried to give him her chilly look, to push him away, but she was so far from cold it wasn't funny, so she glared at him instead and held up the shorts. "I suppose you know how to get these on since you took them off." The thought of him peeling them off her had her hands shaking. She struggled to keep her voice even, struggled to meet his gaze.

He pushed away from the door and came to kneel in front of her, inches from her bare legs, his face nearly on a level with hers. He held out his hand for the shorts. She handed them to him as her gaze roamed the strong planes of his face—his pronounced cheekbones, his strong, faintly stubbled chin. The firm mouth that even now tilted into a sensual smile.

With effort, she tore her gaze away, but his warm scent wrapped around her, sending need rippling through her body.

Damn hormones.

"How you feeling?" he asked.

His words, the movement of those lips, pulled her gaze back to him and she couldn't help but wonder what it would feel like to have that mouth pressed against hers.

How was she feeling? *Like a woman who hasn't had sex in eight years.*

She took a deep breath, struggling to find air, scrambling for an appropriate answer. "Hot. Sore. Definitely sore."

She caught a glimpse of laughter in his eyes before his mouth compressed with sympathy. He set the shorts on the floor at her feet.

"Step in." He rose and held out his hand to her. "Can you stand?"

She wanted to say, "of course," but she wasn't sure. It annoyed her that she might need help, yet she took his hand. "Let's find out."

He gave her a small, approving smile and closed his warm hand around hers. Pure attraction hit her hard. She struggled to keep her face impassive.

"Okay?" he asked.

Her bare feet sank into the soft beige carpeting. "So far, so good."

"The room's not spinning?" A hint of a smile lifted the words.

Oh, yeah, it was spinning all right. Just not the way he meant. She had to get rid of that lethal smile of his before it caused her to do something she'd regret. Like smile back. He could *not* know what he was doing to her. He'd have power over her she desperately couldn't afford to give him.

She met his probing gaze with a glare. "I'm fine," she snapped, pleased with the bitchy sound even as it extinguished the teasing light in his eyes. She felt only a twinge of regret.

With swift, clinical movements, he pulled the shorts up and over her bottom. No lingering touches, no seductive fumbling.

But it didn't matter. Her body was like dry brush ready to ignite. The rough slide of his thumbs over her thighs and hips as he pulled up the shorts, the warm touch of his fingers at her stomach as he fastened the button, set up a throbbing between her legs just below the place he reached for the zipper.

She held her breath against the wave of sensations pricked by his nearness and his touch. If he ever decided to seduce her, she'd be in deep trouble.

Who was she kidding? She was already in trouble. First thing in the morning she was making some calls to get herself a different bodyguard.

Jack met her gaze, his expression enigmatic. "Dinner's almost ready."

Larsen nodded and followed him into the hall, but as he led her into the living room, his hand slipped around her upper arm, gripping her lightly just beneath the sleeve of her T-shirt. His thumb brushed over her bare skin in a soft caressing motion that was too intimate, too pleasant.

She jerked her arm away and winced as harsh discomfort radiated down her arm from her shoulder. "I'm not an invalid," she said tightly. Silence, heavy and reproachful, followed her into the living room.

The room was as masculine as the bedroom, but more fully decorated. Leather upholstery and rustic wood sat against a backdrop of light olive walls and hardwood floors with area rugs reminiscent of the southwest. On the walls were framed prints of sailboats caught on rough seas. The room was simple, yet attractive. Inviting. The kitchen, on the other hand, was plain and functional.

She caught the scent of a mouthwatering aroma and made a small, involuntary sound of appreciation. She hadn't realized how hungry she was until that moment.

He watched her with an expression that appeared almost boyish. "I tried something new tonight. I hope you like it."

Be the bitch, she told herself, but she couldn't do it. Self-protective she might be, but she'd never intentionally crossed the line to cruel.

"It smells delicious."

Though the words were without inflection or an ounce of enthusiasm, the smile that lit his eyes set butterflies to flight in her stomach. Larsen nearly groaned out loud. She might as well admit defeat right here and now. How was she ever going to steel herself against this man's charm? And she must. She couldn't let him get too close.

Jack seated her at the table, then went to fetch their dinner as Larsen's gaze followed him. He moved with an athlete's strength and coordination, every movement controlled and sure. As bodyguards went, she could have done worse. Much worse. Heaven knew, she enjoyed watching him.

If only his sharp eyes didn't have to watch her quite so closely in return.

Jack watched with amusement as Larsen dropped her fork for the second time. She was clearly right-handed, but trying to eat with her left to avoid jarring her injured shoulder. With an exasperated sigh and a wry roll of her eyes, she picked up the uncooperative fork, then dug back into the chicken paprika he'd cut into bite-size pieces for her.

The woman was a puzzle. One moment she was snapping at him for touching her, then minutes later he caught her watching him over her dinner plate with raw feminine interest in those golden-brown eyes. Was the Ice Queen warming up to him at last? Or was she, as he was beginning to suspect, no ice queen at all?

He watched her devour the meal with obvious relish. "You're hungry."

She looked at him with those wide, naturally slumberous eyes as she swallowed. "I haven't eaten since lunch yesterday. And this is—" she made a sound of appreciation deep in her throat "—unbelievable."

The compliment pleased him. He saw an opening to draw her out and took it. "Do you like to cook?"

Her mouth twisted into a rueful frown. "As little as possible. I never really learned. My dad didn't know how and my mom…died when I was eight."

"I'm sorry."

She shrugged. "It was a long time ago. I'm over it." But something moved in her eyes, sharp and fresh, belying her words. He could almost see her pulling back and away, her expression turning into that of the aloof attorney. Conversation over.

Not if he could help it. "My aunt taught me to cook when I was ten. Aunt Myrtle. She was an odd bird, nice in a zany sort of way. Her weirdness drove my mom crazy. She finally went too far when I was sick one time. Myrtle took me to her house, tried to cure me. I don't know what happened—just that she used some heavy woo-woo stuff. My mom took me home and never let her visit again."

Larsen's eyes had lost that defensiveness and had taken on a gleam of interest. "Did she hurt you?"

"No. That's the funny part. When she finished, I was fine."

"You mean, she really healed you?"

"I don't know. My parents wouldn't tell me what happened and I never saw Aunt Myrtle again. Last I heard she was still living in the Virginia mountains, only about an hour away from here. I should go see her one of these days."

When they'd finished eating, Larsen dabbed her mouth with the napkin, then stood. "Thank you. Dinner was excellent."

As she reached for her plate, he grabbed her wrist, blanketing his brain in a calming silence. "Nope. You're company. No touching the dirty dishes."

She stared at him, but to his delight, a twinkle appeared in her eye. "You're just afraid I'll drop your plate like I kept dropping my fork."

Self-deprecating humor. Who would have thought? He grinned at her, coaxing the twinkle in her eye into a glimmer of a smile. "Let's just say, I'm being cautiously hospitable."

A full-fledged smile illuminated her face, transforming the Ice Queen into a true angel, making him ache to pull her close and kiss her.

For a heart-stopping moment her eyes warmed until her expression seemed to be the visual equivalent of his thoughts.

She wanted the kiss as much as he did.

Then golden lashes swept down to hide her emotions. "Do you mind if I watch some television?"

Jack took a deep breath and released her wrist, uncorking the noise in his head. "Help yourself. The remote's on the coffee table." What just happened? *She wanted him.* She wanted him.

Hot damn. He seriously doubted the formidable Larsen Vale ever gave in to such base desires, but a guy could dream.

He carried the dishes to the sink. The soundtrack from a *Friends* rerun and the sweet sound of Larsen's laughter kept him company as he did the dishes. He could do this. Every night for the rest of his life. A woman's company over dinner. Soft, feminine laughter filling his house. *Larsen's* laughter. Hell, yeah.

The sudden jolt of longing startled him. Longing for an honest-to-god life and future with the beautiful woman whose touch could keep the madness at bay.

If he didn't blow it with her first. And he would, if he pressed her too hard about this case. Yet if he didn't…how many more would die?

Larsen rose as the final scene of the James Bond movie slid into the fifteenth car commercial of the evening. She'd paid little attention to the flick, too aware of the cop watching her from the sofa.

"I need a bath," she told him.

He visibly started. "Can't you wait until…tomorrow?"

"No, I feel gross. I'll sleep better after a hot soak." She still had flakes of dried blood on her shoulder and arm. "Can I borrow something to sleep in?"

Jack's eyelids sank over those blue eyes, sending tendrils of warmth snaking down her limbs. "Lady, you can have anything of mine you want. You sure you want clothes?"

"Yes."

"Are you certain you're up for this?"

"I feel fine." And, amazingly, she did. Her brows pulled together. "My shoulder doesn't even hurt anymore."

Jack set his Coke on the coffee table, his gaze skimming leisurely down her bare legs. "Don't get dressed afterward."

She jerked her head to face him. "Jack..."

His smile dawned sexy and playful. "Relax, Larsen. I just need to change your bandage. Wrap your top half in a towel so you don't have to take your shirt off."

She stared at him, scrambling to gather the wits he'd scattered to the wind with his suggestive comments. "Right," she said at last, and spun on her heel toward the bathroom, wondering if she should forego the hot bath and opt for a cold shower instead.

Steamy moisture hung in the air, clinging to the mirror in a wet fog. Standing on the terry bath mat, Larsen slipped into the borrowed pajama pants she'd brought in with her, then wrapped a dry bath towel tight around her breasts, tucking the end under her arm. Clutching it tight to her chest with one hand, she fluffed her wet hair with the other and called to her host.

"Jack, I'm ready for you!"

Larsen groaned as the raw double entendre echoed in her ears, making her cheeks flood with heat, which just flustered her more. She was twenty-eight years old. The *Ice Bitch*, for heaven's sake. Ice bitches did not get flustered over hot cops. They weren't supposed to blush over *anything*.

She heard the doorknob twist. As the door opened, she tried to fake a calm disinterest, but the sexy smile Jack leveled on her sent heat of a different kind flooding her system.

He leaned against the doorframe, teasing lights dancing in his blue eyes. "You're ready for me, are you?"

She tried to look haughty, but failed miserably as she met his grin. "You're impossible."

The worst part was that she *was* ready for him. Never in

her life had she been so aware of a man. But he couldn't know. She couldn't go there with him.

"The bandage, Detective," she said crisply, struggling to hide her reaction to his nearness.

He made a mock face of disappointment that did nothing to dim the smile in his eyes, but his hands busied themselves with the first-aid supplies.

His gaze dipped to take in her outfit, lingering a moment too long on her hands…or what they covered…making her feel hot and damp.

"How was your bath?" he asked, his smile turning friendly.

An answering smile escaped her mouth. She didn't want to like him, but he made it so hard not to.

Larsen tucked the towel in tighter. "The bath felt great. I'm finally clean again."

"No trouble with that shoulder?"

"No. Like I told you, it's stopped hurting."

His eyebrows lifted. "Let's see how it looks, shall we?" He motioned to the closed toilet lid. "Have a seat."

He stood close, his knee brushing her thigh as he carefully pulled at the tape holding the bandage to her shoulder.

"This might hurt." He eased the bandage off her skin. His brows pulled together as he stared at the wound.

"Damn, woman, you heal fast." His expression registered both surprise and approval. Beneath dark lashes, his blue eyes slid to her face.

Larsen shrugged. "It must have been a small arrow."

Jack stared at her shoulder, frowning. "I don't care what size it was. This wound looks like it's been healing for days." He shook his head. "Amazing. Anyway, I think we can probably switch you to a couple of Band-Aids."

"Great. Let me get back in the bath and wash the tape marks off."

But he was already reaching for her. His thumb ran along one of the tape lines, the look that entered his eyes warming her to her toes. "I'll help."

"Yeah, I bet."

He grinned at her. "As much as I'd enjoy seeing you in that tub, we'll do it here." He picked up the washcloth and began to ease the glue from her damp skin.

She stared at the speckles in the tiled floor while he worked. The subtle scent of his aftershave gave an exotic touch to the steamy, soapy smell of the bathroom, stirring her senses, as if his nearness and the rough pads of his fingers skimming her bare shoulder weren't doing enough.

His breathing no longer sounded calm. She glanced up to find him watching her, his eyes hot with wanting. The room turned stifling. Airless.

"Larsen…" Her name was little more than a whisper on his lips. He slid his palm along the side of her neck, sending shivers rippling through her. His gaze held hers captive. Tension built and coiled within her as she waited, breathless. *Wanting.*

Slowly he slid his thumb beneath her jaw and lifted her face, bending toward her. Even as part of her begged to push him away, she reached for him, lifting her hand in turn to slide along his stubbled jaw.

A low growl escaped Jack's throat a second before he covered her mouth with his own. The kiss started out gentle, then turned harder, more insistent, stirring feelings in her that quickly turned raw. Hungry.

How long had it been since she let a man get this close?

She'd forgotten how good it felt to be touched, to be filled with passion and life. And need.

Larsen wrapped her arms around his neck and pulled him closer, opening her mouth on his. A growl rumbled deep in Jack's chest as his tongue swept inside to claim hers. He tasted like heaven, like warm, sinful fantasies.

His hands gripped her waist and he rose, lifting her to her feet and into his arms. She forgot the towel, forgot everything but her need for this man. She lifted both hands to his face, holding him just where she wanted him, that wonderful mouth fused with hers. He pushed her gently backward, against the sink cabinet, pressing against her. He was hard. Aroused.

Reason wormed its way into her passion-fogged mind. Sex. *Too much. Too close.*

She pulled back from the kiss. "Jack…"

He dragged in short ragged breaths as he watched her, his passion-drugged eyes brimming with impatience, an impatience that slowly turned to resignation. Jack sighed and let her go. But as he stepped back, the towel that had covered her dropped to the floor between them. With a gasp, Larsen grabbed it and yanked it over her breasts, but the damage was done. The moment shattered.

"I…need to get dressed." She tried to push past him but he put out an arm to bar her way.

"You still need a Band-Aid."

Embarrassment heated her cheeks. "Okay, but no sexy, lingering touches this time." She couldn't quite meet his gaze.

It was one thing to kiss him. Something entirely different to flash him, accident or not.

To his credit, he didn't say anything that would compound

her self-consciousness. Instead he applied the Band-Aids to her shoulder with quick, clinical movements.

"All done."

She hazarded a glance at his face and found him watching her with amused sympathy.

He lifted one wry, teasing brow. "You do know how to get a guy's attention."

"Yeah. Well…" Her embarrassment melted beneath his gentle humor. "On that note, I'm going to bed. Alone," she added as she walked with forced calm down the hallway to Jack's bedroom.

Larsen closed the door, then sank back against it, her legs refusing to hold her upright a second longer. She struggled to suck air into her lungs, struggled to remember how to breathe after that kiss.

Every nerve in her body hummed with electricity. She could probably light the entire room if she shoved her finger in the light socket. Her fingers went to her lips, trailing over flesh that still tingled.

The man could *kiss*.

With a groan, she closed her eyes and leaned her head against the door. Why had she let him do that? Now he was going to want more. *She* was going to want more.

When what she needed to do was put distance between them.

She banged her head silently against the door at her stupidity. It was time to find that rock-solid control she'd always prided herself on, and find it fast.

The sound of Jack's cell phone ringing in the living room permeated the room, followed by the low murmur of his voice.

With a determined sigh, Larsen pushed away from the

door and grabbed the borrowed sleep tee off the bed. She was just pulling it on when she heard the rap on her door.

"Larsen, that was my partner on the phone. Come watch the news. There may be a break in the case."

Her pulse leaped with a bone-deep if fragile hope. "Thank God." She wrenched the door open and followed him into the living room as the newscasters appeared on the television screen.

"In our top story, two congressional interns are missing tonight. The young women were last seen leaving a pharmacy on Dupont Circle this morning with an unidentified male. The event was caught on the store's security camera."

Larsen watched the screen change to the grainy black-and-white videotape, then gasped as she saw him. *The albino.* His back was to her as he stood in the middle of the tape, but she was certain it was him. The same stark white hair, the same odd clothing.

Her heart began to pound. *She hadn't imagined him.*

In the background, the two young women chatted as they walked into the store. Neither seemed to pay any attention to the white man standing feet away.

The albino lifted his arm and the pair stopped abruptly, going suddenly, unnaturally, still. The purse one carried dropped, unnoticed, to the floor.

Chills raced over Larsen's skin as she watched the evil man step around them and leave the store, the two women turning to follow. As the three exited onto the sidewalk outside, two small figures emerged from the right and followed them out the door.

The station cut back to the newscasters, but not before Larsen got a look at the last two. Though she wore a baseball cap and a different T-shirt, one of them was the cancer girl—the girl who had shot her.

She heard the click of the remote and the television screen went dark. Larsen turned toward Jack, suddenly afraid she hadn't hidden her reactions. Her heart sank when she met his gaze. Gone was her friendly companion of a minute ago. In his place stood an angry, hard-eyed cop.

"I want the truth, lady…and I want it now."

Chapter 4

Jack's sugar-spun fantasy of spending his life with the one woman who could cure his madness crumbled beneath a slug of hard reality. How could he have forgotten Larsen Vale was a liar?

She stood beside him, her fingers gripping the back of his leather sofa, her face pale, her eyes wide with guilty dismay.

He'd called her into the living room to ID the bald girl Henry had seen at the end of the tape. Instead she'd visibly jerked at first sight of the prime suspect, the latter-day Pied Piper who seemed to have led the little group right out the store.

"You know him." The implications ricocheted across his brain.

"What?"

"The Pied Piper. The leader. You've seen him before."

Something pained moved through her eyes. "No." She

unhooked her fingers from his sofa and turned to face him, raising that stubborn chin. "I recognized the cancer girl."

She looked so damned innocent standing there in her soft pajamas, her golden hair damp and curling under her jaw. Another man might have believed the act of innocence, but not a cop. Not him. Beneath those soft golden lashes, her wide eyes crawled with guilt.

Jack slammed the remote on the table. "*Don't*. Don't lie to me. You nearly came out of your seat when you saw him."

Larsen crossed her arms over her chest, her gaze sliding away. "If I reacted to him, it was only because of his weirdness."

He stared at her, feeling the fragile connection between them fray and split. "How stupid do you think I am?"

She froze, then seemed to shake herself loose, her gaze shifting to the blank television screen. "I swear to you, Jack, I've never seen him before."

Dammit. His fingers flexed with the need to grab her and shake her, to scare the crap out of her until she told him what he wanted to know. At the same time, he wanted nothing more than to sink to his knees and beg her to trust him.

He turned away from her, shutting his eyes over the battle raging inside him. "Go to bed, Larsen." Before he destroyed what tenuous connection remained between them, losing his only chance at a life without madness, his only chance at a future.

Larsen paced the darkened bedroom, the room lit only by the soft wash of light slipping under the door from the hallway. She'd been pacing for more than an hour, but she wasn't the only one still awake. Beyond the door she could hear the low sound of the television and knew Jack was still up. And probably still furious with her. What was she going to do?

She couldn't tell him what she knew. As a kid, she'd believed she somehow caused the tragedies she foresaw. The shame and self-loathing kept her silent. Then in college, she'd done some research on visions and premonitions and realized she was just a type of fortune-teller. Seeing the future didn't mean she was causing it. But neither did it mean others would understand, if they knew. It didn't mean they'd accept her, not think she was a freak. It wasn't a risk she was willing to take.

But now she didn't know what to think. The albino saw her. He *saw* her. If she were merely a fortune-teller, merely a seer of the future, that wouldn't be happening. So, what did that make her visions? What did that make *her?*

The old fear that she was somehow to blame clenched like a fist in her stomach. The feelings that she was evil rose like bile in her throat.

She couldn't tell him. She couldn't tell *anyone.* But those cop eyes of Jack Hallihan's saw way too much. He already suspected she knew something. He had an uncanny ability to see right through her lies. He was dangerous. She needed to get away. In the morning, she'd make some calls. She wasn't a prisoner…yet. But he certainly wasn't going to let her walk out of here after she'd given herself away with that video.

No, she needed help. The kind one got from friends in high places, which she happened to have, thanks to her skill in the courtroom. She'd rescued the daughter of a D.C. circuit court judge from an abusive marriage just last month. She had little doubt George would put a bug in the right ear and she'd be free of Jack Hallihan before lunch.

Regret pressed down on her with surprising force.

She'd been attracted to him for months. But that mild infatuation was nothing compared to the attraction that had built over the past couple of days, catching fire in his arms tonight. Strangely, her attraction to him was more than physical. When he wasn't playing cop, he was good company. Fun, sexy.

Her fingers trailed over her lips. And the man could win awards with his kissing. She remembered the way he'd held her, the way he'd pressed her against the sink cabinet until she'd had no doubt of his desire.

A warm rush of longing turned her knees weak and she sank down onto the bed. If only things were different. If only—

Her sight suddenly vanished. Pain split her skull.

Heart lurching with fear, Larsen grabbed her aching head as another vision hit her like a sledgehammer.

She recognized the Old West decor of Tony Jingles, a restaurant on Q Street, not far from the pharmacy where the young intern had been abducted. As before, she watched from above, as if she hovered near the ceiling, wrapped in an unnatural silence.

Dread balled in her stomach.

She didn't want to see this.

She tried to close her eyes, tried to wake herself up or to shake herself out of the scene, but she remained rooted. *Trapped.*

The scene below appeared disturbingly normal. The afternoon sun shone through the slats of the window blinds, illuminating a half-empty restaurant. On the television in the corner, the Baltimore Orioles mascot bounded across the field in what appeared to be pregame shenanigans.

A flash of white caught her eye and everything changed.

The albino strode into the restaurant, turning the patrons

and wait staff to stone. Forks and glasses dropped onto the tables, food-laden trays crashed silently to the floor.

The only natural movement came from a booth nearby. A middle-aged woman with a round, intelligent face stared around her in disbelief. She opened her mouth as if yelling, then began to shake the two people in the booth with her—a man Larsen presumed was her husband and a pretty young woman, probably her daughter.

The woman looked up to see the albino approaching. Her eyes widened with shock, then turned to fear as her husband's hands closed around her throat and he began to choke her. The albino motioned to her blank-faced daughter. The girl climbed out of the booth and, like the bridesmaid before her, stood motionless as he raped her in front of her mother's dying eyes.

With his white hair swirling around his face, his eyes glowing like yellow-green embers, the albino's head jerked up and he met Larsen's gaze. Through his song, he smiled malevolently.

And reached for her.

Jack paced his living room, slapping the television remote against his thigh in an agitated, bruising rhythm as the newscaster droned, becoming just one more voice in his head.

Who was she? Ice Queen or siren? Angel or devil?

Winning her trust was a luxury he could no longer afford.

His last doubt that she was involved in this case had evaporated as he'd watched her react to the surveillance video.

His sanity be damned. His first responsibility was to the people of D.C. It was high time he got to the bottom of Larsen Vale's involvement. Before that bastard committed another murder or assault.

With weighted feet, Jack strode to his bedroom and rapped on the door. "Larsen?" When she didn't answer, he pounded harder. The door, not fully latched, swung open to reveal a figure huddled on the floor in the sweep of hall light.

His heart lodged in his throat. "Larsen, what happened?"

She stared at nothing, her eyes glassy and filled with horror. He crossed to her in three quick strides and knelt in front of her, searching for sign she'd been injured, but he saw nothing out of the ordinary. No arrow sticking out of her. No blood.

He cupped her face in his hands, his palms encountering the cool clamminess of her skin. "Talk to me, Larsen. What happened?"

Long lashes swept up. Tormented eyes met his gaze and slowly filled with tears. Sobs began to rack her slender body.

"Are you hurt?"

She pressed her lips hard together, but shook her head.

His fear slid away. Keen protectiveness warred with frustration even as he pulled her against him in a move that was at once alien and utterly natural. She fit against him perfectly, her arms sliding around his neck, her face buried against his shoulder.

She belonged to him. In a way he couldn't describe, he felt it in his bones.

Jack stroked her damp hair as her crying slowly subsided. She wasn't injured, not physically at least. Whatever tormented her came from within. Was it fear that hounded her? Guilt?

He felt the tension drain out of her as he rubbed her back.

"I need to know what's going on," he said quietly. "I can't help you if I don't know."

Too late, he realized she'd cried herself to sleep. Resigned, he lifted her into his arms and carried her to the bed, then lay beside her, his fingers twined with hers.

Blessed silence filled his head, perhaps for the last time, as he gazed at the woman who stirred so many conflicting emotions in him. Come morning he was going to have to break through her defenses to get at the truth. No matter what it took. Even if it meant earning her hatred, and losing his last chance.

Larsen woke to the smell of coffee and the sound of a soft rain pattering against the window. Her arms, which were always on top of the covers when she slept, were buried beneath a sheet tucked up to her chin, as if someone had pulled the sheet over her during the night.

Jack.

She'd woken just before dawn to find her back pressed against his chest, his arm tight around her. She'd felt so safe, so secure, she'd fallen right back to sleep. Something warm and soft moved in her chest. If things were different, if *they* were different, he might just be a man worth taking a chance on.

But though he might be able to protect her physically, he was, ultimately, a cop who saw too much. And she was a woman with secrets she could never share. Premonitions. Death.

Tony Jingles.

The terrifying memory slammed into her and she struggled from beneath the snug sheet and sat up, heart pounding. The albino would strike again. Another rape. Maybe another death.

She raked her hair back from her face and stared at the plain blue sheet bunched at her knees, her mind spinning. She'd seen her own death at the wedding reception, yet she hadn't died. For the first time ever, one of her death visions hadn't come true. Were these visions different from the ones she'd had as a child, or had she simply never believed she could change things, so never before tried?

Oh God, what if she could have saved her mom from that car accident all those years ago? Her scalp began to tingle with the horror of the thought. *Don't. Don't go there.* What was done was done. She couldn't change the past. But maybe… *maybe*…she could change the future.

The horror charging through her system slowly changed to excitement. What if she could stop the murder at Tony Jingles? What if she could save that woman and her daughter, and possibly end the albino's rampage once and for all?

Sudden restless energy shot down her limbs. With a kick of the sheet, she climbed out of bed and began pacing the room. Jack was a cop. He could stop the attack and catch the murderer.

But how could she tell him what she knew without telling him how she knew it? She'd find a way. She *had* to. For once, just maybe, her death visions could be used for good instead of bringing evil.

Jack poured himself a cup of coffee as he dug his fingers into his scalp, trying to ease the volume in his head. The damned voices were getting louder, as if each day they invited more and more guests into the party.

"Headache?" Larsen said from behind him, entering the kitchen.

He jerked his hand away, nearly spilling the coffee, and turned to face her. She looked soft and delicious this morning, her hair sleep-tousled, her pajamas clinging in all the right places. Blood pooled between his legs as he remembered the feel of her pressed against him during the night. He'd slept. Eventually. But now, with her awake, all he wanted to do was to sweep her up and carry her back to that bed, preferably without those soft, clinging pajamas.

He tore his gaze away from her and shoved the coffee carafe back under the brewer. It was time to play tough cop, not horny fool. But damn, she looked good.

"Do you get the *Post?*" she asked. Her gaze met his, then darted away with a glimmer of fear. She must know he intended to dig her secrets out of her this morning and he hated that she did. Hated that she feared him. An innocent woman would have nothing to fear.

"It's in the foyer," he told her. "The plastic sleeve is wet. It's been raining since dawn."

She returned moments later holding the newspaper in one hand and a folded white sheet of paper in the other. "I think you'd better see this."

At the strained look in her eyes, he set down his mug and reached for the folded sheet. A handwritten note. As his gaze skimmed the bold black letters, the hair rose on the back of his neck.

Tony Jingles. This afternoon. The Dupont Circle Rapist strikes again.

His gaze pinned Larsen. "Where'd you find this?"

"It fell out of the newspaper when I picked it up."

She was lying. He wasn't sure how he knew that. The answer wasn't necessarily in her gaze, which was finally meeting his, nor her erect, self-assured stance. Nor was it in the stubborn, upward thrust of her chin. He simply felt it in his gut. And he'd long ago quit second-guessing his gut. The question was, what was he going to do about it?

He skimmed the note again. Did it matter? Didn't he have what he needed—a way to catch that son of a bitch? If he still had questions afterward, he'd interrogate her then.

He'd know where to find her. Larsen Vale wasn't going to make another move unless he said so.

Larsen's nerves were eating her alive.

She paced Jack's living room, her sandals clipping over the hardwood floor as she waited for word from the Tony Jingles stakeout. The Orioles game was scheduled to begin in twenty minutes unless they called a rain delay, which was a real possibility given the drizzly skies.

The woman cop Jack had sent to babysit Larsen walked through the living room on one of her quarter-hourly rounds. The woman, Sergeant O'Malley, wasn't much in the way of company. Short, stocky and unsmiling, she'd relinquished no more than one-word answers when Larsen tried to engage her in conversation when she'd first arrived. When the cop wasn't making her rounds, she remained firmly by the kitchen door.

Outside, two male cops kept an eye on the house. Larsen hadn't considered the fact that whoever supposedly put the note in Jack's paper obviously knew where he lived. Of course, that person had been her, though she could never tell him that. So she cooled her heels in a protective custody with no means of escape short of outside intervention.

It wouldn't take much to get herself out of here. She was convinced of that. A phone call, maybe two. Heaven knew she'd made enough of them already this morning, apologizing for yesterday and clearing her calendar for the next few days until the police caught the albino and ended this nightmare.

Why was she hesitating? Maybe because if she left now

she'd never know what happened. Larsen stared out the front window at the damp, gray afternoon, the trees in front of the row house wilting with the drizzle.

And maybe the problem was Jack himself. She needed to get away from him. She *knew* that. But it didn't change the fact that she was drawn to him in a way she hadn't been to a man, to anyone, in longer than she could remember. But staying here was foolish. She was playing with fire.

With a sigh, she turned from the window as the clock on the chest in the corner chimed two o'clock. The Orioles game was about to begin. Her heart gave a nervous kick. If she was right about the murder happening pregame, it would happen soon.

Larsen turned on the television and stared as the Orioles mascot ran onto the field exactly as she'd seen him in the premonition. Chills raced over her skin, standing her hair on end. *The murder had begun.* The memory of that vision, that *nightmare,* replayed in her head like a horror film—the restaurant, the albino, every patron hypnotized but one. And she'd sent Jack and the D.C. police into the thick of it. *With guns.*

A sudden, horrible thought struck her. What if he controlled them, too?

Oh, God, what have I done?

Chapter 5

"Sabrina's in love," Henry said, his dark head glistening from the misty rain. "Says she's going to marry the guy."

Jack scanned the street outside Tony Jingles for sign of anything...or anyone...suspicious. The two men were tucked into a doorway across the street from the restaurant. Watching.

Waiting for the Dupont Circle Rapist.

"Fourteen's a little young to be getting married." Jack glanced at his partner. "Who's the lucky kid?"

"I don't know, man. I don't even let her date, yet. Shook me up good."

"What does Mei think?"

"She's laughing at me. Says *she* was planning to marry Michael Jackson when she was that age. She doubts Sabrina's even met the guy, but I don't know. I don't like my little girl talking about getting married. It's not right."

Henry's despondency made Jack smile. He clapped his friend on the back. "Don't sweat it, Hank. Sabrina's a smart kid. When the day comes, she'll pick a great guy."

"I'll still hate him."

Jack chuckled. "Yeah, so will I."

Henry grinned. "That's one of the things I like about you, man. If anything ever happens to me, I know you'll watch over my family. You love my kids near as much as I do."

"Your kids are great, Hank. The best."

For once he didn't feel the usual pang of melancholy that being "Uncle" Jack brought him. Always before, he'd thought this was the closest he'd ever come to being a father. He'd always known he could never have kids of his own. But now he wasn't so sure. A fragment of hope lodged in his chest the day he met Larsen. The day he realized she could stop the voices.

A flash of white caught his attention inside the restaurant. As he peered closer, he realized he was staring at the same stark white hair, the same odd clothes as on that news report last night. His blood went cold.

"He's in there."

Henry pulled his gun. "Where? I don't see him."

Jack yanked out his phone and called Griff and Duke who were inside the restaurant posing as patrons. He could see Griff's red hair, knew he was facing the Pied Piper. Why hadn't he called for backup?

"Griff, he's there. Do you have him?"

"Where? I don't see…"

A sudden crash reverberated through the phone, the sound of breaking glass and shattering plates, followed by an eerie silence.

"Griff? Griff!" In the background he could hear some-one…*singing*. The hair rose at the nape of his neck.

"Come on." Jack snapped his phone shut and dodged through traffic, Henry racing behind him.

Jack pulled his gun and burst into the restaurant, aiming the weapon at the whitest man he'd ever seen. The man wasn't merely blond, but a true albino, skin without color.

"Police! Hands in the air!"

The man turned to face him, still singing the odd, tuneless melody Jack had heard through the phone. A movement in the booth beside him caught Jack's attention.

A man was strangling a woman.

Jack fired at the ceiling. No one seemed to notice, no one reacted at all. Their expressions, to a man, woman and child, were blank. As if every one of them was completely stoned.

He ran and lunged for the strangler, hauling him off his victim. The woman gasped, coughed, then screamed when the man reached for her again.

"Stop!" Jack lifted his gun to shoot him.

"No!" the woman cried as she scrambled out of her assailant's reach. "It's him." She pointed at the albino. "It's his singing."

Jack aimed his gun at the pale man. "Quiet!" When the man ignored him, Jack shot him in the leg. The song stumbled, but never ceased, and the Pied Piper's expression never changed.

Jack stared at the uninjured leg. Had he *missed?* A second shot rang out and a bullet ruffled his hair. He dove for cover as another hit the table beside him. Were they trying to turn this into a shoot-out? Jack lifted his gun in the direction of the shots, and froze.

The only one aiming for him was Henry.

"Hank!"

But his partner's eyes had gone as blank as the others. His partner and best friend fired at him again.

"He's hypnotizing them," the woman shouted, scrambling under the table as a man lunged for her over the back of her booth. "They don't know what they're doing. You've got to stop the white man." Two men surrounded her table and she screamed again.

Pulse thudding through his veins, Jack rolled under another table a second before Henry's shot hit the place where he'd been. Henry was slow, he realized. His reflexes weren't his own.

If he kept moving…

"Stop it!" the woman cried.

Jack's gaze jerked toward the sound and he nearly choked. The Pied Piper was pulling out his dick while a teenage girl pulled down her shorts in front of him.

The rapes. *The victims never remembered.*

Rolling out of Henry's line of fire, Jack took aim at that engorged piece of white flesh and fired right at the base of it, right into the heart of the bastard's groin…and didn't miss.

The man let out a howl that would have done a wolf proud. The gunfire came to an abrupt halt, an eerie silence pressing at the walls of the restaurant. Jack held his breath, his pulse pounding in his ears. As long as Henry was firing, Jack had a fix on him. Without that, he could be anywhere. Creeping up behind him…

Suddenly, as one, the people who'd been controlled sank to the ground, unconscious. Or dead. Jack saw Henry fall with a silent thud and turned back to the white bastard, the man he was now certain was the rapist. This bad guy was *his*.

But as he lunged for him, an arrow missed his face by millimeters. *Damn.* He dived for cover, more arrows clattering on the empty tabletop above him. In the background, the low sounds of the Orioles baseball game provided an eerily normal soundtrack to a bafflingly surreal battle.

Jack fired at the nearest archer, but the shot went high as the small man ducked behind a booth. His gaze swung to the rapist and he found him pushing his dick back into his pants as if nothing had happened. As if he hadn't just been shot.

Jack stared with disbelief at that white flesh. *He wasn't bleeding. Why wasn't he bleeding?*

The albino met his gaze, his yellow-green eyes lit with hatred. "I will kill you."

"Not if I kill you first," Jack murmured, taking aim at the bastard's forehead. He pulled the trigger. A hole appeared in the center of that snow-white forehead…two seconds before it disappeared.

Jack's blood went cold. *No way. No damn way.* He was losing his mind. This could *not* be happening.

Hands shaking, he shot him again.

The white man simply looked at him with venom in his eyes. "I will kill you." Then he turned and walked toward the kitchen as if Jack's gun had been firing nothing but blanks.

Jack stared at him. How in the hell…? He jumped up to chase after him, but a hail of arrows forced him back under the table. When the attack finally ended, he raced after them, but he was too late. By the time he reached the swinging door to the kitchen, they were gone.

His head pounded with questions as he called for backup and returned to the front of the restaurant where the booths and floors were littered with bodies.

He ran to Henry and felt for a pulse. Steady. Strong.

He'd tried to kill him. His partner and best friend had tried to kill him. And if he was right, if this crime scene played out the way the others had, he wouldn't remember. None of them would remember a thing. Hell. How was he going to write up this one? He couldn't tell the truth. Henry would be put on administrative leave and it hadn't been his fault. He hadn't known what he was doing.

Besides, no one was going to believe any of this. He wasn't sure *he* believed it. Had his mind finally snapped?

The big man moved and gave a small snore. "Hank." He shook him. "Hank!"

"You can't wake them," the woman called from the end of the aisle. Fortyish and carrying an extra fifty pounds, she knelt on the floor, fastening her sleeping daughter's clothes.

Jack went to her and squatted in front of her. "Is she okay?"

"I think so. But I can't wake her or my husband." She looked up, her distraught gaze meeting his. "I'm a doctor. An anesthesiologist with Children's Hospital. I put kids under all day long and I've never seen anything like this."

"Can you tell me what happened?"

A host of conflicting emotions crossed her face. "We were eating lunch when the white man walked into the restaurant. He was so odd-looking. I mentioned him to my husband and daughter, but they couldn't see him." Her brows pulled together and an expression that was almost hurt entered her eyes. "Where I pointed, they saw only a normal-looking businessman. Then he began to sing and everything stopped. All the conversation stopped. It was like he hypnotized them. With a song."

She looked at him like a child whose most treasured belief had just been shattered. "How can that be?"

"I don't know. I wish to hell I knew." The only one who might know something was the person who'd put the note in his newspaper. The person who'd sent him here. The person who'd set him up to be killed.

Larsen.

Jack slammed the front door behind him, his face hard, his blue eyes blazing. Larsen's heart gave an anxious lurch as she rose from the chair and watched him toss his sport coat on the back of the sofa without so much as a glance her way, making it pretty clear his anger was directed at her. *He knew.* But what?

He went into the kitchen to talk to Sergeant O'Malley, telling her she and the other cops would no longer be needed.

What happened? It was nearly six o'clock and she still didn't know anything except that things had gotten ugly. Sending him into that without a warning had been a mistake. But how could she have warned him? And if the cops couldn't catch the villain, who could?

She stood rooted as Jack escorted the policewoman to the door, then closed and locked it. Slowly he turned and met her gaze, the hard mask melting beneath his fury, his hands clenching and unclenching at his sides.

A primal fear lodged in her chest as he started toward her, his stride slow and deliberate. Larsen took a step back.

"You set me up to be killed."

"I didn't." *I didn't mean to.* She bumped into the table behind her. "What happened, Jack?"

He closed the distance between them and grabbed her with both hands, his fingers digging painfully into the bare flesh of her upper arms. "What happened is you put that note in my paper this morning, sending me to Tony Jingles where I damned near *died.*" Jack shook her roughly, making her teeth rattle. "How did you know, Larsen? How did you know he was going to be there?"

The air caught in her lungs. "I didn't," she lied. "How could I possibly know something like that?"

"You couldn't." His lip curled nastily. "Not unless you worked for him."

Larsen gaped at him, fear congealing in her chest. "No. Jack... How can you even *say* that? He's a rapist. A murderer."

"And you knew what he had planned."

Had he seen her put the note in the paper? No. He couldn't have. He was guessing.

She forced herself to look him in the eye. "You're wrong. I'm not part of this."

He shook her again. "Quit lying to me. How does he do it, Larsen? How does he control them?" A bolt of pain flashed through his eyes. "My men...my *partner*...tried to kill me."

She caught her breath on a burst of understanding. *Dear God.* He was like her. He couldn't be controlled. And the albino tried to kill anyone he couldn't control.

Jack's mouth grew pinched. "I shouldn't have said that." He released her and turned away. "Henry doesn't even know. None of my men remember any of it." He stared at nothing, his eyes narrowed in thought. "It's just like the murder. And the assaults. No one remembered a thing."

"Did he...was anyone hurt?" The woman she'd watched strangled had haunted her dreams. And her poor daughter...

"No. I stopped a murder in progress and foiled an assault. Barely."

Larsen had to struggle to keep the relief from showing in her face. "What about *him*...the albino. Did you catch him?"

"No. I shot him, but…" His razor-sharp gaze cut to hers. "Why did you call him an albino?"

"What would you call someone that white?"

His eyes narrowed dangerously. "And just how do you know his skin's that white?"

Larsen stared at him, too late realizing her mistake. She wasn't supposed to have seen him except for the security video. And the man had never turned around. She'd known it was him from his hair and his odd clothes. *But not his skin.*

Damn, damn, damn. "That hair…" Her voice cracked and she cleared it. "I just assumed…"

"He's white. Pure unadulterated white. Total absence of color except for his eyes." His own eyes glittered ominously. "There's no way in hell you could know that from that piece-of-crap tape." He veered toward her.

"Jack…" Her heart pounded at the stupidity of her slip.

He stopped a hand breadth away from her, but didn't grab her this time, as if he didn't trust himself. His eyes were no longer burning with fury, but with something far more dangerous.

"You are going to tell me the truth, Larsen," he said with deadly softness. "*All* of it. Right now. Or I'm going to haul your ass to the station and lock you up until you decide to talk. I'm through playing games, lady."

She couldn't tell him how she knew. She couldn't. *Ever.*

She forced herself to meet his gaze without flinching, to stare into blue eyes as rigid as the steel bars of a prison. "I've told you all I can, Jack."

The planes of his face hardened. "Then I'm taking you in for questioning." He reached for her, then stopped midmotion, his body going rigid. *"Hide."*

"What?" But then she heard it, too. A commotion out front. A shout. A child's cry of pain. Running feet.

"*Hide,* Larsen!"

He spun away, leaving her staring after him, shaking, as he pulled the gun from his waistband and ran for the front door.

She had to get out of here. She had to get away from him. He knew too much, or suspected too much. Either way, if he hauled her into that police station, she'd never come out again. Not whole.

As she started for the bedroom, Jack wrenched the door open, revealing a young, dark-skinned girl standing on the porch, a smaller child lying at her feet. Larsen stopped, recognizing the kids Jack had been playing ball with that day at the marina. Was it only three days ago?

"What happened?" Jack demanded as he bent and scooped up the boy.

Words spilled out of the girl's mouth in a quivering rush. "There were two little bald people trying to see in your windows."

Larsen's eyes widened. *Her archer.*

Jack ushered the girl into the house.

"He shot me," the boy said as Jack kicked the door shut, then turned to lock it despite his full arms.

"Where, David?" Jack strode to the sofa and deposited the child gently. "Show me."

The boy lifted his shirt to show an unblemished expanse of brown tummy.

Jack nodded. He speared Larsen with his gaze as he rose. "I'm going after them. Lock the door behind me, then get David and Sabrina in the bathroom where they can't get shot."

"Jack—"

But he was already heading out the door. Larsen stared at the closing door, the blood pounding in her ears. She could leave. For the first time in two days, she was without a jailer.

Behind her, the little boy whimpered. Larsen shook her head. She locked the door as Jack instructed and helped David into the bathroom, the only room without a window. Sabrina followed and perched on the edge of the tub. David curled up on the rug, holding his stomach, tears in his eyes.

Larsen knelt beside him. "It still hurts?"

He nodded, tears sliding down his cheeks to drip on the rug. "He shot me."

"With an arrow?"

"Nah-unh. It was invisible." His face screwed up in a mask of pain. "He flicked it off his thumb."

It didn't make any sense. But she couldn't deny his pain, nor the fact that nothing about this nightmare had made any sense from the beginning. She was all too afraid the little bald people had come after *her*. Why had they attacked the children?

Larsen had badly misjudged the cancer girl. She'd appeared so fragile when Larsen had first seen her in the church. Sweet.

"What are *you* doing here?" Sabrina asked sharply.

Larsen looked up and met the teen's glare. She was a pretty girl, though Larsen didn't much care for the look in her eyes.

"I'm a guest of Jack's."

"Why?" Dark eyes flashed with unfriendliness.

Larsen watched the girl with interest. She knew jealousy when she saw it and decided to answer truthfully. "One of those little bald people shot me with an arrow Monday night. Jack's a cop. He brought me here to keep me safe until he caught her."

"She followed *you,* then. It's your fault David got hurt."

"It's not my fault."

"It's not my fault either! David shouldn't have yelled at them."

The girl's sudden defensiveness took Larsen by surprise.

The teen's face crumpled, tears welling in her eyes. "My dad's going to be so mad."

"He told her…" David began, then gripped his stomach and grimaced. "He told her not to leave the house without him or Mom. But she wouldn't listen."

"It's Jack's birthday," Sabrina said through lips tensed and trembling. "We always surprise him on his birthday."

"Maybe you should have sent him a card," Larsen murmured.

The girl stared at her, then began to cry in earnest.

Larsen sighed. "Sabrina, please don't cry. It won't help anything." But she might as well have been talking to the sink. She rose and went to stand in the open doorway where she might hear Jack when he returned. Finally the rap sounded on the front door.

"Larsen, open up. It's me."

She hurried to the door and let Jack in. "Did you catch them?"

"No." He met her gaze for one brittle moment, his eyes revealing a wealth of anger…and a deep vein of hurt. He brushed past her and went to the bathroom where Sabrina still cried. The bathroom where she'd experienced the most amazing kiss of her life.

She followed him and stood in the doorway, watching him kneel beside David, his dark head bent with concern. Whatever had been growing between them was gone. There would be no more kisses. No more sexy smiles. No more warm arms holding her through the night. All that was left between them was blame and anger and guilt. A fist-size lump of regret lodged in her chest. If only things could have been different. If only *she* were different.

If only she were normal. But she wasn't and she had to get away from Jack and his cops before they figured that out, even if it meant risking another arrow.

While Jack comforted the children, Larsen walked to the bedroom and closed the door, then grabbed her purse. As she eased open the window, the doorbell rang. She tensed until she heard the deep rumble of a second male voice and knew the kids' dad had arrived.

"Goodbye, Jack," she whispered, then slipped out the window and escaped into the night.

Chapter 6

The night air crackled with malevolence. Threat danced on the humid breeze, raking its nails down Jack's spine while mounting questions pricked his skin, itching like new wool. Never in his life had he felt so off balance. He'd dealt with rapists before, and murderers. With thieves and car-jackers and gang-bangers. But never had he faced anyone like this—a villain whose powers and abilities defied logic. How in the hell could a man hypnotize cops with a song? One measly song.

The voices in his head surged as Jack paced the walk in front of his row house, gun at his side, watching Henry load his family into the minivan. His gaze darted up and down the street, searching for sign of the little bald bastards who'd attacked David.

What in the hell had they done to him?

"Tomorrow, man," Henry called with a wave as the van started down the street.

Jack lifted his hand. He hated mysteries. And damned if he wasn't mired in the stickiest of them. Only one person could get him out of this one. Larsen. She knew something. And she was damn well going to tell him what it was. *Now.*

Once the van turned the corner, he retraced his steps into his ground floor apartment in the row house and locked the door behind him. Tensed and ready for a showdown, he strode toward his bedroom, the squeak of his damp soles on the wood floor the only sound in the silent apartment.

Jack pounded on the closed door with the heel of his fist, the sound echoed by the rise of noise in his head, as if the party in his brain had been crashed by yet another dozen revelers. The voices were multiplying. Just what he needed.

"Larsen, open up!"

He longed to take her hand and lose himself in the silence, to pretend he didn't suspect her of sending him to Tony Jingles, of sending him into that death trap. To pretend she wasn't involved in this case up to those finely arched brows.

But he needed answers and he needed them now, even though forcing her hand surely meant forfeiting her quieting touch and, ultimately, his sanity.

Misery weighted his shoulders as he pounded again. "Dammit, Larsen, open this door or I'll kick it in." A truck rumbled by out front but, oddly, the sound seemed to reverberate loudest from inside his bedroom. His eyes narrowed. She'd opened a window.

Damn. He grabbed for the key on top of the door frame and unlocked the door to find the window wide open. *They'd taken her.* But then his gaze took in the screen propped against the *inside* wall.

"Larsen?"

Nothing. The little fool. She knew there were archers looking for her. The next arrow might not pierce her shoulder, but something far more vital.

The ramifications of that thought hit him square in the gut. She preferred to take her chances with the archers than with him. And why did *that* say about her innocence?

He crossed the room and leaned out the window. No sign of her. With a quick tug, he shut the window, then grabbed his keys and ran for his car. He didn't know how deep she was into this thing, but at the moment he didn't care. All he wanted was to know that she was safe. And that meant finding her before whoever was trying to kill her.

Larsen curled up in the small upholstered chair by the hotel window and stared out at the gleaming lights of Crystal City, Virginia, across the Potomac River from her home and her life. And Jack. She should feel relieved to be away from him and his questions and accusations. Instead, all she felt was lonely. And scared.

The musical ring of her cell phone cut through the noisy rumble of the air conditioner. Larsen grabbed it from the table and glanced at the Caller ID.

Jack.

Indecision pulled her in two as the music filled the room. She wanted to talk to him, just to hear his voice. But she knew she'd sealed her guilt in his eyes by running away. There would be no pleasant conversation between them, just more anger and accusations.

Besides, she was afraid if she answered he might be able to pinpoint her location, which might lead to her being picked up for questioning. No, answering a cop's call was definitely not a smart move for a woman officially on the run.

The ring tone continued unabated, clawing at her nerves until she couldn't stand it any longer and shoved the phone under the mattress to muffle the sound.

Finally the ringing stopped. Loneliness swept over her. His strength and warm arms were lost to her now. She didn't dare contact him again, at least not until this was over. And by then, there would be no reason to. For now she was trapped in her solitude, unable to go home. Life as she knew it was lost to her until the albino's reign of terror came to an end.

It was all up to Jack. There was nothing more for her to do but to wait it out and pray Jack caught the guy soon.

Larsen got ready for bed and was brushing her teeth when her vision suddenly went black.

No. Not again.

Pain split her head as the premonition swept her away.

She was in a theater this time, a place she recognized well. The Kennedy Center with its opulent gilt decor, the blood-red carpeting and atmospheric lighting. The theater was full, teeming with kids. A matinee. She vaguely remembered hearing an advertisement on the radio for a reduced-price matinee of *The Lion King* with the proceeds going to some children's foundation. Thursday. The special presentation was Thursday.

Tomorrow.

As she watched, the lights in the theater dimmed. After a short, dramatic pause, the heavy curtains opened to reveal a set right out of the African savannah. The musical began and, just as suddenly, stopped, the actors relaxing their poses as if the director had called for a break, then going still, frozen in place.

In the middle of the orchestra seats, a man rose. An all-too-familiar man with white skin and white hair. The only other movement in the packed theater came from two young children several rows in front of him, a little girl of about six dressed in a pink sundress, her white-blond hair in a single, curly ponytail, and a boy a couple years older who was bouncing on his seat like an escaped jack-in-the-box.

As one, the pair turned to look at the albino, their eyes wide and curious. The man sitting between them, an older version of the little boy, turned, as well.

What happened next was almost a blur in the darkened theater. The audience rose and attacked the small family while the albino grabbed the young woman who'd been sitting beside him and raped her.

As the vision faded, Larsen's gaze focused on one last, horrible sight. Draped across the back of one of the seats lay the lifeless body of the little girl, facedown, her white-blond pony tail hanging from a small head cocked at an impossible angle.

Larsen came back to herself, sitting on the bathroom floor, the toothbrush still in her mouth. She lurched to her feet, tossed the toothbrush into the sink and lunged for the toilet, losing most of her dinner. When her stomach was empty, she sat on the cold tile and leaned her head back against the wall, her body quaking, her eyes squeezed tight against the awful memory.

No more. *Please, no more.*

Tears slid down her cheeks and she buried her face in her hands. Why would he kill children? *Children?*

Because he hadn't been able to control them. Like Jack and her and the woman at Tony Jingles and the man who'd died at the wedding, he hadn't been able to control them. So he'd killed them.

No. He *would* kill them. Unless she stopped him.

Angry determination crowded out the horror and helplessness swirling inside her. She could do this. She could stop him as she had before. But how? She'd nearly gotten Jack killed today and nearly gotten herself hauled in for questioning.

She struggled to her feet, rinsed her mouth and crawled into bed, praying something would come to her as she slept. She needed a plan. A brilliant plan.

And the courage to see it through.

The ruckus in his head grew worse by the day. Jack pressed his fingers into his scalp as he lay on his back in bed, longing for a single moment's respite from the din.

If he'd never met Larsen Vale, he wouldn't know what he was missing. He'd never have experienced the relief of a moment's quiet. Or the delight of an angel's laughter.

Where was she?

He lowered his hands and glanced at the red read-out of the digital clock beside his bed: 2:42 a.m. The night was slipping away, but he was no closer to quieting his thoughts than when he'd gone to bed.

Where was she?

He grabbed his cell phone and punched the redial button. "Answer, Larsen," he murmured in between rings. "Answer the damned phone."

But like before, the voice that came over the line was cool and stilted. "I'm not available to take your call. Please…"

Jack's hand convulsed and he slammed the phone onto the beside table, sending the battery careening onto the floor. He collapsed onto his back, his arm across his eyes as fear overwhelmed him.

The small control he'd maintained over his life was

slipping away, the voices in his head getting worse every minute. His partner had tried to kill him. The one woman who could light the darkness of his mind was gone.

With a punch of his pillow, he rolled onto his stomach and sank his face into the cool cotton. Larsen's scent filled his nostrils. Longing twisted him in knots. If he just knew she was all right he could deal with the rest, even if he never saw her again. But he was afraid he'd never find her if she didn't want to be found. His only choice was to focus on catching that white son of a bitch before he hurt anyone else. Before he got Larsen.

And hope he wasn't already too late.

Larsen stood under the hot shower spray, letting the droplets pelt her with a thousand stinging blows, begging the near-scalding water to wash away the horror that filled her mind.

Over and over, the scene played out in her head. The family destroyed, that little blond ponytail hanging as still as its owner.

Larsen turned the water temperature down and shoved her face under the spray, washing away the tears that burned her eyes. More than anything in the world, she wanted to forget what she'd seen and let Jack solve this case on his own. But he didn't know the albino would be at the Kennedy Center this afternoon.

And she did.

She turned off the water and grabbed a worn, white bath towel. If she took the Metro back into D.C. before she called him, he wouldn't be able to trace her to Virginia. She could claim to be in the Kennedy Center, tell him she'd seen the albino, and let him take it from there.

Safe. Certain. Risk-free.

The perfect plan.

* * *

Nothing ever went as planned.

Larsen paced beneath the soaring ceilings of the crowded Kennedy Center lobby, listening to Jack's answering machine for the fourteenth time. Why wasn't he answering his phone?

The silk scarf she'd bought in the gift store slipped as she tucked the phone into her purse. She grabbed the scarf and adjusted it to hide her hair. It didn't precisely go with the crop pants and T-shirt she'd picked up at the store this morning, but in this international city, a woman with head covering rarely garnered a second glance.

Larsen was counting on it. She knew the albino would show. If he recognized her....

The memory of her own death beneath the feet of Veronica's wedding guests ripped through her mind like talons through soft flesh, immobilizing her. *She couldn't do this.* But the vision of that small girl, her head bent at an impossible angle, shoved aside the other and she knew she could. *She had to. Someone* had to save that family.

Larsen eased behind a large potted fern and scanned for sign of the oddly dressed albino, the bald archer or the little girl in the pink sundress. Moments later, her eyes caught the flash of pink. Her heart lodged in her throat.

The father from her visions, a nice-looking, thirty-something businessman in a shirt and tie, walked between the two towheaded children. The little girl, her curly ponytail swinging, held the man's hand while the boy, a bundle of barely suppressed energy, darted ahead toward the short flight of stairs leading to the ticket-taker.

Larsen took a step toward them and stopped as the cold reality of what she needed to do washed over her. It wasn't enough to warn them not to go into the theater. She had to tell them why. *I'm a freak who sees death. And I've seen yours.*

She couldn't do it.

She *had* to do it, or those kids and their dad were going to die!

The breath froze in her lungs, the blood turned to slush in her veins.

Do it! But her feet wouldn't move.

As if hearing her inner shouting, the dad's gaze swung toward her, punching her in the gut with a fistful of guilt, then swung away.

Her heart thudded against her ribs. *Now!* But as she finally started forward, the dad handed over the tickets and the three disappeared into the theater.

Larsen blinked. *What had she done?*

She grabbed her phone and punched the redial with shaking fingers. "Jack, answer your damn phone!"

The bell rang through the theater lobby, signaling the imminent start of the show. *They were going to die.* One chance to stop them and she'd blown it.

In the soaring hallway, Larsen paced in an agitated little circle, her stomach roiling like a boat in a summer storm. Maybe it wasn't too late. They were still alive. They'd stay that way for another few minutes, but she had to get inside that theater and the show was sold out.

Yanking the scarf off her head, she strode up the short flight of stairs, pinning her most haughty Ice Bitch persona firmly in place.

"Miss…excuse me."

Larsen spared the slightly built retiree collecting the last-minute tickets a cool glance. "I'm checking something for Mr. Wright. I'll only be a minute." Then, without slowing her pace, she brushed by him and into the dark passage that separated the lobby from the gilt splendor of the theater.

At the top of the aisle, Larsen paused and looked out over the sea of heads, the pulse thudding in her ears. They were in here somewhere. *He* was in here. Her gaze zeroed in on the area where she'd seen the albino in her vision. Sure enough, his stark white head shone at its center.

Dread rose from her pores to crawl over her skin like slithering, blood-sucking leeches. *He'd kill her.* If she stayed in this theater, she was going to die. A child's laugh pierced the hum of excited voices. If she left, two children were going to die.

The lights dimmed. The music rose. *She was out of time.*

Larsen took a deep breath as she pulled the scarf out of her purse and laid it over her head, wrapping it around her mouth and nose.

Heart racing like a speedboat on the open river, she started down the aisle. "Ladies and gentlemen, there's been a report of a bomb in the theater. Please move quickly to the nearest exit."

The people close enough to hear her over the music jumped up and began to fill the aisles. For one breathless moment she thought her makeshift plan was going to work. Then she forgot herself and glanced at the albino.

Their gazes locked. Recognition flared.

No. She looked away, but not before she saw him open his mouth and knew it was too late. An eerie singing rose with the music, then became the only sound in the theater as hundreds of audience members, musicians and actors went suddenly, silently still.

Larsen stood trapped in the middle of an aisle clogged

with human statues, fear crawling up her throat. Her premonitions, as horrible as they'd been, hadn't prepared her for the real thing, for the singing that tore at her eardrums and sent terror flooding her heart.

She had to get out of here.

As she turned to run, she caught movement out of the corner of her eye. *The children.* They were staring at the singer just as they had in her vision.

"Run!" she shouted to their dad. "If you can hear me, run for your lives."

But even as the words burst from her mouth, the audience around them rose. With a terrible dread, Larsen knew what would happen next. She'd seen this movie and hated the ending. But there was nothing more she could do. She'd failed. The children and their father were going to die. And she right along with them if she didn't run.

She pushed between a frozen couple and dodged a small knot of teens as she ran up the aisle. Three rows to freedom. *Two.*

A beefy arm hooked around her neck, jerking her off her feet. A silent scream tore through her mind as she struggled in vain to free herself. *Too slow. Too late.* The pressure against her windpipe cut off her air. *She couldn't breathe.* Colored lights swam in her vision. Over the roar in her ears, she heard a child begin to scream.

And suddenly she was free.

The choking arm dropped away. Larsen sank to her knees, sucking in the precious air as the roaring in her ears slowly abated, leaving only the sound of the child's screams.

She pushed to her feet even as the statues collapsed to the ground like puppets cut from their strings. Only then did she realize the singing had stopped. Her gaze sought the source of the screaming, the place where she'd last seen the albino, and locked on Jack.

Jack. He had the white villain by the hair and was shoving a gag in his mouth.

Thank God. He'd gotten her message, after all. But the screaming went on, unchecked. Her gaze finally located the source, capsizing her heart. The little girl in the pink sundress writhed in her father's arms, raking her fingernails down her small face, leaving trails of blood.

The frantic father lunged for the albino, his unharmed son tight against his side. "What did you do to her? *What did you do to my daughter?*"

Jack caught Larsen's gaze and shook his head as if reading the question in her mind. "He touched her forehead," he shouted to the father over the child's screams. "That's it. I saw him do it right before I grabbed him."

He'd touched her. *What had he* done *to her?* What had *she* done by failing to keep them from going into that theater?

"Get out of here," Jack shouted to the grieving father. "Take your kids and get out of here in case I can't hold him. Larsen, you, too."

"Do you need help?" Larsen croaked, her throat raw.

"I've got backup on the way. Now get out of here!"

He didn't have to tell her again. She ran for the lobby feeling like she was still choking…this time on guilt.

"I'm going to kill you, *Sitheen.*"

Jack clenched his fists to keep from decking the white devil sitting across the table from him in the small interrogation room.

"You say that one more time and I'm going to kill *you.*

Now," Jack repeated, "I want to know how you hypnotized those people."

The suspect, who'd identified himself only as *Baleris*, watched him with that faint smile Jack was growing to hate. A turn of the mouth that was little more than a sneer in a face that made his skin crawl. He'd never seen skin so utterly absent of color, nor so…perfect. Not a blemish, not a line, not a hint of beard stubble marred his flesh.

Jack had seen his share of weird characters over the years, but this one took the prize. He ran his palm over his own prickly jaw. Twenty-nine hours he'd been at this. Twenty-nine long hours and all he had was a name. A single name. *Baleris*. And what in the hell kind of name was that?

Jack's patience was gone. He needed a shower and a shave and about forty-eight hours' sleep. He was nearly dizzy with exhaustion. The last time he'd slept at all had been two nights ago, but he'd spent most of that night worrying about Larsen.

The one bright spot in this whole sorry mess was that she was safe. Thank God he'd been in time to save her. He hadn't realized he'd wrecked his phone and she'd been trying to call him, until almost too late. He'd heard Larsen shouting as he entered the theater, a second before the bastard had started to sing.

He'd been in time to save Larsen. But he hadn't been in time to stop whatever had been done to make that little girl scream. And for that he was more determined than ever to nail this guy to the wall.

Baleris shifted in his seat, the gold flecks in his Robin Hood costume catching the fluorescent light. Who *was* this guy?

"You will bring me a ewer of wine."

Jack snorted. "You're getting nothing…*nothing*…until you tell me how you control these people."

He'd been so sure the answers would be obvious once he caught the SOB. But he'd strip-searched him himself and found not one damn thing to explain his ability. Everything pointed to his singing. And that just wasn't possible.

Nevertheless, Jack had ordered the intercom into the interrogation room turned off just in case. And he was afraid to leave him. He'd been so *sure*...

Now he was sure of nothing except that he couldn't leave the son of a bitch alone. Twenty-nine *hours*.

He shouldn't have called for backup. He shouldn't have brought him into the station at all. As it turned out, the suspect had put up no fight. Jack had had the perfect opportunity to disappear with him and to deal with him in any way he found effective. Instead he'd played it by the book. He always played it by the book. That was just who he was. A damned good cop.

But after twenty-nine hours, he was beginning to think he was a fool. All he'd been able to get out of the man was a single name and constant threats. *I'm going to kill you, Sitheen.* And who in the hell was *Sitheen?*

"What did you do to that little girl?"

Again, that miserable sneer.

Anger and lack of sleep were making his hands shake. "I'm going to learn your secrets, you bastard," Jack snarled.

"I am going to kill you, Sitheen."

Jack's temper snapped. He pulled his gun and aimed it at the man's crotch. The sudden flash of fear in the white man's eyes told him he had his attention at last.

"Answer my questions or I'll put another hole in your dick. Now!"

"Jack." The voice came through the intercom.

Dammit. They weren't supposed to be listening.

"What?"

His captain's voice came over, hard and humorless. "Out of there. Now. I want to talk to you."

Hell. He lowered the gun slowly. He was so tempted to shoot the man right between the eyes. But he'd done that once—shot him in the head. And it hadn't done a thing.

"Who are you?" he asked.

"I am going to kill you, Sitheen."

"Yeah, yeah, yeah. You said that already." Wearily, Jack rose to shove the gag back into the albino's mouth, then went out to meet with his police captain.

"Go home, Jack." Captain Greg Wilkins, a tall wiry man with silver hair, clasped Jack's shoulder. "You're going to be useless to us if you collapse from exhaustion."

"Captain…"

"That's an order, Detective. He's not going anywhere. This door will stay locked through the night. You'll be the first one in here in the morning."

Jack clenched his jaw. "Turn off the damned intercom and keep everyone away from the door."

His captain gave him a hard look.

"I mean it, Captain. The bastard's more dangerous than anyone we've ever had in here."

"He looks like a pansy."

"He'd deadly. He has abilities…he shouldn't have. Keep everyone away."

Greg met his gaze, then slowly nodded and handed him a stack of notes. "Some guy by the name of Harrison Rand has been trying to reach you all day. Says he wants to know what in the hell happened to his daughter at the Kennedy Center."

Jack sighed and took the messages. He tried to call the guy

on the way home, but had to leave a message telling him to meet him at the station at ten tomorrow morning. As Jack crawled into bed, he glanced at the clock. He had twelve hours before he faced the father of that little girl. And he intended to spend every second of it sleeping.

Jack almost didn't hear the phone.

His eyes felt like sandpaper as he squinted at the clock. Ten thirty p.m. Thirty minutes of sleep.

Exhaustion pulled at him but the phone wouldn't quit its incessant ringing. He grabbed for it, then forced his bleary gaze to focus on the Caller ID. Hank. *Hell*. Something had already gone wrong.

He flipped open the phone. "What's up?"

"I'm sorry, man."

Jack collapsed into his pillow in a tired heap. "What's happened?"

"I've got to kill you, man."

He blinked, trying to clear his head. "Hank, are you drunk?"

"You've done a terrible thing, Jack. I've got to kill you."

I'm going to kill you, Sitheen. The words knifed through his memory and he sat up, suddenly wide awake. "Who told you to kill me, buddy?"

"There's an APB out on you, man. We've been ordered to kill you. I shouldn't be telling you. We're coming for you now. But you're like a brother to me. Like the white brother I never had."

"Hank…" But his partner of ten years, and best friend, had hung up.

Jack stared at the phone. *I'm going to kill you, Sitheen.* No, the devil was sending Jack's men to do the deed.

Son of a *bitch*.

Chapter 7

Car breaks screeched to a stop in front of his house. Multiple cars. *Police cruisers.* Jack ran for the window, propelled by a surge of pure adrenalin. That white bastard, Baleris, was behind this, which meant Jack didn't stand a chance of reasoning with these men.

As he opened the back window, a volley of gunfire shattered the front. *Damn.* They hadn't called for him to give himself up. They hadn't given him any warning at all. *We've been ordered to kill you,* Henry had said. And that's exactly what they were going to do. Unless he got out of here, fast.

Jack leaped out the window and tore across the small fenced yard in nothing but his boxer shorts. As he dashed through the high gate, he heard the sound of gunfire move into his apartment. If he were a sound sleeper, he'd be dead.

But as he ran down the dark alley, it was fear for Larsen

that twisted his gut. If she was still in hiding, she might be safe. But what if she'd gone home? Baleris knew where she lived. He'd already sent his minions after her once.

Now the evil thing had the cops under his control, and he wanted them *both* dead. If Jack didn't find a way to warn her, it would be Larsen who would die.

She ought to be celebrating. The nightmare was over, the villain caught, the dad and his two kids saved from a terrible death. But as Larsen stood, barefoot, in front of the microwave oven in her houseboat, waiting for the water to heat for a cup of tea, the pulsing, aching knots that twisted her stomach only seemed to worsen.

She pressed her fist against her abdomen and the soft knit shortie pajamas she'd donned for bed. A day and a half since the incident at the Kennedy Center and the ache wouldn't go away. She could still hear that little girl's screams.

The microwave beeped. Larsen dropped a tea bag into the steaming water and carried the mug to the sofa. She couldn't remember when she'd felt so lousy. Or so lonely. She missed Jack. She kept thinking he'd call her. Even his probing questions would be better than this…silence. Had he forgotten her so quickly?

And wasn't that what she wanted? As she took a sip of the hot tea, her cell phone rang. It was nearly eleven. Too late for most callers, but maybe not for Jack? Maybe he hadn't forgotten her, after all. She set down the warm mug and grabbed the phone from the coffee table.

"Hello?"

"He's turned the M.P.D.," Jack said without preamble.

Larsen blinked. "He's what?"

"He's turned the cops. Larsen, *tell me you didn't go home.*"

"Where else would I go? It's over, isn't it? What do you mean he's—?"

"Get out! If they're not there already, they will be at any minute."

He wasn't making any sense. Or maybe her brain was just too tired to make sense of what he was saying, but his urgency came through loud and clear, easing her pulse into second gear.

"Where should I go?"

"Get in your car and drive. Then call—"

The window behind her shattered on a crack of gunfire. A small squeal escaped her throat as she fell to her knees behind the sofa.

"Jack…"

A second shot hit the kitchen light. More bullets sprayed the outside of the houseboat.

"Larsen, get out of there! Into the river. It's your only chance. I'll find you."

Terror pinned her to the floor as bullets took out the lamp beside the sofa, throwing the houseboat into darkness.

Was he crazy? "I can't!" If she stood, they'd kill her.

"Larsen, go!"

Her pulse pounded in her ears as the sound of gunfire shredded her nerves. *They were going to kill her.* Jack was right. She had to try to escape. No one had boarded the boat yet. She'd have felt them. They were shooting from the dock, which might mean she could escape out the back door.

"Oh, hell, oh, hell, oh, hell. I'm going!" Squeezing her eyes closed, she dropped the phone. It was now or never. She sprang up and ran for the back door as bullets peppered the walls and broke every pane of glass in the boat. In one continuous motion, she jerked open the door, ran and dove over the rail without looking, knowing the slightest hesitation would end her life. She hit the water surrounded by a hail of bullets.

Jack's hands gripped the steering wheel of the Toyota Highlander he'd coerced from one of his neighbors as he tore through the streets of D.C. toward the marina, his knuckles white as that devil's skin, his palms slick with sweat.

Larsen. He had to reach her.

The remembered sound of gunfire and breaking glass echoed across his brain, drowning out the normal voices that filled his head, sending a rare pain arcing through his chest. She couldn't have survived such an attack. He'd get there only to find her bullet-riddled body floating in the river beside her boat.

"No." He slammed his hand against the steering wheel. She *had* to survive. He needed her, dammit.

It was his fault. He'd had him. *Had* him. He should have killed the albino when he'd had the chance. Instead, he'd let him turn the tables on him, turn his own people against him. Now he'd sent Jack's fellow cops to snuff out the one light that had begun to shine through the darkness of his life. Larsen.

He pulled into a parking lot across the street from the marina, then slid out into the warm night in nothing but his boxers, palming the car keys. The gravelly asphalt was rough beneath his bare feet, but his fear was too great and his heart too heavy for the discomfort to matter.

Gunfire peppered the stillness of the night, igniting hope within him. If Larsen were dead, they wouldn't still be shooting, would they? He couldn't be sure. They weren't in their right minds.

The irony didn't elude him. He, who had been dealing with encroaching madness all his life, was the most sane man on the force tonight. He crossed the street and eased his way into the shadows surrounding the marina office. Immediately, he felt the presence of another and went for his gun, but his hand encountered nothing but cotton fabric.

"Who's there?" He could just make out a shape pressed against the wall.

"Jack?" The voice, so low it was barely more than a breath on the night breeze, sent his heart soaring.

"Larsen."

He closed the distance between them and pulled her soaked body against him, the voices in his head evaporating as if sharing his joy in her survival. His nostrils filled with the smell of fish and salt water and God knew what else, but he pressed his cheek against her wet hair and held her tight. Never in his life had he felt such knee-buckling relief.

He felt her tremble and eased her away from him. "We've got to get out of here."

"That gets my vote."

His admiration for her swelled tenfold. Despite the trembling of her body, her voice was strong and sure. Grabbing her wet hand, he eased to the edge of the shadows. While the gunfire continued unabated at the water's edge, the pair stole across the street, climbed into the borrowed SUV and escaped.

Larsen huddled in the front seat of Jack's car, wet and cold. Shaking. *Oh, my God.* They'd tried to kill her. They'd shot at her, bullets slicing through her home, zinging through the water around her when she'd tried to escape. She'd thought she was going to die. *Again.* Against the wet leather seat, her body quivered like a building about to implode.

Cold, so cold. Not just her damp, sticky skin or her wet, matted hair. She was cold all the way down into her bones, into her blood. Cold with fear of an enemy who was too strong. An enemy who wanted her dead. And she wasn't even sure why.

A sneeze tore through her as she shivered.

Jack's warm hand brushed her damp shoulder. "How did you get away?"

She wiped her runny nose on the sleeve of her wet shirt, her gaze skimming over the needle-thin Washington Monument rising from a distant pool of light.

"I dove, like you said, then circled back under the boat and two more before I surfaced. They kept shooting where I went in. *Right* where I went in. Like they couldn't figure out I might have swum away. I climbed out and escaped without any of them even looking at me."

"They're hypnotized."

"He's getting stronger."

Jack looked at her sharply. "Why do you say that?"

Her heart lurched. For a moment she thought she'd given herself away again, but then realized she hadn't. "You saw the ones he controlled in the Kennedy Center. They looked like zombies. Your cops were driving, shooting…*almost like normal.*"

The lights of a passing car illuminated the lines of strain on Jack's face. "Except they kept shooting in the exact same spot."

"True. I guess there wasn't a *lot* of brain function."

Jack slammed his fist against the steering wheel. "How in the hell is he doing it?"

How in the hell was any of this happening? She'd thought it was over. Less than an hour ago, she'd sat on the sofa with a cup of tea, for heaven's sakes. Now they were on the run with nothing but the river-soaked clothes on their backs.

Her gaze skimmed over Jack's half-naked form. Strike that. *Not* the clothes on his back. A giggle erupted from her mouth, followed by another, but her giggles quickly turned hysterical. It was just too damn... awful. The D.C. police force was using her for target practice and her beloved boat now had more holes than a window screen. She began to cry in earnest. Not until after Jack crossed the Potomac into the Virginia suburbs did she manage to regain some measure of control.

Finally she wiped her eyes with the heels of her hands and looked at the man beside her. His gaze was fixed on the road, his mouth set in a grim line. "What are we going to do, Jack?"

He reached for her, covering her hand and giving a quick squeeze. His gaze met hers, a fine layer of sympathy softening the hard core of determination.

"We're going to survive, Larsen. The first thing we're going to do is survive."

Chapter 8

Jack pulled the stolen SUV into the parking lot of a deserted industrial park. It was dangerous to stay with the vehicle, but Larsen needed to get warm and at least partially dry before he exposed her to the night air. He glanced at her, huddled against the door, looking as lost as he felt.

Larsen glanced over at him as he pulled the car behind the low white building, parked it in the shadows and turned off the engine. "What are we doing?" she asked, her voice tight. She was visibly shivering.

"We're almost out of gas."

Larsen's head dropped back against the seat with a defeated, disbelieving sigh. "And we have no money." He could barely see her in the dark, but in the glow of the dashboard light he watched the way her lush lips moved with every word.

"No." He got out, came around to her side and opened her car door.

"Where are we going?"

"The backseat." He ushered her into the back and climbed in behind her.

"This is a bit high-schoolish, isn't it?" Her teeth were clattering together.

He pulled her against him, silencing the noise in his head as he wrapped his arms around her. "You want to complain or you want to get warm?"

She tilted her wet head against his shoulder. "W-warm."

A wet strand of her hair brushed his cheek and he pulled her closer. The night was mild enough that he didn't feel the urgency to get her out of her wet clothes. Besides, trying to stay unaffected by her naked body was a hell of a lot more than he could handle right now.

"We need to talk," he said, running his hand up and down her arm. He felt her tense, felt her muscles bunch as if she were about to pull away.

"Larsen…if we're going to get out of this alive, you can't keep holding out on me. I've got to know what you know."

"You already d-do. I swear to you, Jack, if I had any information that might help us get out of this mess, I'd share it. But I don't. Can't you *please* believe me?"

The cop in him didn't want to let it go, but he could feel her body quaking with cold and he knew…he *knew*…she was as much a victim in this little scenario as he was. Trusting her when she wouldn't trust him was damned hard. But his gut told him to do it anyway. Whatever she was hiding wasn't important. Or at least it would wait until later…until their lives were no longer in imminent danger.

"Yeah," he sighed against her hair. "I believe you."

He felt her slowly relax beneath his hands. Her arms went around his middle and she pressed her shivering body tight against him. Hard nipples brushed his bare chest through the thin, damp fabric of her shirt, making every one of his senses stand at full attention.

Her shivering was becoming contagious, but his own body's quaking had nothing to do with cold and everything to do with heat. His hands shook as he stroked her arm, his palm sliding along the raised gooseflesh. Flesh that was slowly evening out, warming beneath his touch.

Larsen pressed her lips against the sensitive skin beneath his ear, sending shards of need slicing through him. If he wasn't such a gentleman, he'd have her naked and beneath him in a heartbeat. Now *that* would warm her up.

Get a grip, Hallihan. She'd been through enough tonight. She didn't need to fend off his advances, too.

Then something warm and damp touched his neck. Jack froze. It couldn't have been. Could it?

There. He felt it again. Definitely her sweet little tongue.

"Larsen…" His voice sounded strangled to his own ears.

"You smell good."

A laugh escaped his throat on a burst of air. "I don't know why. I haven't had a shower in two days."

"Maybe because I smell like the Potomac."

He slipped a hand into her damp hair and nuzzled her cheek. "No you don't. You smell like…like every fantasy I've ever had."

"You must have had some weird fantasies, Detective. Do you dream of mermaids often?"

He put her away from him far enough to frame her face.

In the dim glow of a distant streetlight, their gazes met and locked. "No," he whispered. "I dream of you."

Then he kissed her. He couldn't have stopped himself for any amount of money in the world. Her lips beckoned. Her eyes, her heat. He had to taste her and taste her *now*.

But the moment their mouths came together, he knew it was a mistake. Their near-death experience was acting as a powerful aphrodisiac. As if he needed any additional kindling for the fire that simmered just beneath the surface whenever he was near her.

He devoured her mouth in an explosion of need, drinking her scent, her taste, the very feel of her tongue wrapped around his and the press of her soft breasts against his chest. Too much fabric. He reached for the hem of her shirt and pulled it over her head. If he didn't feel her bare flesh against his, he'd go insane—right here. Right now.

If he didn't bury himself inside her he'd die.

"Jack," she breathed into his mouth as he tossed her shirt against the back window and pulled her against him. Skin met skin, the hard tips of her breasts slid over his chest as she straddled him. Heat built at his groin as his hard arousal strained against his cotton boxers.

He grabbed her buttocks and pressed her hard against him, letting her feel his need. She began to rock against him in her soft little shorts, a whisper of fabric keeping them apart. His thumbs swept under the bottom hems of the shorts to encounter bare flesh. No panties barred his way.

Her small hand reached low between them to cup his erection, setting him aflame and pulling a groan from his throat.

"Larsen…" She was open to him. Wanting him. And, oh, how he wanted her.

Dipping his head, he pulled one bare breast into his mouth, the soft tip turning hard under his stroking tongue. He hadn't been wrong. She tasted like nectar. *Heaven.*

He slid his hand between them, burrowing it under the loose opening of her shorts until he found her moist, hot center. As he pushed his finger deep inside her, she gasped and rocked against his hand. "Jack…" Her passion spurred his own until he was sweating from the need to take her.

Releasing her breast, he shifted his hold on her. His hand shaking with a fine need, his finger deep inside her, he ran his thumb lightly over the nub that would pleasure her most. "Do you want this?"

"Yes." The word exploded on a sigh, wrapping him in rich, hot silk.

Jack squeezed his eyes closed against the pain of his own arousal and the exquisite joy of hers. Her body was tight and perfect, the finest of instruments tuned to his touch. Passion rose to her skin, filling his nostrils, his loins, heating his blood as he stroked her. The noises in her throat built until whimpers grew to the sexiest little shouts he'd ever heard.

He kissed her, swallowing her scream of satisfaction as she exploded, feeling the hard contractions around his buried finger and the quaking of her body as she came unraveled in his arms.

Larsen pulled back, wrenching her mouth from his. "Jack," she gasped. "I want you. *Now.*"

Every cell in his body, every molecule, strained to give her what she wanted. What he *craved.* Never in his life had he wanted anything more than to bury his hard erection deep inside her wet, hot sheath, to bring her to another climax as he found his own.

His hands shook with the need to push himself into the

opening of her shorts and pull her down on him. So simple. Never had anything been so simple. Or so complicated.

"We can't, Larsen." The words shredded his throat. "We don't have a condom." And he would not risk bringing a child into this world that would suffer from the madness that killed his father and was slowly killing him.

She stilled. Then with a harsh exhale, she collapsed against him. "You don't travel very well prepared, Jack Hallihan."

He ran his palm up her bare back and into her soft hair. "Honey, if I'd had any idea I'd need a condom tonight, I'd have gone to sleep with one taped to my butt."

She laughed and patted his cheek. "Nice visual, Detective." On a groan, she slipped her arms around his neck and he gathered her tight against the raging need of his body. "The one time I actually *want* to do it."

Slowly, he felt her melt against him and knew she was falling asleep. For a long time he held her, feeling the gentle rise and fall of her bare chest against his, the soft whisper of her breath against his neck. Holding her not only quieted his brain, but soothed the aching fear in his chest, filling him with a surprising tenderness.

He would do whatever it took to keep her safe. He wouldn't let anything happen to her. He couldn't. She was becoming more important to him by the moment, in ways he'd never anticipated.

"Damn!"

Larsen reared back, startled out of a deep sleep, still in Jack's arms. "What's the matter?" she asked, trying to pry her eyes open. It wasn't exactly daylight, but it was no longer dark outside.

"Get dressed quick," Jack said, sliding her onto the seat

beside him. He reached for the door handle. "I can't believe I fell asleep. It's almost sunrise. We've got to get out of here before someone finds us."

Memory came back with a rush, nearly swamping her. The bullets flying through her houseboat, her dive into the cool Potomac, Jack's finger deep inside her.

She groaned silently, knowing she'd acted like a horny teenager, begging him to do her in whatever way possible. Heat burned her cheeks.

She'd let him get too close. Under the circumstances, after all they'd been through last night, she could probably be excused for the lapse, but bottom line, she didn't let *anyone* get that close, emotionally or physically. Since she couldn't put the physical distance between them—they were stuck with one another until they found a way out of this mess—she needed to widen the distance between them some other way.

While she struggled back into her damp top, Jack fished a large, old-fashioned cell phone out of the glove compartment.

"Is that the one you used to call me?"

"Yeah. I found it after I stole the car."

Larsen gaped at him, but ignored the hand he offered and scrambled out on her own. "You did not steal a car. You're a cop."

The morning was damp. Dew seemed to hang in the air, coating everything it touched. Even the asphalt beneath her bare feet felt wet. At least her clothes and hair had mostly dried during the night.

"Well, it wasn't armed robbery, but I probably scared five years off the life of the eighty-year-old owner. I told him I needed the car on urgent police business."

"Yeah, well, I guess things couldn't get much more urgent." She shoved her mussed hair off her face and licked dry, salty lips as they crossed the narrow drive to the trees beyond. "So, if you can steal a car, why not steal a tank of gas?"

Jack sighed. "Don't think I didn't consider it. But most gas stations have security cameras. They'll be able to pinpoint our location and potentially capture us before we get much beyond the gas station. The way it stands, no one knows where we are. For now. They'll be looking for the SUV by now. That's why we've got to get as far away from it as we can."

"We need help, Jack. We've got the phone. Why don't we call someone?"

"I meant to do that last night, then fell asleep." Jack made a sound of frustration. "Honest to God, I don't know who I can trust anymore. Not the M.P.D. I could call one of my neighbors, maybe, but how do I know the bastard isn't controlling them, too?"

"We need someone he *can't* control. What about the dad at the Kennedy Center?"

Jack stopped abruptly. *"Damn."*

"What?"

"I told him to meet me at the station this morning."

"The *police* station?"

"Yeah. If that son-of-a-bitch sees him, he'll kill him. He already knows he can't control him."

"We've got to warn him."

"I don't have his number." But his eyes narrowed with concentration. "Maybe I can remember. The first three were the same as mine. But what were the last?" he asked, muttering to himself. "Four, four something. Or maybe four, five. Eight seven. The last two were eight seven. Definitely eight seven. Or seven eight?"

Larsen watched with bemused anxiety as he dialed the

numbers on the oversize phone. That man and his kids could *not* die. Not after all they'd been through.

"Hello? Is this Mrs. Rand?" A moment later he pulled the phone from his ear. Larsen could hear the virulent Spanish from where she walked, several feet away. "I guess not," Jack muttered, disconnecting the call.

They were deep in the woods by the time Jack found the man they were looking for. The volume was set so high on the phone, he had to hold it away from his ear, allowing Larsen to hear both sides of the conversation.

"Mr. Rand, this is Detective Jack Hallihan from the Metro Police."

To Larsen's surprise, the man didn't question the early hour of Jack's call. "Thanks for getting back to me, Detective. Are we still on for ten?"

"No. It's not safe. In fact, it's imperative you and your family leave your home at once. Leave town for a couple of weeks, if you can manage it."

"What in God's name is going on?" Harrison Rand demanded, his voice hard.

"The man who hurt your daughter is somehow controlling the minds of the entire police department just as he did the audience in the Kennedy Center."

"How?"

"I wish I knew. Only a handful of us can't be controlled. He sent my own men to kill me last night. There's every reason to believe he'll try to get to you and your kids, as well."

The man on the other end of the phone went momentarily silent. "My kids aren't here. My ex-wife swooped in and grabbed them out of here yesterday."

"How's your daughter?"

"I don't know." Even from a distance Larsen could hear the pain and frustration in those words. "We had to drug her to stop her screaming. She hasn't spoken a word since she woke up. Doesn't even seem to know us. That's why I wanted to talk to you. I want to know who that son of a bitch is and *what in the hell he did to my daughter.*"

"You and me both."

"What *do* you know?"

Jack met Larsen's gaze. "Tell you what. I need a ride back into town for myself and another who's caught up in this."

"The woman in the scarf?"

Jack's brows dipped in confusion, but Larsen made a wry face and nodded.

"Yeah. Apparently so. Come get us and we'll fill you in on the way back."

"Deal."

Jack gave him their location, though how he knew it from the surrounding woods was beyond Larsen, then hung up.

She looked at him thoughtfully. "We're trusting a complete stranger, you know."

"I know. But Rand's got as much at stake in this as we do, and he can't be hypnotized. That alone is reason enough." He made a rueful twist of his mouth. "My gut says I can trust him."

Larsen heard the certainty in his tone and glanced at him, meeting his gaze for the first time since she woke. Something leaped between them. Awareness. *Memory.*

She tore her gaze from his and cleared her throat. "Aren't we putting him in danger by involving him?"

"He's already in danger. Just the fact he wasn't controlled makes him a prime target."

"Then what about…" She stopped herself and thought

about what she knew before she said too much yet again. "Was there anyone else, anyone at Tony Jingles?"

"Hell," he said. "Brenda Kettering. I've got to reach her, too." He made a few phone calls and warned the woman Larsen had watched strangled by her own husband—a premonition that had, thankfully, not come entirely true.

The sun rose over the horizon, spearing through the trees as the pair walked in silence. Larsen strode gingerly over the painful twigs and rocks, her feet soft and uncalloused. Jack didn't try to take her hand again. Neither did he try to draw her out. Finally, through the trees, a school came into view.

At the woods' edge, Jack brought them to a halt. He called Harrison Rand and told him where to meet them, then tossed the phone on the ground and sat beside it, looking up at her.

"How did you sleep?" he asked.

Larsen raised a brow. "Fine." After that amazing release of tension, she'd slept like a baby. "Why?"

"I slept well enough, but those four hours barely made up for all the sleep I've lost the past few nights. Do you feel up to keeping watch while I nap?"

He'd be asleep—she wouldn't have to wonder what he was thinking…what he was remembering. "Absolutely. Sleep away."

Something warm, yet guarded, moved in his eyes. "Can I use your lap as a pillow?"

"Jack…" She was trying to regain some distance between them. This wasn't the way to get it.

His gaze wrapped her in cotton. "I won't sleep unless I know you're safe."

She gave up the fight. How could she possibly argue with him over that? He wanted to lay his head in her lap so that he'd know she was safe. To protect her.

He was making it awfully hard to retain any distance.

Larsen sighed. "Suit yourself." She sat beside him, leaning back against a thick oak where she could watch for their ride.

Jack rolled sideways and laid his head in her lap. "He has a royal blue convertible," he said, closing his eyes.

"Perfect," she said dryly. "A car that won't draw attention."

A smile appeared briefly on his mouth. "He'll drive through the parking lot twice. Wake me up when you see him…or anything else that looks or sounds suspicious."

"Aye, aye. Now go to sleep."

He took her hand and slid his fingers between hers. But as he pulled their joined hands against his heart, Larsen's vision began to waver. *No.* She tensed for the onslaught of another premonition.

"What's the matter?" Jack stared up at her.

"Nothing." This vision wasn't like the others. No splitting pain. No complete blackout. Over Jack's face was superimposed a tiny bedroom of sorts, small and sunlit and very, very rustic. Straw littered the floor and the window was simply a hole in the wall, open to the outside, allowing the sun to stream in.

"I think I left the iron on," she told him. "But I guess it doesn't matter now. Go to sleep." She consciously worked to slow her speeding pulse. She didn't know what was happening, only that Jack could never find out.

The vision became clearer and, oddly, noisier as her real vision faded. Unlike her death premonitions, she could hear sounds in this one. She could hear chickens squawking. And the sound of a girl crying.

A door opened and two women bustled in, middle-aged women dressed like peasants from long ago, their dresses long and drab, covered by stained aprons, their hair completely covered by white fabric. Wimples? Was that the term? They looked like they'd stepped out of the Middle Ages.

It seemed so real. She could almost feel the sun pouring into that small room.

The women crossed to the bed and Larsen's vision followed, allowing her a view of the owner of the tears. A girl of perhaps ten or eleven, she was sitting on the edge of the bed, her head in her hands, her fingers digging into her scalp. The women began to speak, but the words were in an old language Larsen couldn't understand. Gaelic, perhaps?

One of the women knelt in front of the girl and pulled her hands from her head. The girl, a pale thing with a narrow face and a smattering of freckles, looked at her with an expression filled with dread. But the older woman was there to do a job and she didn't seem the least concerned about the girl's fear.

She motioned the girl to lie down, but the girl shook her head fearfully. The other woman grabbed the child and held her while the first woman placed her thumbs on the girl's temples and began to chant, the same odd words over and over.

Eslius turatus a quari er siedi. Eslius turatus a quari er siedi.

The girl began to writhe and scream. The women held her, ignoring her terror.

And then it was over. The girl stilled, her eyes wide. Her expression turned to wonder, a grin blossoming on her thin face as she began to talk excitedly to the woman who'd caused her so much pain.

The woman smiled at her with warmth and love, grabbed the child's face in her hands and planted a kiss on her thin cheek.

Larsen came back to herself with a smile, a smile that quickly died. She blinked and looked around, afraid something had happened while she'd zoned out, but all was still and quiet as before.

Jack snored softly on her lap.

What just happened? It wasn't a premonition. Was it? Premonitions foretold the future, yet everything in that sun-filled room had screamed the distant past.

Heaven help her.

She dropped her head back until it hit the tree with a soft thud as tears stung her eyes.

All she wanted was to be normal. To live a life without lies and secrets and subterfuge.

Without visions.

Instead, her visions were spinning out of control, multiplying, transforming. Minute by minute her life was growing stranger, more frightening.

More deadly.

Chapter 9

"You're not going after Baleris with me."

Jack stormed across the small, sparsely furnished living room of the borrowed Massachusetts Avenue apartment. His bare feet tread the worn carpet, while a car horn blared on the street four stories below, ratcheting his blood pressure another notch.

As promised, Harrison Rand had picked them up several hours earlier and deposited them in his brother Charlie's currently unoccupied apartment in Adams Morgan, not far from Dupont Circle. Then he'd gone to snatch his kids out of his ex-wife's hands before the albino managed to turn her, too. He'd promised to return tomorrow, leaving Jack on his own to attempt another capture of the Pied Piper.

No, not on his own. Larsen wanted in on the action, but he refused to put her in that kind of danger.

She sat on the stool at the counter that separated the small kitchen from the living room, smelling like soap-scented heaven and looking like a queen despite the oversize T-shirt and men's jeans she'd borrowed from the dresser drawer. Her damp hair curled around her jaw.

"You're staying here where you'll be safe," he told her. Right here, where no one could find her or shoot at her. Where he wouldn't come close to losing her yet again.

"Jack, you're not being reasonable. The only way to catch him is to stake out the police station, and you can't do it. Every cop in that place will recognize you. You need my help."

"I'll find another way."

She crossed her arms over her chest. "I'm going with you."

Damned stubborn woman. Her chin was high, her full mouth set and determined. And he wanted her with a fire that hadn't dimmed since he'd nearly made love to her last night before coming, screeching, to his senses.

Her golden brown eyes weren't flashing with passion this morning, but with the light of battle. A battle he didn't intend to let her win.

"You're staying here."

"You can't go after him alone."

Jack turned away, running a hand through his hair. Why did he even try to argue with her? She was a lawyer, dammit. A professional arguer.

He stalked into the kitchen and rooted through the cupboards until he found a glass, then filled it with tap water and drank it in one long gulp.

He needed Harrison here to back him up. In more ways than one. The man was all right. He'd left them with money and the keys to his brother's car, since his brother, Charlie, was out of the country on some top-secret gig. Harrison wanted the white devil caught, hung and castrated every bit as much as he and Larsen did. This time they'd do it themselves.

Meanwhile, he and Larsen were on their own. Alone. In an apartment with condoms. He knew because he'd looked in the medicine cabinet. Heat coiled low in his body. How in the hell was he supposed to stay in the same apartment with her when all he could think of was making love to her until she came again, this time with him buried deep inside her?

Unfortunately, she didn't seem to be having any such problems. Sometime between falling asleep in his arms and waking up this morning, she'd retreated behind her walls. She was acting as if nothing had happened between them last night. Or as if she wished nothing had. Which was so much worse, dammit.

He wanted her safe in his bed. She wanted to fight at his side. She was killing him on every front.

"I'm not risking your life, Larsen." She belonged in the courtroom, in neat lawyer clothes, protecting abused women and children, not running from a band of murderers. Certainly not confronting them.

He set the glass in the sink. The discussion was *over.*

As he turned, Larsen hopped off the bar stool and came around the counter. "All I need is a bit of a disguise. Maybe some hair dye." She ran a hand through her damp gold locks. "I've always wanted to be a brunette."

His gut tightened and churned at the thought of putting her life in danger yet again. How had she, in just a matter of days, become so vital to him? She was the key to his sanity. But when he thought of losing her, he felt the ache not in his head but deep in his chest.

"No, Larsen. N-o. You're staying safe if I have to tie you

to the bed." He groaned at the picture *that* put in mind. With a frustrated yank, he opened the refrigerator door and stared at the nearly empty shelves. A half-full jar of dill pickles, an inch of ketchup and a chunk of fuzzy green cheese were all that occupied the fridge. Not only wasn't Charlie here often, he hadn't been here in a while.

"I can certainly get a lot closer to the albino than you." Larsen peered over his shoulder. "Yikes. I guess we won't be eating in."

"I'm going to have to do some shopping. *You're* staying here."

"What are you trying to do, make me your prisoner?"

Tempting. So tempting. He turned on her, grabbing her upper arms, causing the noise to evaporate from his head. *"I'm trying to keep you alive."*

She looked at him calmly, almost pityingly, and lifted that eyebrow. "By getting yourself killed?"

"By not getting *you* killed."

Her eyes softened, the hard edge of stubbornness melting.

"Jack, this is a war, whether you've noticed or not. You need to think of me as one of your soldiers."

The spicy scent of her newly clean hair wrapped itself around him as he slid his fingers over the soft flesh of her arms, his gaze falling to her lush mouth. His grip tightened as the need to pull her against him nearly overpowered his control.

"You've got to forget I'm a woman," she said, her voice low. Husky.

"Like hell." He hauled her against him and kissed her like he'd wanted to all morning. As he'd wanted to since the first time he'd seen her. With passion and fire and little gentleness.

For a few joyous moments she rose with him, meeting his tongue thrust for thrust, digging her slender fingers into his hair. Victory surged through him on a burst of hot need. He wanted her. He wanted her gasping and moaning the way she was last night, but this time he'd be buried deep inside her, their bodies slick and naked when she came.

Larsen lifted her soft hands to his chest and pushed him away. He nearly sank to his knees, ready to beg. She retreated to the other side of the counter, putting an effective barrier between them.

She rested her forearms on the Formica and leaned toward him. "So, tell me this, Jack Hallihan. You want to go off and play cowboy—"

"Cop. I want to play cop."

Her mouth, still damp and swollen from his kiss, twitched. "All right, so you want to play cop." The flicker of humor evaporated from her eyes. "What am I supposed to do if you're caught? If you're killed?"

He mirrored her position, covering her hands where they touched, leaning forward until he could see the flecks of gold in her eyes. "I'm not going to get killed."

Her gaze searched his face, a gaze that burrowed inside his chest. "If you die, I'm the next line of defense. If you die, I've got to fight them alone."

"I'm not going to die."

She rolled her eyes on a sigh of exasperation and pulled her hands from his. "Right. There's no danger. Which is why you won't let me go with you."

She crossed her arms over her chest. "What general fights a battle one soldier at a time? His men would just get picked off that way. There's power in numbers. You know that. Let's maximize our chance of success right from the beginning."

Her eyes glowed with earnest determination. The worst of

it was, he knew she was right. If she were anyone else, he'd agree. But he couldn't bear the thought of losing her.

With a sigh, he pulled away from her and straightened. She was right.

"You win. We'll go after him together." He saw the flash of victory in her eyes. "But..." He crossed his arms over his chest, mirroring her stance. "You're not going anywhere without a disguise, and I mean a disguise so perfect your own grandmother wouldn't recognize you."

She nodded soberly, but he saw the sparkle in her eyes. "I'll need some supplies."

"Make me a list." Her mouth opened to argue, but he held up his hand. "Just the things you need for your disguise."

Larsen nodded. "Okay. But if you're not back in half an hour, I'm coming to search for you."

And he knew she would.

Larsen stared at the business section of the *Washington Post* spread out in front of her, her hands clasping the hot Starbucks' cup so hard she was half afraid she was going to crush it. She forced the air in and out of her lungs in a slow, steady pace, desperately trying to ignore the two cops behind her ordering lattes. Two cops who probably read body language as well as Jack. Two cops who, if they realized who she was, would kill her.

Of course, the chances they'd recognize her were slim. Jack's little shopping trip had netted her a snug-fitting black T-shirt, black cargo pants and flip-flops, along with hair dye, eyeliner and lipstick all in the same dark shade.

Look calm. Casual. Not guilty.

She glanced out the window at the police station across the

street, taking as normal a sip of her sixth cup of coffee as she could manage. She'd been sitting here drinking and reading for nearly two hours and still no sign of the albino. Her hand shook only slightly as she set the cup on the table in front of her and went back to pretending to read the paper.

She'd been so determined to help Jack with this stakeout. What was she thinking? *She could get herself killed doing this.*

Then again, Jack couldn't very well have done it. For the past two hours a steady stream of cops had paraded in and out of the little shop, grabbing espresso, cookies or frozen coffee confections. And while a bit of black—a *lot* of black—had turned her from lawyer to Goth queen, no disguise was going to keep Jack's fellow cops from recognizing *him*.

No, this was the right plan. The only plan.

When she got a glimpse of the albino, she'd call Jack and he'd take it from there. She'd quit arguing about not being included in the take-down. Just the thought of going anywhere near that white lowlife again made her heart thud with fear.

Out of the corner of her eye she saw the cops leave. She took a deep breath and let it out slowly, thankfully, then jumped when her new cell phone vibrated against her hip. She grabbed it out of her pocket.

"Hello?"

"I'm stuck in traffic two streets over," Jack said, his voice sharp with frustration. He'd spent the past two hours circling the neighborhoods nearby, prepared to tail the albino if he left by car, or to ditch the car and follow him on foot. "Some idiot hit a garbage truck. You doing okay?"

"Peachy."

"Bored out of your mind?"

"You could say that." Though terrified was probably more accurate.

Jack chuckled. "Stakeouts are the worst. Just don't get so bored you forget to watch."

She sank into the rich, calming sound of his voice. "Yeah, well, I can't imagine missing what *I'm* looking for." A startlingly white man in a tunic and leggings tended to stand out in D.C. "I'm getting hungry. Thought I might go grab a sandwich."

"Don't they have sandwiches at Starbucks?"

"Sure, but…"

"You've been there too long already. Time to move on."

"Exactly."

"There's a deli at the other end of the block."

"You're reading my mind." Which was a good thing since she had to be careful what she said out loud in the small, always-crowded coffee shop.

She started to fold the paper. "I'll give you a call when…" Her gaze flicked toward the station just as a familiar figure stepped out.

"Jack…"

"What's happening?" Jack demanded.

"My little buddy with the bow."

"The girl who shot you?"

"That's the one." Her pulse, already racing from an overload of caffeine and adrenaline, hit the accelerator. "She's just leaving."

The small, barefoot figure skipped down the steps of the station sporting a Nationals baseball cap and her usual uniform of Redskins T-shirt and oversize jeans.

"Alone?"

"Yes."

"I can't get there. I'm going to have to…" A car honked in the background. "*Hell.* Does she appear to be armed?"

"No. At least not the way she was last time." She lowered her voice. "That T-shirt could hide anything."

"Follow her. I'll be there as soon as I can. Larsen, keep your distance and don't go inside any buildings, do you understand? Watch where she goes and I'll take if from there. If she makes you, get out of there."

"Got it, chief." Larsen snapped her phone closed and rose on trembling legs, her pulse pounding in her throat. She now understood why she'd never thought about being a cop, never even considered going into the military.

The rush of fear was something she absolutely detested. Unfortunately she'd fought long and hard to win a place on the front line of this battle when Jack had wanted to keep her safely behind the scenes. But safety was an illusion. If they didn't catch the albino, they'd both be dead before the week was out.

Taking a deep breath, she pushed open the door and stepped out onto the sidewalk and into a blast of humid heat. Police cars lined the street in front of the station, making her feel like a duck in a shooting gallery. Were the guns even now rising…aiming…?

Stop it. If she didn't quit thinking about it, she was going to make herself sick. If someone had a gun trained on her, then her life was over. Period. There wasn't anything she could do about it except hide. And hiding wasn't an option.

She had a bald girl to follow.

Larsen hurried her pace and pushed through a small knot of suited businessmen until she was close enough to keep a good eye on her.

She still had a hard time reconciling the shy girl sweetly wistful over a slice of wedding cake with her cold-blooded assailant. To Larsen's relief, the girl never once glanced over her shoulder, but walked with quick if uncertain steps, looking neither right nor left. When she turned down a side street, Larsen followed, but allowed a little more space between them. The street was more residential than commercial and lacked the pedestrians of the main road.

Larsen was half a block back when the girl started up the short walk to an old brick apartment building and pulled a card out of her pocket. A key card. *Damn.*

Once she was inside, they wouldn't be able to reach her unless someone else came along and let them in. Larsen's footsteps quickened and she managed to close the distance between them as the girl pulled the door open and slipped inside without a backward glance. Larsen grabbed the open door, heart pounding. *She'd done it.*

Jack was going to kill her.

With her foot propping open the door, she called him and gave him the address. "I'll be waiting for you inside." She hung up before she had to listen to his rant, then eased into the building, praying her disguise would be enough to keep her alive.

Jack reached her seconds later, after the longest two hours of his life. If one of his men had recognized her…

He'd never forgive himself if something happened to her.

Luck, for once, was with him and he found a parking space behind the building, though he'd have ditched the car in the middle of the street if he'd had to. His only concern was getting to Larsen.

As he climbed the steps to the building, she opened the door for him. Her black hair and makeup startled him anew. Even dressed as a Goth, she was sexy as hell.

Relief filled her coal-rimmed eyes when their gazes met. He had to resist the urge to pull her hard against him. Instead he took her hand, feeling the dampness of her palm and the faint vibration of nerves as he closed his fingers around hers, her touch silencing the voices in his head.

"Where are they?"

"Second floor." Larsen pointed to the door on the right, above them. "I saw two of them, but there may be more. The second was an older male version of our cancer kid. Just like Sabrina described."

Probably the little punk who'd shot at him in Tony Jingles. She started to pull him toward the stairs but he stopped her.

"Larsen, you're not going up there. I want you outside where she can't shoot you again."

"You don't even know what you're walking into." There was fear in her eyes, he realized. Fear for him as well as herself. "At least let me wait in here. You may need me."

With a quick squeeze of her hand, he let her go. "All right. But stay here." Jack quickly climbed the stained linoleum stairs, then paused outside the apartment door, heart thudding against his ribs. *Be here, you white bastard.*

He took a deep breath, then with a swift, hard kick, broke down the door and swung inside, gun drawn.

"Police!"

Two women sat on the sofa watching an old *I Love Lucy* repeat, the smell of popcorn circling around them as the light in the darkened room flashed and changed with the television. Their backs were to the door, but neither so much as glanced behind at Jack's shout. As if they hadn't heard him.

Unaware. *Controlled.*

He heard something to his right and swung toward the sound, gun raised. Running toward him, knife in hand, was the little bald man from Jingles. Barely five feet tall, his lined and weathered face wore a look of cruel determination.

"Freeze!" Jack aimed his gun at his chest but the man never slowed. "Stop or I'll shoot." But he might as well be talking to a shrub.

Hell. If he shot the little devil, he'd never get any answers. Jack shoved his gun into his waistband and braced himself for the attack. As the small man lunged for him, Jack shot his hand in and under the knife, grabbing the man's small wrist, immobilizing the deadly weapon.

Stronger than he appeared, the little man kicked and struggled against Jack's hold and it was all he could do to keep that knife from a lethal swipe.

"Jack, watch out!" Larsen yelled from behind him.

"Get out of here!" he shouted, but his gaze swung up in time to see a second assailant, the cancer girl, running for him in an awkward, loping run, a butcher knife held in both hands above her head. *"Larsen, run!"*

Terror for her surged through him, lending him the added strength he needed to quell his small opponent. He clipped him hard under the chin, sending him sprawling, unconscious.

Then Jack grabbed his gun and swung toward the girl, prepared to shoot her down before she hurt Larsen again. But the girl, her bald head glistening with sweat, seemed to be locked in some kind of invisible battle, her limbs jerking, her muscles corded with tension.

"Flee!" she shouted, her cry anguished. "Flee or I must kill you."

"Stop right there. Drop the knife!"

"I cannot. He orders me to kill you and I must obey." She continued forward in that same awful gait. If she wasn't fighting every step, she was a damned good actress. "You must flee. Or stop me."

"If I shoot, I'll kill you."

Tears filled her eyes. "Do what you must. I wish you no more harm." Her gaze fixed on Larsen. "Forgive me. He bade me shoot you with my arrow." A flash of rebellion tightened her mouth. "I shot you in the shoulder so you would not die, and tipped the arrow in healing dust so your wound would heal quickly."

Healing dust. Jack remembered his shock at how quickly Larsen's shoulder had healed. Despite the girl's protestations, she was still advancing with the knife, but after what he'd seen the past few days, he could too easily believe she was being controlled. He was going to have to stop her—without hurting her, if such a thing were possible.

"Is Baleris here?"

"Nay. He is with your guard. Your M.P.D."

The police station. "Are there any more of you? Anyone else who's going to rush me with a knife or arrow?"

"Nay." She was almost upon him and the tears were running freely down her cheeks now. "You must stop me."

Jack shoved his gun into his waistband again, then circled behind her. With a single swift motion, he grabbed her arms and wrenched the knife out of her hands, then pinned her hard against him, absorbing her struggles.

The voices in his head went berserk, screeching like banshees.

"Damn." Jack ground his teeth, struggling against the press of noise on the inside of his skull, half afraid the very bone would crack.

"Jack?" Larsen looked at him with worry in her eyes. "What's the matter?"

"I'm okay." Hell, no, he wasn't okay. It was as if the voices were pressing their mouths to his ear, blasting him with everything they had. He could hardly hear through the screaming. Could hardly think. He had…to…get…control. With everything he had, he fought the noise, pushing at the voices with his mind until he could…almost…think again.

"Jack, you're hurting her."

"What?" He focused on Larsen, saw her staring at the girl he still held. The girl's gasps for breath reached his ears.

Hell. He was crushing her. Jack loosened his grip, but not enough to let her escape, and handed Larsen the knife.

"If the little man wakes up, kill him. This one and I are going to take a look around."

"Tarrys," his captive said, struggling against his hold.

"What?"

"I am called Tarrys. I am slave to Baleris, but that one—" She spat in the direction of the man lying prone on the carpet. "Yuillin serves our master willingly."

"All right then, Tarrys. Let's you and me have a look around." He half carried her, half pushed her around the sofa until he could see the two women clearly. Recognition kicked him in the chest.

"It's them." His gaze met Larsen's. "The two congressional interns kidnapped from the pharmacy."

Larsen's eyes went wide. "We've got to get them out of here."

"See if you can move them while…Tarrys and I finish our tour."

He lifted the small woman off the ground, tucking her still-struggling body beneath his left arm. She weighed next to nothing, but the roaring in his head was going to crush him.

"You are in danger," the girl said as he carried her down the short hallway. "Your people. You cannot let him return to Esria with the Lost Stone."

A memory poked through the screams that filled his head as he checked the bathroom. "The Stone of Ezrie?"

"Aye."

"What's the Stone of Ezrie?" Larsen asked behind them.

"I thought you were going to get the women out of here."

"They won't budge. I couldn't even drag them away."

"I'll have to carry them out." He grunted as Tarrys's elbow slammed into his gut. "The Stone of Ezrie was the name of the artifact stolen from the Smithsonian the morning of the first rape," he told Larsen.

"Baleris stole it," the girl said. "'Twas what called him through the gate. The stone has great power. You must not let him take it."

"Where is it now?"

"Baleris wears it around his neck."

As he approached the bedroom he heard a sound and raised his gun. "I thought you said there were no more of you."

"She is controlled. 'Tis her home."

He eased into the bedroom where a thirty-something Hispanic female sat on the overstuffed chair in the corner, staring straight ahead as if heavily drugged. A quick search of the room assured him there was no one else.

"Is she in danger?" he asked his captive.

"I feed her and the other females. Baleris has not harmed any of them."

"Yet," Larsen said.

Jack met her gaze. "We've got to get them out of here." He set the still-struggling girl on her feet and turned her to face him, his hands clamped on her shoulders to keep her still. "How does he control them?"

She looked at him as if she didn't understand the question. "He is Esri," she said as if that explained it all.

The Stone of Ezrie.

His hands convulsed on her shoulders as the screams tore apart his brain. "*What* is Esri?"

The girl winced. "Do you not know? They were much feared by humans in the old days before the worlds were sealed from one another. They stole into your world at midnight to enchant your virgins and steal your children. The humans once called them elf. Or faerie."

"Are you kidding?" Larsen whispered, wide-eyed beside him.

Jack scoffed. "Don't be ridiculous. She's not a damned elf."

"Nay, I am not." She squirmed in his grasp, still fighting him. "Baleris is Esri. I am Marceil."

Jack shoved her against the wall. "I want the truth!"

"Jack, you're hurting her."

Larsen grabbed his arm, blessedly ending the scream fest between his ears until her fingers slipped away and the banshees once again took up residence.

"She's playing us for fools."

"Why?" Those dark, coal-rimmed eyes of hers snapped with excitement. "Maybe this is the answer we've been looking for—the reason he's so much more powerful than he should be."

Denial shot through him, sharp and hot. No way was he believing in elves. He already had one foot caught in the quicksand of madness. He wasn't about to shove the other in there, as well.

"Wrong." He glared at the girl. "You said the worlds were sealed, yet here you are."

Despite his rough treatment, the girl showed no fear, but looked at him with eyes that seemed somehow old and infinitely sad.

"Baleris stumbled upon a threshold, hitherto unknown, deep in the Banished Lands. One that had never been sealed. If the Lost Stone is returned to Esria as Baleris intends, all the seals will open and the humans will be at the mercy of the Esri once more."

She was talking nonsense. Fairy tales. But the cop in him demanded answers. "Where is this threshold?"

"I…do not know. It was dark. I did not see."

"Convenient."

Larsen grabbed his arm again. "Do you hear that?"

Silence. Silence suddenly overlaid by the chilling sound of sirens. *Police.*

He met Larsen's wide-eyed gaze, his pulse suddenly pounding. "We've got to get out of here."

"What about the interns?" Larsen lifted her hand from his arm and the noise roared back, nearly buckling his knees.

The sirens came to a screeching halt out front.

"No time."

"You must hit me like you did Yuillin," Tarrys cried. "Or I will be forced to follow you until I kill you."

Jack balled his fist, then stopped, a sudden thought exploding through the screams in his head. David. Henry's son.

"What did you do to the boy when you tried to get in my apartment?"

"The brown boy?"

"Yes." He shook her. "Tell me what you did to him."

"Yuillin shot him with…*elfshot.* 'Twill turn him to stone from the inside out. Without a cure, he will die."

"What's the cure? What do I have to do to save him?"

"I do not know. There were once humans with the gift for healing. You must find one."

More sirens came to a halt outside.

"Jack, we've got to go."

He needed answers, dammit! But they were out of time.

With a swift upper cut, he clipped the girl under the chin, then lowered her, unconscious, to the floor. The moment he released her, the screams turned back into voices. Loud, frantic, excited voices, but just voices.

He grabbed Larsen's hand and the noise ceased altogether. "We're going out the window."

She threw him a wide-eyed stare. "It's the second story!"

"You want a broken leg or three rounds through the chest?"

Her jaw dropped, then snapped closed. "Good point."

As the sound of pounding feet filled the downstairs entry to the apartment building, Jack wrenched open the bedroom window, swung out until he was hanging from the sill, then dropped onto the grass with a bone-jarring impact. When he looked up, Larsen was crawling out the window, an expression of terror on her face.

Come on, angel. His heart thudded in his chest. Any second, the cops would burst into that bedroom, guns blasting. He shouldn't have left her behind, but he'd wanted to get on the ground first, to break her fall.

She glanced at him and he held out his hands. *Jump,* he mouthed. He couldn't shout, couldn't take a chance on alerting the police they were escaping. With a grimace, Larsen nodded and eased herself out until she was hanging from the ledge.

Come on, Larsen.

Finally she let go and he caught her as she reached the ground, breaking her landing, pulling her hard against him.

"Are you okay?" he demanded.

"Yes," she said breathlessly.

"Then let's get out of here."

But as they ran for the car, his head spun with the girl's—Tarrys's—words. *Elves.* What kind of idiot did she take him for? Elves were little dwarflike people. Fairies were little more than insects. Baleris sure as hell wasn't either. He was a man. Just a man. Nothing more.

They jumped in the car and took off before the cops saw them.

The son of a bitch *had* to be a man. Because if he wasn't, if he honestly had magical abilities…they were in deep trouble.

Chapter 10

"It's bull," Jack said from behind her.

Larsen stood at the window of the borrowed apartment, watching the early afternoon sun flicker and flash off passing cars on the street below. They'd made a clean getaway, but she couldn't shake the fear that the cops were coming anyway. She couldn't bring herself to abandon her lookout position.

"There's no such thing as elves," Jack said vehemently. Since she wasn't arguing the point one way or the other, she could only assume he was still struggling with the idea, trying to convince himself.

She glanced at him, at where he sat on the sofa, his fingers digging into his hair. He wore a pair of jeans and a dark red polo he'd borrowed from Charlie's closet.

He looked good. He always looked good.

Not a minute went by that part of her wasn't remembering

the way she felt when he kissed her, the way heat moved through her like warm lava, weakening her limbs. Or the cataclysm of coming apart in his arms.

The intense attraction wore at her. She couldn't figure out a way to shut it off. Leaving him again was out of the question, so her only choice was to suck it up and ignore it. And try to keep Jack from realizing just how attracted to him she really was.

If he knew what he did to her, she'd never be able to maintain the distance she needed. She couldn't let him get that close to her again, close enough to see too much, to learn the secrets she couldn't share. To see the strangeness, the evil deep inside her, the devil's sight she was cursed with.

"Maybe Tarrys was telling the truth."

"There's no such thing as elves."

"Why isn't it possible?"

He looked up, his expression incredulous. "You can't honestly tell me you believe that crock."

She shrugged and stepped away from the window. "I don't know what to believe anymore. The albino does things he shouldn't be able to do, Jack. His being nonhuman actually makes some sense."

"It makes *no* sense." Jack scowled. "All you have to do is to look at him to know he's no elf. Elves are—" he held his hand out, palm down "—little dwarflike people. *And they don't exist.*"

"Maybe they're not elves. What if elves aren't real…but the Esri are?" She tapped her fingers on her thighs. "I wish I had my computer."

"There's one in the bedroom."

Larsen's eyebrows lifted with interest. As one, they headed for the bedroom.

The room looked like a college dorm room…before the students moved in. Other than the computer and the dark green fitted sheet that covered the mattress, there wasn't a thing in sight that said an actual person laid claim to the space. An old dresser, an equally decrepit desk and a mattress and springs were all the furniture in the room. The walls were white and bare of pictures. The windows covered only by cheap shades.

As Jack turned on the computer, Larsen raised the shades. "I can't believe anyone really lives here."

"Charlie's a spook," Jack said. "Or maybe special ops. I'd bet money on it. Either way, he probably only needs a place to stay for a few days at a time when he's between missions and an address to collect mail."

"What are we going to do if he shows up suddenly?"

The computer screen lit and Jack began typing. "We're going to hope that doesn't happen."

"Maybe we should hope it does."

"Why's that?"

Larsen sat on the end of the bed, her knees brushing the back of Jack's desk chair. "Because Harrison and both his kids were immune from the albino's control. Maybe it runs in his family."

The clack of the computer keyboard ceased abruptly. Jack turned sideways in his chair and looked at her. His eyes narrowed, his brows pulling down in thought. "Maybe, but it doesn't always work that way. The woman I saved at Tony Jingles was there with her daughter. The girl was controlled."

"Maybe she was adopted. Or just didn't inherit whatever gene we seem to possess in common. The gene that makes us immune to mind control."

Jack pursed his mouth. "You're right. If Charlie *is* a spook, we could use his help no matter what. Maybe Harrison can get word to him. It's worth a try."

As Jack pulled out his phone, Larsen nudged him from the desk chair and took his place. Jack left Harrison the message while Larsen typed.

Esri. Nothing. *Elves.* Too much and most of it garbage.

"Anything?" Jack asked, coming to stand behind her. She could feel his presence like a living thing wrapping around her from behind.

"I've got a list of cures and protections against enchantment."

"Enchantment?" Jack scoffed.

But a chill skimmed down Larsen's spine. "Mind control. That's exactly what he's doing, Jack." She read the few things on the list she recognized. "Salt, holy water, iron, four leaf clovers and holly branches are all supposed to protect against elf mischief."

"Superstition."

"Sure. But sometimes superstition is based in fact if you go back far enough. We've got to start somewhere."

"It's hogwash." His hands rested on her shoulders. "See if you can find anything on the amulet that was stolen from the Smithsonian, the Stone of Ezrie."

"The one Tarrys said will open the gates between the two worlds?"

Jack grunted. "Duke said there was some legend attached to it. The girl probably read it, too."

The feel of his hands, heavy on her shoulders, was thoroughly distracting. Her fingers stumbled, but a moment later the screen revealed the news report of the theft and a small picture. The blue amulet wasn't large, about the size of a man's thumb and shaped like a pear.

Larsen squinted and looked closer. "There's a symbol on the stone."

"A seven-pointed star. See if you can find anything on the legend."

"There's nothing here. But one of my college roommates works at the Smithsonian. Autumn McGinn. If she wasn't the one Duke talked to, she'll know who was. I'll send her an e-mail."

As she typed, she heard the mattress behind her creak under Jack's weight.

A minute later she turned in her seat to face him. "Done." Larsen folded her arms over the back of the chair. "If it makes you feel any better, I don't want to believe he's an elf any more than you do." She rested her chin on her arms. "What are we going to do if he really has magic?"

For once, Jack didn't scoff. "I don't know." Then he scowled and raked his fingers into his hair. "I can't believe in elves, Larsen. I just can't."

"Then don't. That's not what's important."

His brows dipped low. "I thought you were convinced they're real."

"No, I'm convinced the albino is real. And I'm convinced he has abilities we can't comprehend. All that matters is we don't deny what he can do. What you call him doesn't really matter. Call him whatever you like. Elf, Esri, bastard...*zoodopper.*"

A funny smile broke over his face. *"Zoodopper?"*

Larsen smiled weakly. "That's my point. Who cares what you call him? We know what he can do."

Jack reached out, touching her hair, trailing his fingers down one thick lock. "You're right."

He looked at her with eyes that lacked the probing intensity, the distrust of so many of his gazes and were instead filled with a tenderness and understanding that went straight to her heart. This gaze caressed and comforted, lifting some of the suffocating worry and filling her with a strange fluttering lightness like a butterfly on newly formed wings.

Why was she so drawn to him? How could he tear down years of defenses with a single look? She was Larsen Vale. The Ice Bitch. A woman who didn't—*couldn't* let people get this close.

Slowly, the look in his eyes changed, heated. His gaze dropped to her mouth and she knew he wanted to kiss her. Her pulse sped with a sudden longing to be in his arms again.

A longing that scared her. She'd struggled all day to push him away, to put some distance between them. If she gave in to the need to touch him now, she'd undermine everything. He'd never again believe she was uninterested in him. He'd know the truth, that she wanted him, had always wanted him. And he'd get too close, see too much.

Her secrets would never be safe again.

As desperately as she wanted to wrap her arms around his neck and kiss him until she forgot everything but the taste of his lips and the feel of his tongue stroking hers, Larsen forced herself to unfold her legs, stand and walk away.

Jack watched Larsen leave the bedroom without a backward glance. He'd give his right arm to know what was going on inside that head of hers. One moment her eyes were soft and warm, the next they were hidden behind that cool wall.

She wanted him. No, she didn't want him. That was the problem. She was drawn to him but she didn't want to be. For a reason he couldn't figure out, she wanted nothing to do with her attraction to him. Or maybe she just wanted nothing to do with *him*.

The thought sank to his stomach like a brick. How would he survive the rest of his life without her, without her quieting touch, if she left him?

"I'm going to make a sandwich," she called from the kitchen. "Do you want anything?"

You. Just you. He rose from the bed and followed her into the living room.

"I'll get one later," he said, picking up the phone and dialing Henry's number. "I want to check on David, first. Make sure he's okay." He needed to set his mind at ease. The magic, the enchantment, the immortality—none of it turned his blood to ice like the possibility that David might have actually been harmed by the little archers outside his apartment the other night.

"Hello?"

"Sabrina, this is Uncle Jack. I need to talk to your mom."

"Hi, Jack. Mom's not here. She's at the hospital with David."

The blood drained from his head, driving him down onto the sofa. "Why? What's the matter with him, sweetheart?"

She made a frustrated sound. "It's that little bald man's fault. He did something to David, but no one's listening to me. You should tell them, Jack. They'll listen to you. I know my mom will."

His fingers gripped the phone until the instrument bit into his flesh.

"What's the matter with him, Sabrina? What do they think is wrong?"

"No one tells me anything," she said on a huff. "But I hear things. My mom's crying all the time. Last night she called my grandma who's on a cruise and told her to fly home right away if she wanted to see David again. She said his organs are shutting down, hardening like they're turning to stone. All of them. The doctors are giving him forty-eight hours, tops."

He felt a knife go through his heart. "Where is he, Sabrina? Which hospital?"

"Children's. Uncle Jack?" she asked in a small voice. "I'm scared."

"I know, honey. Just do what your mom wants, okay? She needs that right now."

"I know. Is he going to be okay, Jack?"

She wanted assurances he couldn't give. *Dammit.* Damn the bastard. Damn his little bald minions.

"The doctors are doing everything they can, Sabrina."

"Okay."

But what if it wasn't enough? What if David really had been elfshot? Modern medicine wouldn't stand a chance.

He said goodbye to the girl and hung up, the terrible mass of emotion he'd held in check free at last. He surged to his feet and stormed across the room, then back again, pacing at a furious tempo.

"*I'm going to kill him.* I'm going to rip out his heart with my bare hands and feed it to the dogs."

Larsen came around the counter. "Jack, what's happened?"

Rage burned through him as his feet pounded across the room, roaring in his ears, raising its voice in unison with the voices yelling in his head. He was fighting an enemy he couldn't beat, an impossible enemy who was hurting those he loved.

Jack paced the living room like a wounded tiger while Larsen watched, helpless.

"Jack, please, tell me what's happened."

Her words finally seemed to penetrate the haze of anguish

that surrounded him. He sank onto the sofa and buried his face in his hands.

"He's dying."

"Oh, Jack." This was all her fault. The archers had come for *her* and hurt David instead. And it was tearing Jack apart.

She went to him, joining him on the sofa. When he didn't respond to her presence, she ran her palm across his back, over and over, returning the comfort of touch he so often shared with her. Finally he dropped his hands and turned to face her, his eyes bleak.

"Forty-eight hours. That's all they're giving him."

Larsen gasped. "What do they say is wrong with him?"

"His organs are turning to stone. Just like Tarrys predicted." Something broke in his eyes. "How can this be happening?"

Larsen slid her arms around his neck and he met her halfway, pulling her tight against him and burying his face in her hair. She could feel him shaking beneath the torrent of grief and outrage, and she held him, stroking her fingers through his thick, dark hair as he clung to her.

Finally his grip loosened and he pulled back, his eyes so full of despair it made her ache. Without thinking, she slid her palms over his cheeks and kissed him, driven by a need to offer what comfort she could. He responded with a strength that startled her, wrapping her in a tight embrace as he kissed her hard, communicating his need for comfort, for forgetfulness, for *her.*

Passion flared between them in a torrent of need and desperation. All day she'd tried to deny this attraction, tried to pretend there was nothing between them. But after a single fiery kiss, she was lost.

Their teeth clicked as Jack's tongue swept inside her

mouth, filling her with the taste of pleasure and heat, filling her with emotions she couldn't name.

"I need you," he murmured against her lips as his warm hand slipped beneath her shirt, trailing a hot path over her heated skin until it reached the barrier of her bra. "I need to touch you, Larsen." His voice shook, but this time with desire.

"Yes, Jack." She spread a path of kisses from his lips to his cheek, to his ear. "Yes." She nipped at the lobe, drawing a violent tremor from him.

His hands grabbed for the hem of her shirt, his elbow bumping the sofa back, but they got it off her, followed quickly by her bra.

Jack hesitated, his gaze probing hers, his eyes filled with grief and fire and question. Slowly his hands lifted to frame her face. "I want to make love to you."

Years of defenses shook and crumbled beneath the desire his touch stoked inside her and the raw need she felt to share herself with this one man. She covered his hands with her own, then pulled them away from her face and lowered them to her breasts.

The feel of his large hands covering her, her nipples cradled in his palms, sent shafts of pleasure spearing through her. She arched into the touch, pressing his hands harder against her as her head fell back.

"Larsen…" His lips touched her neck, his tongue sliding along the sensitive line as his fingers encircled the hard tips, twirling them between the pads of his fingers and thumbs, sending a hot current of electricity shooting downward to the juncture of her thighs.

She groaned with exquisite pleasure as his lips slid down over her collarbone to cover her breast, taking the pulsing, tingling flesh into his mouth. His tongue stroked where his fingers had moments before, the sensation delicious but maddening as it did everything to increase the urgency filling her loins and nothing to quell it. Small, helpless noises were coming from her throat.

Larsen dug her fingers in his hair, at once pressing him closer and pulling him away. "Jack...*please.*"

He pulled back, yanked his shirt over his head, then pulled her beneath him on the sofa, his jeans-clad hips pressing hard against hers, the soft furring of hair on his chest tickling her sensitive nipples.

He lifted his head to stare into her eyes, his own shining like jewels. "I need you, Larsen." Holding her gaze, his hand slid between them, between her thighs, and pressed against the very center of the flame.

She gasped, pressing against his hand, mindless with the need to quell the ache. She wasn't a virgin, though her sexual experience had been limited. Never had she felt like this. Never had she longed to take another so deep inside of her.

"Do you want me?" he asked, his breath ragged, blue eyes gleaming with desire.

"Yes. *Yes.*"

Triumph flashed in his eyes and he pulled his hand from between her legs, gripping her hands as he pressed the hard ridge of his erection against her through their clothes, mimicking the act of mating, starting her on a slow, upward climb. Her pulse raced, her head began to spin...

Larsen froze. Her heart lurched in her chest as she realized the spinning had nothing to do with what Jack was doing to her. She was fading into another vision as she had this morning, under the trees. Through the blur of Jack's head, a bedroom appeared, very different from the modern room that surrounded her for real.

The one in the vision was, like before, a different time, if not quite as far back as before. The walls were papered, the window had glass, but it was thick and opaque, reflecting the flames from the hearth. Clearly nighttime; the hearth flame was the only light in the room.

On the small bed in the center of the room sat a boy of maybe twelve or thirteen. He was moaning, his head in his hands, his brown hair hanging loose to his shoulders. He was dressed in a plain off-white linen shirt with pants that ended at his calves, revealing bare feet.

An old woman bustled into the room followed close behind by a man in an old-fashioned black coat with a white ruffled collar. They spoke to the boy in something that might have been French, or maybe Flemish.

As with the girl in the previous vision, while the man held him down, the old woman put her thumbs on the boy's temples and chanted.

As before, the woman chanted the same odd words, over and over. *Eslius turatus a quari er siedi. Eslius turatus a quari er siedi.* And as before, the boy began to smile, as if cured from whatever was causing his pain.

"Larsen."

The vision dissolved and Larsen blinked to find Jack no longer on top of her, but beside her, one palm on her face. He was looking down at her with tight concern.

"What's the matter, angel?"

Oh, God. "Nothing. I'm fine." Clearly the biggest lie ever told.

Why did she keep seeing these? They weren't death visions. For once she was seeing things that seemed to end well. But why? What *were* they? What did they *mean?*

She pulled away from him and scrambled off the sofa, but he grabbed her arm and held it in a gentle vise.

"Larsen, don't." His gaze, when she met it, was sad, not angry. He sat and pulled her down beside him. "I'm not going to hurt you, you know that, don't you?"

"Yes, of course." He thought she was afraid of him? "I just...changed my mind."

His gaze bore into hers. "I think somewhere along the line someone hurt you."

It wasn't true. And yet... Tears pricked the backs of her eyes. She did hurt. She hated being like this, hated the visions and the fear that she was touched by evil. Hated that she was afraid to let anyone get too close.

"No one's hurt me."

Jack sighed. "Maybe not physically. But someone destroyed your trust in men."

She dropped her gaze to her lap, unable to meet his probing eyes. He was wrong. It wasn't someone but some *thing*. And it hadn't just destroyed her trust in men, but in everyone.

She felt his hand brush over her hair.

"I would never do anything to hurt you, Larsen. Believe that if you believe nothing else."

The tears burned harsher now and she felt one escape to slide down her cheek.

The pad of his thumb brushed it away. "I won't pressure you. I'd never push you to do something you didn't want."

She didn't respond. Couldn't lift her gaze for fear of dumping more tears. But she didn't pull away when he gathered her gently against him and pressed her head to his bare shoulder.

He held her like that, stroking her bare arm, giving her only comfort and the assurance he thought she needed, asking for nothing in return.

Something warm grew inside her, bursting on a rush of

tenderness. Within his arms, she felt as though she'd finally come home. But the feeling was just an illusion. She had no home. Nowhere she could reveal herself. Nowhere she was truly safe.

She eased out of his embrace and went to retrieve her bra and shirt. When she was dressed, she turned to find him lying on his back on the sofa, his arm flung over his eyes, his mouth a tight line of despair.

David. Their love-making had been a way to forget—at least for a moment—that the boy was dying, but she'd stolen even that from him.

She sank onto the nearest chair. "I'm sorry, Jack."

"I can't let him die," he said, confirming her suspicions. He sat up again, meeting her gaze with hard, tormented eyes. "I've got to do something."

"The bald girl, Tarrys, said we need to find an ancient healer. Maybe a Chinese doctor or someone with holistic training could help him."

He shook his head, denial in his expression. Then suddenly he stilled, his eyes widening. "Aunt Myrtle."

"The one your mom sent packing after she did some woo-woo number on you?"

"Yeah." He shoved to his feet and reached for his phone, then stopped. "Nah. Can't call her. Too risky considering our current status as D.C.'s Most Wanted. We need to get David to her."

"Jack, they're never going to release a dying kid from the hospital."

"Then we'll have to break him out."

"Maybe his mom…"

He made an impatient swipe with his hand. "His mom

can't be involved. I can't be sure she hasn't come into contact with that devil's power."

"Are you sure about this? We don't know he's been elfshot. You don't even believe in elves."

He met her gaze. "Weren't you the one who said it doesn't matter what we call him as long as we accept what he can do? Well, I've accepted he's done something to David. The doctors can't help him. Maybe Myrtle can."

Larsen let out a deep, worried breath. "Okay. But how are we supposed to kidnap him from a hospital?"

A tight, determined smile formed on his mouth. "I've got an inside connection. The woman I saved at Jingles is a doctor at Children's."

"I thought you told her to leave the area."

"I did. But I've still got her cell phone number."

He made the call while Larsen watched him pace the bedroom. When he hung up, he looked like a man reborn, his eyes shining with the light of battle.

"She's still in town, just staying with a friend. She's going to meet us at the east service entrance at 2:00 a.m."

"I can't believe she agreed to this. It's kidnapping."

"She knows what we're up against. She knows I'm rescuing him." He closed the distance between them and took her shoulders in his hands as grief tightened his mouth. "She knows we're his only chance."

"Hello, Jack," Brenda Kettering said, bending to talk to him through the car window. It was 2:00 a.m., the hospital service entrance all but deserted. She handed Jack a small bundle. "David's clothes," she said by way of explanation. "We have a small problem."

Now, why didn't that surprise him? If anything went right at this point, it would be a cause for major celebration.

"His mom's sleeping with him," Brenda continued. "I'm going to ask her to come down to the nurses' station to sign some forms for me. When I get her out of the room, you need to be waiting in the shadows, ready to whisk him away."

Jack turned off the ignition. "Can do."

"Do you want me to wait here?" Larsen asked.

"No." He lifted his hand to reach for her, but stopped himself. He needed to back off and to let her come to him even if it killed him. Though he longed for a moment's peace from the noise in his head, her touch was so much more. Light, strength, warmth. She was becoming far too important to him to risk scaring her off.

"Come with me," he said. "As you pointed out earlier, we're safer together."

He stepped out of the car and into the humid night air. The area around the hospital was well-lit, illuminating them like a trio of bull's-eyes. God knew who—or what—watched from the darkness, but they entered the hospital without incident and followed Brenda into the elevator. The three stood facing each other as the elevator engine sounded noisily against the quiet of the hospital.

"I've already disconnected him from the wires and tubes, so he'll be easily moved."

"Are you endangering your job doing this?" Larsen asked the woman.

Brenda eyed her squarely. "Sure." A look of compassionate determination warmed her round face. "But I can't let a child die if there might be a way to save him. I nearly died a few days ago." She glanced at Jack. "If not for Detective Hallihan's timely intervention, I would have."

"I'm just glad I was there," he told her.

Brenda cleared her throat and continued. "I'm willing to do whatever it takes to stop this villain. And I mean *whatever it takes*."

The elevator door swooshed open and Brenda led them into an empty hallway. "His is the second room on the right. I've looked into his condition. Carrying him out in your arms is unlikely to do any additional damage. Give me a couple of minutes to call his mother away."

Jack nodded. "Thanks, Brenda. I owe you big time for this one."

The woman smiled sadly. "I think we're even. But all that matters is saving that child. Do what you can, Jack. And I'll do the same."

As Brenda walked the short distance to David's room and disappeared inside, Jack slipped his hand around Larsen's arm and pulled her into the shadows beside him, wrapping his head in blessed silence.

Beneath his fingers, her muscles ached with the tension of a new recruit on his first stakeout. "Relax, Larsen. Your heart's pounding so loud it's going to give us away."

She looked at him, startled, then scowled. "It is not." But she leaned into his touch and it was all he could do not to pull her into his embrace.

Moments later, Brenda reappeared followed by an Asian-American woman of medium height and the look of someone whose world was crumbling around her. Mei.

His heart went out to his friend. She would hate him for what he was about to do.

When they disappeared around the corner, Jack squeezed Larsen's hand. "Come on."

They eased into the room and found David in the bed, but not alone, as he'd expected. In the chair behind the door, his sister, Sabrina, slept. As they walked into the room, she opened her eyes and blinked at him.

Hell. He froze, hoping she wasn't really awake. But she stretched and smiled up at him sleepily with that mouth full of braces.

"Hi, Jack."

Now what was he going to do?

He went to her, squatted in front of her chair and took her hand.

"Sabrina, honey, I need you to keep a secret. I know someone who may be able to help David, but I can't tell your parents."

"Why not?"

"It's complicated."

She stretched long, coltlike legs and straightened. "Jack, what's going on? My dad's acting like you're the bad guy or something."

"I know. But I'm not. You've got to trust me on this." He squeezed her hands. "Sabrina, I've got to take your brother without your mom knowing. She's going to be mad at me, but it's the only way to save him."

She looked at him with dark trusting eyes. "Okay."

He stood and squeezed her shoulder. "That's my girl." Then he turned and went to the bed where David lay, not asleep, but unconscious and dying. His heart nearly ripped in two as he gathered the boy into his arms.

He would not let him die.

As he crossed to Larsen, who was waiting for him just inside the door, he met Sabrina's tired gaze.

"Go back to sleep, honey." Then he slipped into the hallway, Larsen by his side, and into the elevator without incident. Larsen sagged against the elevator wall across from him as the doors swooshed shut, her gaze tense but relieved. They'd done it. The first step—springing David—had been a piece of cake. But when the elevator reached ground level, they stepped out to find Sabrina flying out of the stairwell and running toward them.

"I'm going with you," she announced.

Jack groaned. "No, sweetheart. You're not. It's way too dangerous."

But the teen's dark eyes flashed with stubbornness. "I *am* going with you. Or I'll start yelling until my mom comes."

As well as every security guard or cop in the building.

"Sabrina…"

Her chin jutted, her eyes starting to glisten dangerously. "I'm going with you, Jack."

Larsen touched his arm. "We've got to get out of here."

Damn stubborn females. "All right," he snapped.

He loaded them into the car, Larsen in the back holding David, and Sabrina in the front with him, then took off. He circled D.C. long enough to be certain they weren't being followed, then headed into the Virginia suburbs once more.

He pulled out his cell and called Mei.

"Jack! My kids are gone."

"I have them. I'm the one who took them."

Silence.

"I won't hurt them, Mei. You know I won't. I know someone who may be able to save David."

"Then you should have taken me with you!" Her voice was filled with fury…and tears.

Jack sighed. "I couldn't. Henry can't find us, Mei. He's not himself. I think you know that."

"Jack, so help me…" Her voice clogged with tears.

He listened to the woman he loved like a sister crying, and it broke his heart. "I won't hurt them. I didn't even mean to take Sabrina. She insisted on coming along."

A small, choked laugh sounded on the other end. "That one has a mind of her own." She sniffled. "What's happening, Jack? What's the matter with Henry? He's okay unless I ask about you, then he gets this awful look on his face and it's as if someone else is talking through his mouth."

"That about sums it up. Mei…I can't explain. I'm not entirely sure I understand what's going on myself, but his mind is being controlled. The entire M.P.D. It's not their fault, but they could be dangerous. Don't talk to Henry about me. And don't tell him I have the kids. *Please.*"

He waited, knowing she was trying to deal with what he'd said.

"Mei, I don't know if I can save David. But the doctors can't and I wouldn't be able to live with myself if I didn't try. Trust me."

"I do. I always have."

"I may not be able to keep in touch. I can't take a chance on Henry tracking us down."

"I'm scared, Jack."

"Me, too, Mei. Me, too."

"Can I speak with my girl?"

"Sure." He handed his phone to Sabrina.

"Yeah?" Sabrina paused. "Mom…" She let out a put-upon sigh as only a teenager can. "I will. Love you, too."

He was doing the right thing. He was doing the only thing. But fear for the three precious lives in the car with him turned his knuckles white as he headed out of the city and toward the mountains of Virginia.

Chapter 11

The unconscious child lay across the backseat, his head heavy in Larsen's lap as they headed west on I-66 into Virginia. Larsen felt for the pulse at the base of the boy's warm neck. Steady, but weak.

It wasn't fair. He was just an innocent victim, a cute kid who didn't deserve this.

She remembered his apologetic grin the first time she saw him—after he'd accidentally hit her with the football. He was a likable kid. A kid Jack adored. And he was dying because of her. Because the albino—the *Esri*—saw her in that vision and sent his minions after her. It was all too much to take in.

In the front seat, Sabrina chattered away, seemingly oblivious to her brother's plight.

"So, anyway, Emily's phone bill comes and she has almost three thousand text messages. In one month! Her dad got so

mad, he took the phone away. But he forgot to turn it off."
Sabrina giggled. "Emily's friends kept texting and before the
battery died there were almost two hundred new texts!"

Larsen bit back her annoyance at the girl's callousness, then
sighed. She was just a child—a child who believed Jack would
take care of everything. Larsen wished she could do the same.

"And her dad had to pay the bill because it wasn't even her
phone anymore."

"I guess that taught her dad a lesson," Jack said.

"Yeah. It taught him to turn off the phone."

Jack chuckled and glanced at the girl, fondness warm in
his eyes. She was distracting Jack from his fear for the boy,
and for that Larsen was grateful.

But when he turned back to the road, Sabrina continued to
gaze at him—not with the innocent adoration of a kid, but
with the lovesick look of a fourteen-year-old girl.

Sabrina turned her head suddenly, catching Larsen's stare.
Her eyes turned hard, her expression telling Larsen, in no uncertain terms, to *stay away. He's mine.* Then she turned back
in her seat and looked out her side window.

Oh, boy. Poor Jack. He thought of the girl as a daughter.
Larsen was certain he didn't have a clue Sabrina harbored very
undaughterly feelings for him. She felt sorry for both of them.

Finally, Sabrina stopped talking and soon her head was
leaning against the window as if she were asleep. Larsen
tipped her own head against the headrest, listening to the low
hum of traffic.

The next thing she knew, the car was slowing down. She
blinked and looked out the front as they took the exit ramp
off the interstate. They shouldn't be getting off for more
than an hour.

"What's the matter?" she asked Jack.

"We're almost there."

She rubbed her eyes. "I must have fallen asleep."

Jack met her gaze in the rearview mirror. "How is he?"

Larsen felt for David's pulse against his warm throat. "The same."

Jack turned onto a two-lane road. A car passed, illuminating the hard, worried lines of his face.

"What if I screwed up, Larsen?" His words were low and raw.

He'd probably been tormenting himself with doubts for the entire ride. "What if I've signed his death certificate by taking him out of there?"

Her heart clenched with sympathy. Even after all they'd been through it was this—the danger to his partner's son—that threatened to break him.

"You're doing the right thing, Jack. You're doing the only thing."

She reached over the seat and laid her hand on his shoulder. "Would you believe me if I said everything's going to be all right?"

"No." But he reached up and squeezed her hand. "God knows how this could turn out okay." A hint of a sad smile whispered through his voice. "But keep saying the words anyway."

As he gripped her hand like a lifeline, tenderness filled her chest for this strong, determined man. And she realized she was going to have to take some serious measures to protect her heart.

Jack turned off the road onto a long twisty drive that led up a treed hill. He'd never been so afraid in his life. What if Myrtle couldn't help David? What if she wasn't even here? His stomach churned until he tasted bile in his throat.

How was he going to live with himself if David died in his arms instead of his mother's? How was he going to live with himself if David died at all?

With a burst of fury, he slammed his hand against the steering wheel. If it was the last thing he did, he would kill the bastard responsible.

At the top of the hill, the car lights illuminated a modest, two-story Colonial home with a narrow porch, white siding and black shutters. A home he'd been to once before, long ago.

"This is it?" Larsen asked behind him.

Though she'd leaned back as they climbed the hill, the remembered weight of her hand on his shoulder lingered, calming the torment that raged inside him, quieting the storm in his head. What would he do without her?

"This is it." He turned off the ignition. "I suppose I should call her so I don't scare her half to death." The porch light went on and he winced. "Guess I should have done that before I drove up the drive."

"At least she's home."

"Yeah." *Thank God.* But what were the chances she'd actually be able to help David? How could he have thought she'd be able to save a boy the doctors had given up on?

Larsen's hand patted his shoulder. "We're here. Let's do this."

Jack pulled himself together and got out of the car as the front door opened and his aunt stepped out onto the porch, her gray hair in rollers, a red silk bathrobe tied at her slender waist.

"Aunt Myrtle? It's Jack."

The woman's curious face lit up with a huge smile. "Jack! How nice of you to visit."

It was three-thirty in the morning. The irony struck him funny, coaxing a much-needed smile from his mouth. He went to her and embraced her, feeling a surge of affection for his father's sister, a woman he barely knew. She was of medium height, and had to be over seventy, but she was strong and erect and hugged him hard.

He pulled back and shook his head at her. "You shouldn't have come outside. I could have been anyone."

She waved her hand. "Oh, I don't worry about those things. No one makes it all the way up *my* hill unless it's important." She smiled broadly at him. "And I was right, now, wasn't I?"

Myrtle's sharp gaze moved behind him. "Hello, dear," she said as Larsen joined them. "Why, Jack, you didn't get married without inviting me, did you?"

Larsen's eyes widened.

A hard, startling longing to say *yes* rocked him.

"No, Aunt Myrtle. Larsen's just a…friend."

"How nice. Any friend of Jack's is family, I always say."

Larsen gave him a bemused look and Jack grinned. He hadn't seen her for decades.

"So, what brings you out here in the middle of the night, nephew?"

The brief respite from his worry for David evaporated as if it had never been. "I need your help."

She turned and waved at him to follow. "Then come in, come in."

"I've got to get the kids."

"You have kids?" she exclaimed.

"They're not mine." As Jack walked back to the car, Myrtle followed. "One of them is very sick."

Myrtle's eyes widened. "You think I can heal him."

Jack shook Sabrina awake, then reached in and lifted David into his arms.

"I don't know," he admitted, straightening, fear tightening his chest. "What I do know is the doctors have given up on him. You're his only chance."

"What do they say is the problem?"

"His organs are hardening. They're not sure why."

Myrtle touched David's forehead, then met Jack's gaze with shrewd sympathy. "This boy means much to you."

"Yes. He does."

"I can't make any promises. I haven't done any healing in years. It brings the wrong sort around, if you know what I mean."

He didn't, but it didn't matter. All that mattered was that she help David.

She turned and motioned him to follow. "Bring him inside and I'll see what I can do."

He followed her into the dark house, David in his arms, Sabrina and Larsen close behind. Myrtle turned on one of the lamps, revealing a living room that didn't appear to have changed from the last time he was here. The house even smelled the same, like musty age and lemon oil. In the corner a grandfather clock chimed the quarter hour like a sentinel reminding him he was out of time.

Myrtle led them up the stairs to the same room where he'd lain as a boy—a frilly room with white ruffles, flowers on the walls and the same musty smell.

"Put him on the bed, Jack. I'll get my things."

Jack laid the boy in the middle of the white bedspread. Sabrina sat, crossed-legged at David's feet. Larsen moved to look out the window, standing alone with the demons that haunted her.

Myrtle returned with a lace-trimmed basket filled with an assortment of things. She set the basket on the bed and Jack peered into it with dismay. Rocks, a bottle of oil and candles. Nothing that looked the least bit useful in saving a dying child. The slim light of hope that had ridden with him into the mountains sputtered and dimmed.

His mother always said Myrtle was crazy. Jack was suddenly all too afraid she was right. Heaven knew, madness ran in the family. If that's all she was—just a crazy old woman—David was doomed and Jack would burn in hell for stealing the dying boy from his mother. Pain lanced his chest. He berated himself for his stupidity as doubts tried to suffocate him.

"Take his shirt off, Jack." Myrtle waved one bright red fingernail toward the child.

"Will this hurt him?" Sabrina asked.

Myrtle smiled at the girl. "No, it won't hurt. Jack can tell you. He's been through the ritual before."

Sabrina turned and eyed him curiously.

He took a deep breath, fighting for control. He'd brought David here to be healed. There was nothing more to lose by letting Myrtle try. In the morning, he'd take him back to his mom. There should still be time.

Before he died.

A vise clamped around his heart, but he cleared his throat and forced his voice to sound normal before answering Sabrina.

"I don't remember much about it," he told her truthfully. "Other than the oil smelling bad."

Myrtle unstoppered the oil and the pungent smell of decaying animal filled the room.

Sabrina pinched her nose closed. "Euw."

"Bad?" Larsen said behind him, the word more choke than sound. "That's like calling the Arctic a bit cool."

"Hush, children," Myrtle said softly. She poured a small

The Silhouette Reader Service™ — Here's how it works:

If offer card is missing write to: The Silhouette Reader Service, 3010 Walden Ave., P.O. Box 1867, Buffalo, NY 14240-1867

NO POSTAGE
NECESSARY
IF MAILED
IN THE
UNITED STATES

BUSINESS REPLY MAIL

FIRST-CLASS MAIL   PERMIT NO. 717-003   BUFFALO, NY

POSTAGE WILL BE PAID BY ADDRESSEE

SILHOUETTE READER SERVICE
3010 WALDEN AVE
PO BOX 1867
BUFFALO NY 14240-9952

Play the Lucky Hearts Game

and get...

2 FREE BOOKS and
2 FREE MYSTERY GIFTS...

Yes! YOURS to KEEP!

I have scratched off the silver card.
Please send me my *2 FREE BOOKS* and
2 FREE mystery GIFTS. I understand that I
am under no obligation to purchase any books
as explained on the back of this card.

Scratch Here!
then look below to see
what your cards get you...
2 Free Books & 2 Free
Mystery Gifts!

338 SDL ELWG

238 SDL EL3S

FIRST NAME

LAST NAME

ADDRESS

APT.#

CITY

STATE/PROV.

ZIP/POSTAL CODE

(S-N-04/07)

Twenty-one gets you
2 FREE BOOKS and
2 FREE MYSTERY GIFTS!

Twenty gets you
2 FREE BOOKS!

Nineteen gets you
1 FREE BOOK!

TRY AGAIN!

puddle of oil on David's bare chest and laid two rocks on top of the glistening liquid.

Then she handed the stack of candles and a pack of matches to Jack. "Replace the other candles in the room with these please, nephew, then light them. Larsen, please turn out the lights, then no more talking."

Jack struck a match, the sharp scent barely cutting through the oil's stench, then lit the first candle and each of the others from it.

Soon the silent bedroom flickered with candlelight. Jack stood back from the bed and motioned Sabrina to join him to give Myrtle room. The girl crawled off the bed and came to him, wrapping an arm around his waist as he pulled her against his side.

His aunt sat on the bed, her bloodred robe a startling contrast to the white bedspread. As she placed one hand on the rocks and the other on David's forehead, she began to hum, then sing a soft wordless melody under her breath. At times Jack thought he heard words, but he couldn't be sure.

The air turned thick with hope and promise, and he found himself holding his breath, praying with everything inside him. *Please let this work. Please spare this boy.*

But David remained motionless and Jack cursed himself for his stupidity in believing, even for a moment, that his aunt had some kind of special gift.

Larsen stepped beside him and rested her hand on his shoulder. He slipped his arm around her and pulled her hard against his other side. Both the noise in his head and the turmoil in his heart found a moment's peace within the whirlpool of despair that was sucking him down.

Sabrina pressed her head against his other arm. Poor kid.

He'd made promises he couldn't keep and given her hope where there was none. Idiot.

A pair of gasps sounded in stereo from either side of him, and he blinked at the sight in front of him, his flesh rippling with chills. David's warm brown skin had turned luminous, as if a light were rising to the surface of a dark, still pond. Larsen straightened in his hold. Sabrina pressed herself harder against him. Myrtle hadn't moved. Her eyes were closed as she sang softly.

Jack stared in disbelief. David was glowing. He was flat-out glowing. Sabrina started to cry softly, her shoulders trembling beneath his arm. The light that filled David's body rose to the surface of his skin, then higher, hovering over the boy in a rainbow of harsh, sparkling color.

Larsen gasped. Chills molded and remolded Jack's flesh.

In a sudden flash the hovering light exploded, blowing out the candles in a rush of charged air that blew over his skin like a foul wind. And then it was gone.

Jack stood rooted, not breathing, his mind reeling. *He'd witnessed a miracle.*

"Mommy?" *David's voice.*

Emotion stung his eyes. *She'd done it.*

"It's okay, pal." He disentangled himself from Sabrina and Larsen and moved through the dark toward the bed. "I'm here." But when he reached for the boy, his hand encountered a head of curlers.

"*Myrtle?* Larsen, get the light switch."

Light flooded the room, making him squint against the sudden brightness. David blinked at him, confused and groggy, but very much alive—*thank God*—while Myrtle lay draped across him, unconscious. Or worse.

David smiled at him sleepily. "Hi, Uncle Jack."

"Hey, pal." Jack scooped up Myrtle, but as he was lifting her off David, she took a shuddering breath and her eyes fluttered open.

The fear eased in his chest and he grinned down at her. "You did it."

She smiled weakly. "Did I?" As he started for the door, she lifted her hand. "Where are you taking me?"

"To your bed. You need to lie down.

She waved a wrinkled hand. "No, no, just put me in the chair by the window. These things always take a bit out of me, though I must say, this one took more out of me than usual."

He did as she asked and set her on the overstuffed red chair, then squatted in front of her, taking her wrinkled hands. "Maybe this was a tougher healing job than you've ever had to do. I should have warned you."

Aunt Myrtle looked at him quizzically. "Warned me about what?"

Elfshot.

Elves.

Insanity.

He squeezed her hands and released them. "We need to talk." Excitement pounded through him. He needed to know what she'd done. She'd used magic to counter magic. He might have finally found the weapon he needed, right in his own backyard, so to speak.

Larsen's hand slid over his shoulder. "I'll see to her. David needs you."

Jack straightened and pulled Larsen to him, kissing her hard, needing an outlet for the harsh joy that threatened to blast him into a million pieces.

She pulled back and touched his face, tears sliding down her cheeks. "Go."

As he turned, he found Sabrina staring at him with an unhappy look on her face.

"He's going to be okay, sweetheart." He turned to David. "Aren't you, pal?"

David's gaze followed him. "Where's my mom?"

Jack sat beside the boy on the edge of the bed and took his wrist. His skin was warm, his pulse strong.

"She's at home, David. I'll take you back there tomorrow. Your mom's going to be so glad you're feeling better."

Jack couldn't wait to call Mei, but he couldn't risk it. If Henry traced the call, he could pinpoint their location to Front Royal. And Henry knew Jack had an aunt out here. It would be too easy for his friend to get a fix on him.

Too dangerous.

Though Jack hated putting Mei through this misery, he *had* warned her he wouldn't be in touch. With any luck, he'd have the kids back to her tomorrow, whole and healthy, and she'd forgive him everything.

Jack's thumb ran over the soft underside of the boy's wrist. He looked tired and not entirely healthy—his skin tone still a tad grayish. But his eyes were clear, his pulse strong.

The boy was going to be fine.

It was himself Jack feared would never be the same.

Chapter 12

Larsen sat on one of the cushioned ladder-back chairs at Myrtle's kitchen table and watched the older woman pour three cups of coffee. Both kids were upstairs, sleeping peacefully on the frilly bed. Her gaze slid to Jack where he leaned against the counter. Half a dozen feet separated them, yet she could see the hair on his arms standing on end.

Magic. Honest-to-goodness magic.

It was crazy, exciting, and terrifying.

For some reason she'd found it easier to accept the albino wasn't human than the sparkling lights. Maybe because he looked human. Almost normal. And glowing little boys just didn't.

"Anyone want a shot of whiskey in their coffee?"

Larsen raised her hand. Two shots? Maybe three?

Jack shook his head. "None for me, thanks."

"Not like your father, are you?" Myrtle said, giving Jack a shrewd look.

"No, and I'm not going to be." He met Larsen's gaze. "My father was an alcoholic."

"I'm sorry."

"Yeah." He gave her a rueful look. "Me, too."

Empathy traced the pathways of her heart. With dismay, she dipped her gaze to the yellow daisy place mat in front of her. She was starting to have real feelings for him. Strong feelings.

Feelings she didn't want to have.

The only way she'd survived her solitary world this long was by not needing anyone, by relying solely on herself.

Caring meant needing, and she wanted nothing to do with either one. But what could she do about it? Nothing but stay away from him as she'd vowed to do before. Caring about him didn't change anything. It didn't change what she could do. It didn't change what she was.

Jack brought two of the mugs to the table. As he handed her one, their fingers brushed. Their gazes met and locked, and she found herself drowning in the warmth of his blue-eyed gaze.

Myrtle joined them, startling them apart.

"You said we needed to talk, nephew," she said, taking her seat at the head of the small table.

Jack sat on the chair at her right.

Larsen watched the expressions move over his face as his fingers ran up and down the sides of his coffee mug. He seemed unsure how to start. Finally, with a deep breath, he dove in.

"We think David may have been elfshot."

Myrtle's eyes widened, her gaze going from Jack to Larsen and back again. "Well, I'll be. Of course he was."

Jack scowled, his gaze swinging to Larsen. "Why am I the only one having trouble believing elves are real?".

Myrtle leaned forward and patted his arm. "They were always real, sweetheart. What shocks me is that they're back. There haven't been any elves in the human world for close to fifteen hundred years."

Jack stared at her. "How do you know that?"

"Why, Jack, we have an elf in our family tree. Did your father not mention him?"

Larsen nearly spewed her coffee.

Jack's eyes widened, but Myrtle wasn't through.

"And a Gypsy," she said. "And witches from your great-great-grandmother Hubbard's side."

As she talked, Jack's expression turned from surprise to bemusement to faint impatience, though Larsen was sure the older woman would never notice the latter.

Jack's fingers rapped impatiently on the table. "Aunt Myrtle," he began when she paused for air. "I need to understand your magic."

"Magic?" Myrtle glanced at him in surprise. "Why, Jack, I don't have any magic."

Jack frowned. "What do you think you did up there?"

"Why, healed him, of course."

"And you don't call that magic?" Larsen asked.

Myrtle smiled. "It's just healing."

Glowing children, sparkling lights. If *that* was healing, she'd been going to the wrong doctors, Larsen decided, taking another sip of the spiked coffee.

"Where did you learn to do that?" Jack demanded.

Myrtle smiled. "Why, I've always known. I can't tell you how. No one taught me, if that's what you're asking."

"You just…knew?"

"Yes." Her expression turned wry. "I'm sure that's not what you were hoping for, but gifts have always run in our family. I had an aunt who read minds and an uncle who could talk to his turnips, which was nice. There's a story that one of my great-great-grandmothers claimed she could talk to her ancestors. Or, rather, they could talk to her. Unfortunately she was locked away in a crazy house for that revelation. Never saw her children again, so the story goes."

"Maybe that's where my dad's insanity came from," Jack murmured.

Myrtle shook her head. "I'll never believe he was crazy, Jack."

"He thought he was."

"Yes, well, perhaps the alcoholism did more damage than I knew."

Jack laid his hand on Myrtle's arm. "Do you have any other…gifts, Aunt Myrtle? Other than healing?"

She covered his hand and sighed. "No, nephew. I'm afraid that's all I know. I've often wished my talents were more interesting. Wouldn't it be fun to be able to move objects with your mind or to make your lost car keys appear on a whim?"

Larsen leaned forward, the whiskey making her feel as if she were floating. "Myrtle, do you know of any tricks that might break enchantment?"

"No, dear. I'm afraid I don't know anything about that."

Jack's gaze flicked to Larsen, disappointment stretching between them.

Myrtle stood and carried her mug to the sink. "Well, now, I want to do a couple more oil treatments on the boy just to make sure we've got everything. Nothing so dramatic as the last time, so the two of you may as well sleep." She gave them a knowing look. "Or if you'd like to take a walk in the moonlight, there's a pretty little creek at the bottom of the hill out back."

Jack watched his aunt like a puzzle that had just thwarted him. With a sigh he turned to Larsen and met her gaze with the lift of a single dark brow. "You up for a walk?"

She should say no. No was definitely the right answer. She needed to stay away from Jack. But she'd had just enough whiskey to forget why. Besides, drinking coffee at this hour pretty much guaranteed she wouldn't sleep a wink if she tried to go to bed.

"Okay." They rose as one and let themselves out the sliding-glass door. Larsen kicked off her flip-flops on the deck. Sabrina had left a pair just like them beside David's bed, where she'd fallen asleep.

"Jack…" The full moon cast an otherworldly glow on the landscape. "Have you noticed a difference in the way Sabrina's been treating you lately?"

"No." He glanced at her. "Why?"

The grass felt soft and damp beneath her feet as she stepped off the deck. "I'm pretty sure she has a crush on you."

"What do you mean?"

"I mean, she thinks she loves you."

"Of course she loves me. Both the kids do."

"I'm not talking about loving you like an uncle. She thinks she loves you like a man."

"She's just a kid."

"She's a teenager. It's natural enough. I just thought you should know."

"Thanks," he said as they started down the sloping backyard, past the bushes that lined the yard. "But I don't think it's anything to worry about."

There was nothing more she could say. It probably didn't matter one way or the other.

The night was warm and humid. The scent of honeysuckle floated on a gentle breeze as they made their way down the steep, grassy hill toward the creek below, side by side. Not touching. Which was pretty silly considering she liked him. A lot.

She hooked his arm with her own and leaned against him as they walked toward the creek below, which fluttered across the landscape like a glistening ribbon below. Beyond the creek was a thick wood that gave the impression that Myrtle's house was the only one on the mountain. But the not too distant sound of a car engine accompanied by the thump, thump, thump of newspapers landing on driveways gave lie to the feeling of true isolation.

She could almost forget they were being hunted, could almost believe they were safe, hidden away in a special world. A world of moonlight and magic. With Jack at her side.

As they reached the creek, one of the bushes caught her eye.

"Holly."

"What?"

"There," she said, pointing to the bush eerily illuminated by the full moon. "A holly bush. That article online said holly might ward off enchantment. We should take a few sprigs home with us, just in case."

"I'll cut some in the morning." But his voice sounded distracted. He turned to her, watching her with eyes that shone with a fire that burned through what was left of her reserve. Eyes that promised heaven.

She wanted this. She wanted him. Need filled her veins with a joyous, sparkling warmth. As an owl hooted nearby, she hooked her hands around his neck and pulled him to her, feeling safe so far from those who hunted them.

The night was magic.

Jack's arms went around her, pulling her hard against him as their mouths met in a frenzy of need. She felt free from her skin, floating in a haze of desire beneath the moonlit sky.

He pulled back, cupping her face in his hands, his gaze boring into hers.

"Angel...*I want you.* I want you more than I've ever wanted anyone in my life. If we're not going to finish this, we need to stop it here. Now. While I can still walk."

The thought sent heat running hotly through her veins. "I don't suppose you taped a condom to your butt?"

He didn't laugh. Didn't even crack a smile. "I have one in my pocket. But don't tempt me unless..."

"I won't run this time. I promise." And prayed her devil's sight didn't make a liar out of her yet again.

He took a step back and pulled off his shirt. "Take off your clothes, sweetheart. If you have any trepidation about going through with this, I want to know it now."

Her breath caught at the fire that flared within her. "You want me to strip for you?"

His teeth gleamed white in the moonlight. "Yeah. My fantasy come true."

With unsteady hands, she pulled her T-shirt slowly up her torso, feeling the night air brush her bare skin and slide between the lace to caress her sensitive breasts. She pulled the shirt over her head and tossed it on the grass, then looked up to find him watching her. For the first time she understood the true power of being a woman. Her fingers met at the button of her pants and slowly, so slowly, she lowered the short zipper and slid the pants over her hips until they fell with a whisper to her ankles. She stepped out of them and kicked them toward the shirt.

"Enjoying yourself, Detective?" she asked coyly.

"You're killing me." There was no humor in his words, only raw need that sent heat spiraling low in her body.

"You can take over whenever you want."

"Not for all the tea in China."

She smiled. "Good." She felt wonderful. Powerful. Lust and whiskey making her bold. She reached down and ran a single finger between her legs, over the soft cotton.

Jack made a sound that was half groan, half choke, making her even more bold. She reached for the front clasp on her bra and unfastened it with a snap. Inch by inch, she peeled back the cups, exposing her breasts fully to the night air. Then she dropped the bra, too, on the small pile of clothes and stood in front of him in nothing but her panties.

"You're beautiful," he breathed.

She watched him, heard the truth in his voice. "I've been told that all my adult life. But I never believed…or never cared…until now."

As she hooked her fingers inside her panties, he closed the distance between them.

"You don't want me to finish?"

His warm hands gripped her waist. "Do it."

Slowly she pulled the panties over her hips. His hands followed, his fingers splaying over her buttocks, rocking her with sensation as his fingers dug into her bare flesh. The insides of her thighs grew damp with wanting.

With a low growl, he abandoned the game and knelt on the grass in front of her, sweeping her panties down to her ankles in a single glide of his hands. When her panties had joined the rest of the clothes, he grasped her calves and began a slow upward climb, his thumbs sliding along the insides of her thighs until they reached the fire at her core.

Larsen shuddered, passion exploding outward at his intimate touch. He pressed his face against her abdomen, kissing her, his finger burrowing deep inside her.

With a gasp, she dug her fingers into his hair. "Jack…"

Slowly he withdrew his finger and rose in front of her. As his hands went to his waistband, she reached for him and brushed his hands aside.

"Let me." She unbuttoned his jeans and smiled. "I'm starting to get into this undressing thing."

"You can undress me—or undress in front of me—anytime you like."

"I'll bet." She slid his zipper down over the hard length of his erection, pulling a groan from his throat. He was so hard, so ready. She slid her hand inside the elastic waistband of his boxers to feel the soft damp tip straining toward her. Her fingers slid over the velvet smoothness, down the hard length of him until she held him firmly in her hand.

"Sweetheart, I think you forgot something. The undressing part."

She leaned forward and kissed his bare shoulder. "I'm getting there." Her fingers trailing a silent retreat, she knelt in front of him and pulled his jeans down his legs, then his boxers until he stood in front of her like a god in the moonlight.

He bent and removed a small foil packet from the pocket of the jeans. Then he grabbed her and her world tipped. Larsen found herself flat on her back in the cradle of his arms.

Tenderness poured through her as she wrapped her arms

around him. Her breaths were ragged. Her hips were growing restless, moving. *Needing.*

"Jack, I want you."

"Honey, I've never wanted anyone or anything more." He kissed her temple, then rose, straddling her legs. The night sky framed his head with a smattering of stars as he covered himself with the condom. He came to her and she opened herself to him. He entered her with one smooth thrust. Nothing had ever felt so perfect. So right.

Exquisite sensation exploded from her center outward until she could think of nothing, remember nothing but this moment, this man and the hard thrust of his hips, then fullness filling her and retreating and filling her again. She pulled his face down to her and kissed him deeply, curling her tongue around his, wrapping her legs around his hips, wanting him closer. Deeper. Hers. *I need you. I need you.*

With every hard thrust, he drove her higher. Higher.

His mouth trailed over her jaw. His head lifted and he looked down at her, their gazes meeting, locking. One.

"Fly for me," he whispered.

"And you for me."

The climax burst within her, shattering her into a million blinking stars. As she floated back to earth, Jack thrust hard once, twice more, then on a deep growl of satisfaction, collapsed against her.

But as she cradled his head on her shoulder, running her fingers through his hair, another scene began to overlay the dark night. The harsh daylight of another vision.

Larsen didn't freeze this time, recognizing this vision as one of the odd bedroom scenes, not one of her horrible death visions. But she wasn't in a bedroom this time. She was in the back of a hay wagon.

A woman lay in the wagon, her hair soaked, her round face damp with sweat and gray with nearing death. A second young woman, wearing a pioneer-style bonnet, sat beside her, holding an infant to her breast, crying.

"See?" the second woman said through her tears. "She's healthy. Your daughter's eating already, Sarah. She's going to be fine. You're both going to be fine."

"Jenny." The prone woman touched the other woman's arm. "My blood soaks the hay. You must raise her as your own." She gripped the woman's wrist. "When she reaches first womanhood, there is something you must do, Jenny. It's important. You must bring her into her voices."

"Her what?"

Sarah squeezed her eyes closed as if in terrible pain. "If she's Esri-touched—true to my line—she'll possess a gift—a wonderful gift that will turn on her and destroy her without help. She has a gateway within her head to her forefathers. As a child she'll hear their voices as mere noise. She'll not understand them. Without intervention, as she becomes a woman the noise will grow worse and worse until it tears apart her mind. You must help her, Jenny. When she reaches womanhood you must perform the Ritual of Understanding."

"Sarah…I don't know what you want of me."

"It's simple, Jenny." Moment by moment, Sarah's voice grew weaker. "Press your thumbs to her temples and say these words over and over. *Eslius turatus a quari er siedi. Eslius turatus a quari er siedi.* Promise me, Jenny."

The woman named Jenny nodded, the tears falling freely down her cheeks. "I…I'll try."

"Tell her she'll feel like she's falling, but she must not fight it. When the falling ends, the noise will cease. The voices will speak to her, clear and true, and only when she has need of them."

Sarah's hand fell away from Jenny's wrist. "You must do this for her, Jenny. Promise…"

The woman—Sarah—died.

Jenny's tears turned to sobs. "I don't understand, Sarah. I don't understand. But I'll do as you ask."

And suddenly the scene shifted to a modern bedroom and a young man sitting on a twin bed, head in his hands, his fingers pressed to his head. He was older than any of the others she'd seen. Nearly an adult. Posters of past baseball greats lined the walls behind him.

"Shut up," he said, low and angry. "Just shut up. Leave me alone." With a growl of frustration he looked up with tormented blue eyes and Larsen stared into the face of a younger Jack.

And then her vision cleared. Once more she was lying on the ground, the night air sliding over her heated skin. Jack's warm, naked body was spooned at her back, his hand stroking her arm.

Heart pounding, Larsen's mind swirled with Sarah's revelation. Was it possible? My, God. *He had the voices of his forefathers in his head.* Just as Myrtle claimed her own ancestor had. *Jack's* ancestor.

His arm tightened around her. "Shh, sweetheart. You're safe, Larsen. You're safe with me." He thought she'd frozen on him again.

Without intervention, the noise will grow worse and worse until it tears apart her mind.

Is that what was happening to Jack? Myrtle said her ancestress with the voices in her head was institutionalized and never saw her children again. She wasn't there to pass down the Ritual of Understanding, to teach them to use their gift. To keep future generations from going insane.

The knowledge had been lost.

Until now.

Realization fell into place like the tumblers of a lock. Somehow Jack's ancestors had found a way to communicate with *her,* through the one sense she possessed that others didn't. Her second sight. Her devil's sight.

A hard shiver tore through her.

His lips brushed her bare shoulder. "You're safe, angel."

"I know, Jack. I'm okay."

But she felt like she'd jumped off a cliff in the dark, unsure if the ground stood inches below her feet…or miles. Every time she got one of these visions, the non-death ones, she and Jack had been touching. The first time was beneath the tree as they'd waited for Harrison Rand. Jack had clasped her hand and fallen asleep. The second time they'd been in the bed in Charlie's apartment, as Jack clasped her hands over her head. And just now as they'd joined in the most intimate of embraces.

His ancestors wanted her to help him. They'd shown her the way. Taught her the words.

Oh, God. It was insane. Impossible.

Yet it all fit. She'd seen Jack grip his head as if he were in pain. His younger self had done the same, as had the other kids in the visions. Each episode had shown her the same thing— how to perform the ritual. How to bring Jack into his voices.

Panic flared beneath her rib cage. She couldn't tell him. The very thought of telling him about her visions—*any* of her visions—sent cold dread spiraling deep and heavy inside her.

He wouldn't understand. He wouldn't accept elves, how could he accept *her?*

As his warm hand stroked the heated skin of her abdomen and breast, one thought careened through her brain: she had to try to help him before his mind collapsed beneath the weight of the noise. Now. Before she forgot the words.

She brushed her cheek against the muscled arm that cradled her head as fear clutched her stomach. How could she tell him what she had to do without explaining how she'd come about the knowledge?

Maybe she didn't have to tell him. The ritual was simple enough. With any luck, she could bring him into his voices without him ever knowing she was involved.

Her gaze sliding across the star-studded sky, she prayed this night had room for a second miracle.

Chapter 13

"How about a back rub?" Larsen asked.

Jack propped himself on his elbow, wanting to see her face. "I didn't scare you?"

She rolled onto her back and looked up at him, the moon's glow like twin diamonds in her dark eyes. "You didn't scare me."

But raw, subtle tension vibrated off her in waves.

Would she ever trust him enough to share her private demons? Could he ever trust anyone enough to share his own? Perhaps some things simply had to remain secret. He supposed he could live with that. At least this time she hadn't frozen on him until *after* they'd made love.

God, she'd been amazing. Sensual, abandoned, everything he'd ever dreamed of. Just thinking about that little moonlit striptease was enough to get him hard again. But her passion hadn't lasted. He'd barely finished coming inside her when she'd turned, shaking and unresponsive, as if she'd been sucked into some nightmare world. He wished to hell he knew what was going on in that head of hers. How could he protect her if he didn't know what haunted her?

And he had a sudden, overpowering need to protect her.

"Jack…?"

He trailed his fingers down her face, from her temple to her jaw line. "Hmm?"

"Can I give you a back rub?"

His lips twitched and he leaned down and kissed her, brushing her lush, cool mouth, drinking the sweet taste of lingering passion. "You can rub me any place you like."

She gave a small, feminine snort and patted his shoulder, then rolled out from under him. "Lie down."

"The grass is wet."

She made a sound of amused disbelief. "Hypocrite. You were happy enough to have me lying on it."

A burst of joyous laughter caught in his chest and he grabbed her and upended her back onto the grass, his naked body once more covering hers. He grinned down at her. "I like you lying on it…as long as I can act as your blanket."

Her arms snaked around his neck and she pulled him down for a thorough, mind-destroying kiss. With every stroke of her tongue, every caress of her fingers against the back of his neck, his joy grew stronger, filling him until the air seemed to squeeze from his lungs.

She was his, dammit. *His.* And he wanted to shout it to the moon. She was his mate. His partner.

His love.

He froze, mid-kiss. *Love.*

Hell.

Larsen pushed at his shoulders. "Lie down, Jack. I want to give you a back rub."

He was too stunned to argue. When in the hell had he fallen in love with the woman? Yet he had. There was no denying he wanted her, not just for this moment, but for always. Forever.

Head spinning, he let her push him onto his stomach on the damp grass where she wanted him. He felt her straddle his hips, her soft sex brushing his buttocks. A groan escaped his throat as need surged through him all over again. Dammit. He'd only brought one condom and he was ready to make love to her all over again.

Wonder filled him. How many times had he thought he'd made love to a woman? More times than he could count. Only now did he understand the difference. With the others, he'd had sex. Just sex. He'd truly made love to only one woman. Larsen.

"Relax," she said, then began to rub his shoulders with quick, tense motions that were anything but relaxing.

He grinned into the crossed arms that pillowed his head. She didn't have the first idea how to give back rubs. But as long as she was touching him, he was a happy man. He closed his eyes and gave himself up to whatever she wanted to do to him. Then it would be his turn. Oh, *yeah*.

Her hands clasped his head. "Facedown. I'll give you a head massage, too."

Jack smiled and rested his forehead on his arms. "I'm your willing slave, sweetheart."

Her fingers dug through his hair, then down to his temples where she began to press and murmur something beneath her breath.

"Hmm?"

"Nothing." But she continued her murmurings. Maybe some kind of prayer. He hadn't taken her for a...

Searing pain split his head, tearing a yell from his throat, ripping him from his body and sending him tumbling into blackness.

Terror swirled through him, raking him with razor-sharp claws as he free fell through madness, an inky blackness that had no form. Voices all around him. He could feel them, not just hear them. They ripped at his skin from inside, as if clawing to get out. Pain seared every nerve ending, every cell and molecule of his body.

Falling.

Stop. He had to stop.

He struggled against the insanity that swallowed him. Was this it? The moment he'd feared all his life? The moment he went completely, utterly insane?

No. Climb out. Out. Or be lost.

"Jack!"

Larsen.

She needed him. Fear for her twined with his terror, expanding them into one until his mind threatened to explode like a balloon with too much air.

Where was she? Where was *he?*

Falling.

The voices joined in with the pain and surged into a riot of sound that would have exploded his eardrums if he'd had any. If he'd been anything more than pure pain.

"Jack! I'm sorry. Come back. Come back."

Larsen needed him. He had to reach her. But how? He had to stop falling. He had...to...stop.

The sensation of falling ceased abruptly.

The feeling of drowning in a thick black fog took its place. Voices screamed at him from every side. Voices that threatened to tear him apart.

"Jack!"

Larsen. He had to get to her.

"Jack."

He followed the voice. *Keep calling, Larsen. Keep calling.*

"Jack, wake up. *Jack.*"

And suddenly he was back in his body, lying facedown in a bright pool of agony. He rolled over and blinked up at her, gripping his head against the slicing pain.

In the early dawn light, he could see the tears in her eyes and he reached for her face.

"I'm sorry," she whispered. "I'm so sorry."

"Larsen?" Why was she sorry?

"I didn't know, Jack. I swear I didn't know. I thought it would help."

He closed his eyes and tried to control the pain enough to think. He was losing his mind. Suddenly, terribly.

Not now. Not when he finally had something—*someone*—to live for.

"I'm so sorry."

He sat up with effort, his stomach aching as though he'd been sucker-punched, every muscle taut and bruised. She was sorry.

"Why?"

Larsen stared at him like a doe in the headlights, tears glistening in her brown eyes. "I thought I could help you understand the voices."

Her words tore through his chest like a bullet. He grabbed

her wrist, suddenly, *horribly* clearheaded. "What did you say?" No one knew about his voices. He'd never told a soul. No one!

"I...I was trying to help you."

"*By nearly driving me to the brink of madness?* Why did you think I needed help?"

"You...talk in your sleep." Her eyes shifted sideways, just a flicker, but it was enough.

She was lying. Unbelievable—she was lying to him again! "What in the hell did you do to me?" She winced and he loosened his hold on her, but grabbed her shoulders and pulled her close. "I want the truth, Larsen. For one blasted moment, give me the truth. What in the hell did you do to me?"

"I don't know. I thought it would help you, but it didn't."

"Help me *how?*"

She tugged against his hold on her arm. "Let me go, Jack."

"*Answer me.*"

"I can't explain." She stared at him with those dark, secret-filled eyes.

"You'd damn well better start. You've been lying to me from the beginning. From the moment you left that church, you've been lying." Yet he'd chosen to ignore it. *Fool.*

The evidence of her duplicity swirled around him, pummeling him from every direction, ripping his heart to shreds. "Your touch....every time I touch you, the voices quiet. It's magic, isn't it? You're quieting the voices with magic. You're one of them."

"No!"

His angel. God, he was a fool. He gripped her arm until she winced. "What did you do to me? You tried to steal my mind."

"No! I...had a dream. I think your voices were talking to me. They told me what to do and I tried to do it. I was trying to help you."

And then it hit him. His fingers were wrapped around her bare skin, yet the voices were as loud as ever. Her touch no longer quieted the riot.

The final betrayal. Denial clawed at his throat.

"You've stopped quieting them. After pulling me through hell, you've taken even that from me." Despair crashed over him. His mind was almost gone. The one who might have saved him had turned on him.

He released her, suddenly unable to touch her. She reached for him.

"Stay away from me." Pain. So much pain. She'd discovered his madness. No one knew. *No one had ever known.* Everything was wrong. Every single thing in his life was wrong.

He pulled on his clothes and headed for the house alone, leaving his heart shattered and bleeding by the creek.

What had she done?

Larsen hugged her knees to her bare chest as tears burned the backs of her eyes. She'd tried to help him.

Stupid, stupid, stupid.

Why had she thought it would work? Why had she thought her visions could ever be used for good? They'd always brought death and misery. Poor Jack. The sound of his cry of pain lashed through her memory. God, what had she done to him? For a moment, she'd thought she was losing him.

In the end, she had.

A misty rain began to fall as even the stars abandoned her. Larsen pushed herself to her feet and struggled into her clothes, hands shaking, her heart shriveling at the memory of the way he'd looked at her just before he left, just before the clouds covered the moon's glow, leaving her in darkness. In his beautiful eyes she'd seen disgust. *Betrayal.*

Yet it was *she* who felt beaten and betrayed.

Every time I touch you, the voices quiet.

Pain lanced her heart as the meaning of his words tore through her anew. For the first time, she understood why he touched her so often. Touching her had quieted the voices in his head as his ancestors tried to communicate through her visions.

All she'd been to Jack was a cure for the noise. A tool to quiet his head. The soft touches, the romantic little gestures had never had anything to do with his feelings for her. He'd have been all over the kitchen sink if stroking it had had the same effect.

Unhappiness twisted her into knots of dull misery. She wanted to hate him for using her, but she'd seen the kids in those visions. She'd seen Jack hold his head in pain. Touching her had brought him some relief. It wasn't fair to blame him for that.

Yet it was clear the relationship she'd thought was growing between them was a sham. He'd needed her, but not the way she was starting to need him.

The tears slipped down her cheeks. How many years had she kept others at bay knowing—*knowing*—nothing good could ever come of letting someone else get close?

She didn't need Jack Hallihan. She didn't need anyone.

And maybe if she repeated that over and over and over, her chest would stop feeling like it was cracking apart. Her heart would no longer feel like it was breaking.

Pain pounded the inside of Jack's head, pummeling him like a million brass-knuckled fists until he expected the bone to crack and shatter. The pain should have stopped. Never before had the voices actually hurt. But two hours had passed since he'd left Larsen at the creek and the pain remained fierce.

What had she done to him?

He watched the light rain fall like a mist outside the guest room window. Behind him, the familiar beep-beep of a *Road Runner* cartoon triggered David's infectious giggle.

David. The one bright spot in his nightmare of a life.

The boy had woken a short while after Jack returned to the house, his color a rich, healthy brown, the gray cast gone as if it had never been.

Jack turned to where the boy sat up in bed, pillows stacked behind him. He still looked tired, the circles beneath his eyes pronounced, but no more so than any kid who'd been through a tough illness and was well on the road to recovery.

Tonight, he'd take him home. Both the kids. Mei had to be frantic by now, but he had no way to contact her that couldn't be traced. After dark, he'd take them back. He and Larsen.

His gut clenched anew at her betrayal. He wanted to hate her for it, but he'd seen the horror in her eyes. Heard the devastation in her voice. He didn't know what she'd done to him, but his heart, mind and gut all told him one thing. She hadn't meant to hurt him. But it didn't mean he had to forgive her. He wasn't sure he could, not the way he felt now.

He heard a sound in the hall and turned to find Sabrina standing in the doorway, watching him. She started to turn away when he met her gaze, but not before he'd glimpsed the look on her face. The lovesick look of a teenage girl.

Damn. Larsen was right.

The girl strolled into the room and sat on the end of the bed, ignoring him.

"Sabrina, move," David complained. "You're in the way."

"Too bad." She glanced at Jack, then away. "Where's *Larsen?*" Her tone was laced with jealousy. What happened to the little girl he'd known and loved for so long?

"Asleep," he told her. He'd heard Larsen come in soon after he'd left her at the creek.

"Are you going to marry her?"

Jack opened his mouth, then closed it slowly. He didn't know what to tell her. Yesterday he might have said yes, if Larsen would have him. But today? Now? His heart still shouted yes but his mind…

Sabrina's eyes widened. "You are! You hardly even know her."

Jack grimaced. He wasn't sure his head could take any more, but clearly he was going to have to do *something*. He started for the hall and motioned Sabrina to follow.

She hesitated, then jumped off the bed and stalked after him. The look she gave him broke his heart. Her chin jutted stubbornly, defiantly, but her eyes ached with feeling and vulnerability.

"Sabrina, honey, I'm old enough to be your father."

The girl gasped.

"You may think you have feelings for me, but…"

"I don't! I don't have feelings for you." Her eyes welled with tears. "I hate you! I hate you!"

"Sabrina…"

She ran into the bathroom and slammed the door, probably waking both Larsen and Myrtle. What just happened? He'd hardly said anything.

Her sobs carried to him, tearing his heart to shreds. He was a monster. And he didn't even know what he'd done.

God, his life was screwed.

He went back into the guest room where David watched cartoons and sank down on the chair by the window. His head pounded. Tipping it against the upholstered back, he wondered what else could go wrong.

Larsen woke to the sound of David's childish laughter and rolled over to grab her phone. She squinted, bleary-eyed at the tiny time readout. Almost nine. Three whole hours of sleep. After the debacle with Jack at the creek, she was surprised she'd managed to fall asleep at all.

The memory of what happened rushed over her like an acid wind, searing her skin all over again. She hadn't seen Jack when she'd come in. How was she going to face him now?

She could avoid the inevitable confrontation a little while longer. Better to sleep and escape, if she couldn't forget.

But then she noticed someone had left a message on her phone. Her brows knit in confusion. This was a new phone. A new number. She hadn't given it to…no wait. She had. She'd given the number to Autumn, her friend at the Smithsonian, when she'd sent her the e-mail. Suddenly wide awake, she sat up and returned her old friend's call.

"Autumn, it's Larsen. You got my message."

"Hey, girlie. Where in the heck have you *been?* I haven't seen or heard from you in *ages.*" There was a note of mild rebuke in her friend's tone and Larsen was sorry for putting it there. Autumn had been a great roommate in college and would have been a close friend if Larsen had let her. She was one of the few people Larsen regretted keeping at arm's length. "So how's the lawyering?"

"Great," Larsen replied. "We'll have to have coffee and

catch up." *If I survive long enough.* "Were you able to dig up anything on the Stone of Ezrie?"

"Yes. Quite a bit, in fact. There's an interesting legend attached to it that says it's the key to the elven world. *Elves,* Larsen. Isn't that a hoot?"

Larsen made a noncommittal sound, every muscle in her body tensing.

Autumn continued. "More specifically, it's the elven key to *our* world. We have it. If they get it back, we're supposedly doomed. I dug a bit further into the legend and found a writing by a monk in the twelfth century. He believed there used to be a dozen gates between the two worlds. Each opened only once a month for about an hour. He says that in the sixth century the gates were sealed, but there was reason to fear one was never found and never sealed. The monk warns mankind to be ever vigilant, lest the elves find that unsealed gate and return for their key."

Larsen pressed her hand to her forehead as the thoughts in her head swirled, trying to get out. It was true. It was all true. Elves and elf gates and other worlds. Chills raced over her skin.

"Larsen, what's all this about? Are you representing the thief or something?"

Larsen choked on a laugh. "No. It's complicated, Autumn. *Unbelievably* complicated." She wished Jack had been on the line to hear all this. "So, the gates open once a month. Does it say when?"

"At midnight of the full moon."

"The full…" Her heart gave a lurch and she stood, suddenly rigid. "The moon's full now."

"Almost. I can check." She heard the clacking of Autumn's keyboard. "Tonight, Larsen. Tonight is the full moon."

"Damn. Thanks, Autumn, but I've got to go." She ran for the door, thankful she'd never bothered to undress, and went to find Jack. She found him snoring softly in David's room, slouched low in the chair by the window, looking tired, his mouth tight.

"Jack, we've got a problem," she said none too quietly as she crossed the room. He came awake with a start, then grabbed his head and grimaced, his eyes lanced with pain. Guilt punched her in the stomach. Her fault. She'd done this to him.

"What's the matter, Larsen?"

She told him what Autumn said, praying he'd believe her, that he wouldn't hold what happened at the creek against her in this. But as she spoke, she could see the doubt in his eyes.

"Jack, you read people better than anyone I know. Am I lying to you now?"

A muscle leaped in his jaw. "No." He looked away, his expression growing more grave, more grim by the second. Finally he turned back to her and met her gaze with hard cop eyes. "We've got to get back. If she's right, we're out of time."

Larsen nodded. "I agree."

He stood and grabbed his phone. "I'll call Harrison. Maybe he's had some luck reaching that spook brother of his. We're going to need all the help we can get." He grimaced. "Would you tell Sabrina we need to leave? Last I heard she was slamming the bathroom door."

Larsen crossed the hall and knocked. "Sabrina?"

"Go away!"

"Sabrina, we're leaving. We're going to take you home."

"I'm not going with you," the teen shouted.

Larsen sighed. "Sabrina, you can't stay here."

"I'm waiting for my dad. He's coming to get me."

Larsen's jaw dropped, her blood turning to ice. She heard Jack behind her and turned to meet his shocked gaze.

He brushed past her to pound on the door himself. "When did you call your dad, Sabrina? I need to know."

But the question became irrelevant as the sound of sirens carried on the wind.

Chapter 14

"*We've got to get out of here.*"

The blood pounded through Jack's head, driven by the jackhammer Larsen had somehow unleashed on him and the realization that Sabrina had unwittingly turned traitor.

He met Larsen's wide eyes as he slammed his fist against the bathroom door. "Sabrina, open up!"

"They could be fire trucks," Larsen said, but he heard the thread of fear in her voice.

"Are you willing to risk it?"

"No."

The sirens were getting closer every minute and by the sound he'd guess there were at least three cars. The idiots! Sirens were hardly the way to surprise the enemy. Then again, Jack wasn't the enemy. Maybe somewhere beneath the Esri's enchantment, his men still knew that.

"We'll never get down that driveway in time. We're going to have to escape on foot. Get Myrtle and get going," he told Larsen. "She'll need the extra time. I'll bring the kids."

Jack pounded on the door, every beat of his fist vibrating in his head until he thought it would explode. "Open up!"

"No! Go away."

Fury and fear blew away his patience and he kicked in the door. Sabrina huddled on the floor fully clothed and stared at him, her mouth agape.

"Come on. We're leaving."

"No." She scooted away from him, until her back was pressed against the tub. A hint of fear glinted in her eyes that tore at his soul. "I'm waiting for my dad."

"Your dad is not himself, Sabrina. His mind is being controlled by an evil…person. He'll kill you and not even know he's done it until it's too late."

"I don't believe you," she whispered, her eyes truly frightened now.

"Then you'll die."

She didn't move. The sirens were getting louder.

"Sabrina…" Tension vibrated through him. Every second they delayed could cost them their lives. "Have I ever given you a reason not to trust me?"

"No."

"Then come with me. Please. Just in case things aren't what you think."

The stubborn look returned, but she rose and stomped toward the door. "Fine."

Thank God.

He swooped David off the bed and followed Sabrina down the stairs and out the back door. A light rain fell as they started down the hill. Just what they didn't need, though maybe it would discourage their attackers. Assuming enchantment could be discouraged.

Ahead of them, Larsen was helping Myrtle down the steep, slippery hill. They'd gotten a head start, but not nearly enough. Myrtle was spry for her age, but much too slow to outrun a cop.

How was he going to keep them alive if Henry and the others came after them? They needed to find a place to hide.

Sabrina ran ahead and caught up to the two women. Jack, with David in his arms, reached them a minute later. "Aunt Myrtle, do you have any neighbors who would hide you and the kids?"

Myrtle's face was red with exertion, her gray hair drooping around her face, her eyes wide and frightened.

"Oh, Jack. No. I pretty much keep to myself up here. Besides, I'd have to know someone very well indeed to ask them to hide me from the police."

The sirens ended abruptly as the little band reached the creek.

"Hurry!" he urged. "We've got to get into the trees."

They quickly crossed the creek together. As they reached the woods on the other side, the sound of gunfire exploded from the direction of Myrtle's house.

Myrtle gasped. Sabrina turned to him with wide, frightened eyes as they made their way through the trees.

"They don't know what they're doing, sprite. That's why they're so dangerous. They'd never in a million years hurt us if they had a choice."

"They sure do waste a lot of ammunition this way," Larsen muttered.

"They're like zombies," Jack said. "They're given an address and they destroy it."

"Will they keep searching when they realize we're not in there?" Myrtle asked.

"I don't know. They didn't when they came after us a couple of nights ago." They'd emptied their guns into the water where Larsen disappeared, never once looking for her elsewhere. "But he seems to be getting stronger. There's no telling what he's capable of."

Behind them a shout rang out. "Find them!"

"Hell. They're searching. Let's go."

They pushed their way through the woods until the trees thinned, a housing development sprouting up on either side.

"Sabrina," Larsen said. "Help Myrtle. I need to get something."

"What do you see?" Jack asked, coming up behind her.

"We need the holly."

"Jack," Myrtle gasped. "You…go on. I can't…keep up."

"I'm not leaving you, Aunt Myrtle." He spotted a good-size wooden shed three houses down, set far back from the house at the edge of the tree line. Assuming he could get into the thing, maybe it would work. They were out of options.

The house itself had a closed, "on vacation" look to it. The shades were drawn, the back porch light still on midmorning. Jack set David on the ground, told them all to wait, then slipped around to see if he could get into the shed. To his relief, the door was open. He saw why when he opened it.

The shed was filled with junk—rotting lumber, a couple of rusted bikes, half a dozen rakes and shovels, along with a lawn mower, a fertilizer spreader and a wheelbarrow. Not a lot of room for five people, but it would have to do.

He motioned to Larsen and went to grab David, but the boy waved him off. "I can walk, Uncle Jack. I'm not sick anymore."

With a nod, he ruffled the boy's tight curls, then helped Myrtle maneuver over the tree roots without tripping, and ushered them all inside. The smell of rotting grass and fertilizer nearly overpowered his sinuses.

He pulled the door closed, blanketing them in darkness.

"It stinks in here," Sabrina whispered.

"Hold your nose," David said.

"Shh, you two. Larsen, open the door, just a crack. I need some light."

She did as he asked. He lifted the wheelbarrow and set it on its side, then did the same with the spreader, leaving a small space in between.

"Kids," he whispered. "Lay down between these."

"It's gross," Sabrina whispered.

"Get down, Sabrina," he said sharply. He loved the kid, but she was trying his patience. "If bullets start flying, you'll have some protection."

"Bullets?"

Okay, maybe honesty wasn't the best policy when it came to kids, but he damned well didn't have time to filter his words.

"Get down, both of you. Myrtle, come here." He helped his aunt into the corner on the other side of the wheelbarrow.

"What about the lawn mower," Larsen asked in a whisper. She stood silhouetted in the doorway, a couple of sprigs of holly sticking out of her back pants' pockets like prickly tail feathers. "Could we tip it, too?"

"It's probably still loaded with gas."

Her eyes widened and their gazes met. In those golden-brown eyes he saw perfect understanding. It would blow sky-high if a bullet struck it. Then again, if the bullets started flying, there wasn't a lot of chance of survival for any of them.

Regret softened her eyes before she broke the contact. Regret for what might have been? Or for what she'd done to him? He couldn't know. None of it mattered now. All that mattered was staying alive.

He stepped over a pile of rotting lumber to join Larsen by the door. "Close it, Larsen, and move to the side, away from the door."

The only sounds now were the occasional sniffle—he suspected Sabrina was crying—and the sound of a dog barking in the distance. All normal neighborhood sounds had been silenced by the crack of gunfire.

Seconds ticked by like hours, the minutes an eternity. He stood facing the door in clothes damp from rain and sweat, his gun hanging at his side, ready to kill the men he'd sworn to give his life for.

If they survived this, if *he* survived, he'd kill that son-of-a-bitch Esri.

A twig cracked heavily near by. A single crack. Someone approached.

Fear tasted like cardboard on his tongue. *Go by. Ignore the shed.* If that door opened, he was going to have to shoot. How could he do it? How could he shoot one of his own men?

No choice. He had to protect the lives inside the shed. And he had to survive long enough to stop the Esri.

The steps moved closer, toward the door. Heavy, slow, careful steps. Cop's steps.

Jack's breaths echoed in his ears. His heart thudded in his chest until he was sure the sound would give them away. Never in his worst nightmare could he have imagined being put in this position. Fury ate through his heart like acid. The albino was going to die for this. If Jack survived the next few minutes, the albino was going to die.

The steps drew closer. Jack raised his gun.

The door vibrated as someone gripped the handle, then flew open in a wash of hazy daylight. In the doorway, a cop looked down the barrel of his revolver.

"Hank."

Jack was going to die.

Fear slammed into Larsen's chest, pounding through her veins like a jackhammer on a city sidewalk. The cop had his gun pointed right at Jack's chest and Jack wasn't moving. He couldn't pull the trigger on his friend. With desperation, she reached for the closest thing that could act as a weapon, her hand closing around a long-handled shovel.

Her muscles bunched and strained as she swung the shovel upward with all her might connecting, with a thud, with the big cop's gun arm. A shot fired at the ceiling, sending a spray of wood chips and dust raining down on them. Jack dove for the man's legs, tackling him, sending him crashing onto the piles of rotting lumber.

Larsen reached for one of the prickly holly sprigs she'd stuck in her back pocket and shoved it up the cop's pant leg before he could roll away. The man stilled instantly. Larsen dragged breaths into her lungs as if she'd run a five-mile race, her heart thudding in her ears.

Jack pressed the barrel of his gun into Henry's neck. "Freeze!" The two men were awash in the misty daylight flowing in from the open shed door. Beads of sweat ran down Jack's temples.

Henry tried to move, but Jack pushed the gun harder into his neck. "Don't move! Drop your gun, Hank."

"What's the matter with you, Jack?"

"Drop it."

"Sure, sure. No problem." He dropped the gun onto the ground beside his head.

Jack grabbed the weapon, flicked something on it, then tossed it behind him, Henry staring at him as if he'd lost his mind. "Get it, Larsen."

She picked up the heavy gun, the first she'd ever touched in her life.

"Now will you get the hell off me?" the bigger man said.

Larsen backed up, cradling the gun, half afraid it would go off if she so much as moved it.

"What are you doing here, buddy?" Jack asked softly.

"I'm…" Henry stopped. Confusion, then a flash of fear entered his eyes. "I'm…supposed to…heaven help me. I'm supposed to kill you."

"Do you know why?"

The big man's eyes narrowed with thought and no small amount of horror. "No. Just that…*Baleris*. He's the one calling the shots now."

"And what are you going to do about it?"

The cop scowled. "You're my partner, man."

Jack nodded. "That's more like it." He pushed to his feet and held out his hand to the other man and helped him up.

"What's going on?" Henry asked, his face still a mask of confusion and disgust. His gaze swung to her and narrowed as if he couldn't quite place her. The dark hair was doing the trick.

"Daddy?" Sabrina sat up from behind the wheelbarrow.

Henry jerked toward the sound. "Sabrina?"

David popped up beside her. "Hi, Dad!"

"Davy? But…what are you…? I thought…"

As the kids started to rise, Jack stepped between them and aimed the gun at their father. "Get down, both of you!"

"But—" Sabrina began.

"Now! Hank, I'm sorry, but Baleris has your mind and I can't take a chance on you hurting your kids."

Henry nodded, his eyes wide. "Do as Jack says."

"But, Dad…"

"Sabrina," Henry barked. "Down. Now."

"Yes, sir." The girl knelt, her expression sullen even as tears sprang to her eyes. Larsen felt a stab of sympathy for the girl. Sabrina was having a rotten day. She needed reassurance that her dad wasn't going to hurt her. But they couldn't give her that.

"What's going on, Jack?" Henry raised his hands even as Jack lowered his gun.

"It's Baleris. Hank, are any other cops with you?"

His dark brows pulled together. "No. We split up back at the house." His dark skin positively paled. "We…you…you were all in there?"

"Not when you were shooting. We ran when we heard the sirens."

"We riddled that place, man."

"I know. That's why I want you to keep your distance from your kids until I'm sure you're safe."

Henry's shoulders sagged, his expression melting. "What's he done to me?"

Jack let out a heavy breath. "It's a long story, but the bottom line is, he's controlling the minds of the entire M.P.D. You're his own private hit squad."

"Damn."

"We've got to get out of here before any more cops come after us."

"How?" Henry winced and shook the holly branch out of his pant legs. "Do you have a plan?"

"Yeah. Come in and shut the door."

"Wait," Larsen said. "The holly."

Henry's hand shot out toward her. "My gun." As the big man's gaze swung up to meet hers, she saw the hard calculation in his eyes.

The enchantment.

"Jack…" As Henry lunged for her, Larsen leaped backward, slamming her back into one of the wood studs that held up the wall.

Jack brought the butt of his gun down hard on the back of his friend's head. With a heavy thud, Henry collapsed at her feet.

"Daddy!" Sabrina cried, and ran for her father.

Jack shoved his gun into his waistband. "The holly didn't work."

"It worked while it touched him. But it only dampened the effects of the enchantment. It didn't break it."

Sabrina knelt beside the prone man and turned horrified eyes on Jack. "You killed him."

"No, baby." He knelt beside her and pressed his fingertips to Henry's neck. "Feel his pulse, Sabrina. It's good and strong."

But the girl stared at him as if she hadn't heard. "I hate you!"

Jack sighed. "Sweetheart, if I'd meant to kill him, I wouldn't have used the *handle* of the gun, now would I?"

Sabrina threw herself on her dad.

Jack picked up the holly sprig and shoved it back up Henry's pant leg. "This is scratching the hell out of his leg."

"I know," Larsen said. "But I don't know if it's the branch or the leaves that do the trick, and something worked. We can experiment later."

"I agree."

Larsen looked around. "We need a length of rope or something to keep it from falling out again."

Jack pulled a small pocketknife out of his pocket and tossed it to her. "There's a sled back there with a cord."

Larsen retrieved the cord and retraced her steps carefully over the piles of lumber and junk. She handed it to Jack and watched as he tied it carefully around Henry's leg at the ankle.

"Nice work with the shovel," he said without inflection.

"I was afraid he was going to shoot you."

"Me, too." He glanced at her, then away, a hint of self-loathing in his eyes. "I hesitated. I could have gotten us all killed."

"But you didn't." Compassion eased through her, a need to comfort and to reassure. She laid her hand on his arm. "You've spent years protecting your partner. I'd be more worried about you if you hadn't had any qualms about killing him. He wasn't attacking you on purpose. And, good grief, his kids were watching. How *could* you have pulled that trigger?"

"That doesn't help a lot." He met her gaze and made a rueful twist with his mouth. "But it does help."

He held out his hand. "Give me the gun and I'll show you how to use it."

"How do you know I'm not a crack shot?"

"Because you're holding it like it's going to explode."

"Yeah, well, maybe you're right." She laid the gun carefully onto his outstretched palm. "Are you sure you want me handling this thing?"

"Positive. You're my backup if anything goes wrong."

The thought was at once reassuring, that he still trusted her, and infinitely depressing. If she was the backup against a dozen cops, they were in deep trouble.

Jack showed her the basics, then handed the gun back to her. With trembling fingers, she set the safety and shoved the gun into the waistband of her pants.

"What do you think?" she asked, holding her arms out at her sides. "Do I look like a cop now?"

His gaze slid slowly down her body as something warm and carnal moved in his eyes.

"You want to play cop for real?"

She dropped her hands. "What do you mean?"

"We need a getaway car. And I can't leave Henry."

Larsen swallowed. "What are you saying?"

He handed her Henry's badge. Larsen's eyes widened. "You want me to impersonate a police officer?"

"We need a car. You can either appropriate it with the badge, or the gun. Your choice."

She stared at him in disbelief. "You're serious."

He nodded once, sharply. "Dead serious. If we don't stop Baleris, we could be facing a much larger threat than one lone Esri. We're the only ones who can stop him. He's shoved us outside of the law by sending the police after us. We're going to have to work out of here for now."

The thought of resorting to car-jacking sickened and terrified her. What if something went wrong? What if someone got hurt?

"Jack, I don't think I can do this."

He grabbed her shoulders. "You can do it, angel. If there's anyone I trust to get the job done—any job done—it's you."

She searched his eyes. "I don't know how you trust me after what I did to you."

Something cool and guarded moved through those blue depths. He dropped his hands. "I don't seem to have a choice."

Larsen sighed. "When you put it that way…" Still, she'd

give anything if she could give the job to someone else. But there wasn't anyone. She could either get the car, or try to keep Henry from killing them all. "One car, coming up."

He reached for her again, then dropped his hand, his expression turning cool and guarded. "Be careful out there." For a moment something warm passed like a shadow through his eyes. "I need you."

Larsen swallowed and nodded. "Here goes nothing." She eased out of the shed and into the drizzle, the safety of the world riding squarely on her shoulders.

Chapter 15

"Dad, it was so cool." David leaned over the armrest of the car seat. "Sabrina says there were lights and everything."

"Lights?" Henry's expression was one of classic disbelief. The two men sat in the far back of the minivan; Henry was bound, hand and foot, the ropes then tied around the bench seat. If he tried to go anywhere, he'd be taking the car with him.

"It's true, Dad," Sabrina said from the second captain's chair. "David was glowing, then the light rose out of him and turned colorful and sparkly."

Henry's disbelieving gaze swiveled to Jack.

Jack nodded slowly. Quick movements just made the pain in his head worse. "Hank, if you're looking for logical, forget it. We left that station about a hundred miles back."

Rain fell lightly outside, the soft swish of the windshield

wipers a whisper against the riot going on in his head. They were on I-66 heading east toward D.C. Larsen was driving, her grip on the wheel white-knuckled and rigid. Beside her, Myrtle talked animatedly as if they were returning home from a family vacation instead of attempting to elude capture and death in a stolen vehicle.

Larsen's dyed hair swung around her chin as she turned at something Myrtle said, her expression preoccupied. Her gaze swiveled toward him, and for a single heartbeat their gazes met before she turned back to the road. He felt the touch of her gaze like a kick to his solar plexis. She was so damned beautiful. Even after what she'd done to him, he wanted her with an ache that was a living, pulsing thing inside him. An ache that would never be eased.

His dream of a future with her was gone. Whatever she'd done to him had accelerated the course of his madness by months, probably years. And her touch no longer gave him the respite he needed to ever hope to stay sane. No, his days were numbered. He just had to hang on to his sanity long enough to catch the Esri. And save the world.

"They said I was going to die, Dad," David said as if talking about nothing more than a cut on his knee. "I heard them. Uncle Jack rescued me and Aunt Myrtle healed me."

Henry's gaze went from Jack to his son and back again. His eyes narrowed as if turning inward, digging for memory. "You kidnapped him out of the hospital?" His eyes cleared as memory apparently returned. "Mei was frantic."

"Yeah. I'm sorry for putting her through that, but the docs had given David up for dead. I had to try to save him."

"And you did." Henry's eyes narrowed with wonder and gratitude. "You risked everything for my son."

"I'm glad it worked." An understatement if there ever was one.

"I owe you, man."

"You've already paid." Jack pressed his palm to his forehead as if he could push the pressure down. "Do you remember calling me the night you shot up my house?"

Henry blanched. "Shot it up?"

"Yeah. You've been busy, Hank. Anyway, you called me and woke me up. You saved my life. You told me you had to kill me and that you were sorry." Jack felt his mouth twitch. "I was the white brother you'd never had."

Henry grinned, the slash of white across his dark face familiar and welcome. "The white brother I never had, huh? Not to be confused with my blue or green brothers." His eyes turned sober. "I saved you? Really?"

"You did. I was so tired, I'd never have heard the cars in time if you hadn't woken me. I'm just saying…you're the brother *I* never had. And your family's mine."

Henry nodded, then turned to look out the window, blinking a little too fast. "Tell me what's going on, Jack. All of it."

As the wipers rubbed lazily against the windshield, Jack told him. About the Esri, the enchantment, the Stone of Ezrie, and the deadline of the full moon. The traffic began to slow as they neared the D.C. suburbs, though they were still a good twenty miles from the city. The car's air conditioner blew steadily, ruffling the edges of his hair.

"Hank, what do you know? What is Baleris doing in the police station?"

Henry shook his head. "I don't…" Suddenly he grimaced, his expression turning pained.

"What's the matter, Hank? What's hurting."

"Nothing. Everything. I just remembered."

"Tell me."

Henry tipped his head back, his mouth grim. "He's turned the interrogation room into his private quarters. Pillows everywhere like a sultan's palace. He's got us bringing him food and wine at all hours of the day and night. And every morning a…"

He squeezed his eyes closed, his face a mask of grief. Finally he turned toward Jack and mouthed, "A virgin. A college kid." He said the last, his voice filled with pain. "And we're helping him."

"You don't have a choice, Hank. You don't even know what you're doing. I'm amazed you remember. No one else has been able to."

"It must be the holly," Larsen called back. Obviously the entire car was eavesdropping on their conversation.

Henry lowered his voice to barely a whisper and leaned toward Jack. "He feeds off the taking of them. The blood strengthens his magic."

"How do you know they're…" Jack grimaced. He really didn't want to know the details.

"He can tell just by looking at them. Says they glow."

"So you…what? Bring him several girls to choose from?"

"No." He made a pained sound deep in his throat. "We're rounding them up. We've got more than a dozen in the holding cells. We bring them in and he says which stay and which go."

"If they go…"

"We release them."

"And if they stay he assaults them."

"One a day."

Jack considered that. "Then he's planning to stay awhile."

"No. He's planning to take them with him when he returns to his world."

"Like hell."

Henry closed his eyes with a grimace. "I'm not sure about any of this, Jack. He's messed with my mind. Maybe I'm right. Maybe not."

"Unfortunately it sounds all too likely." The bastard needed virgins for strength. Why not take a dozen for the road?

"We've got to stop him."

"How?"

"I was hoping *you* could tell *me.*"

Henry's eyes narrowed in concentration.

"Do you know how to hurt him, Hank? Or how to break the enchantment. With the M.P.D. guarding him, he's untouchable."

"No, man. Nothing like that. But you've got the holly."

Jack snorted. "Damned near useless against an armed fighting force. I can't very well jump every man out there and shove a sprig of holly down his shirt."

"Do you have any other ideas?"

"Not yet. I'll think of something."

Henry dropped his head against the headrest. "I can't go home like this. God knows what I could do to Mei or the kids." He lifted his head and met Jack's gaze. "If you need a guinea pig, I'm volunteering."

Jack smiled. "I was hoping you'd say that."

"Dad…" Sabrina complained. "You can't stay with *him.*" She turned hard, angry eyes on Jack.

"Sabrina Mei Jefferson!" Henry scowled at his firstborn. "What in the world has gotten into you?"

Sabrina's eyes sprouted with tears, but the look she turned on Jack was more mortification than real venom. Beneath the tears was a plea not to tell her father the real trouble between them—that her feelings for her uncle Jack had grown beyond the familial.

Jack rested his hand on his friend's shoulder. "Take it easy, Hank. She's just being protective of you. She thought I'd killed you in that shed. It's been a real tough couple of days... for all of us."

Jack felt the tension go out of Henry's shoulder. A slow, sad smile formed on the man's mouth. "So my kitten's grown claws. That's all right, I guess. If we're in a battle, it's better that way." He pinned his daughter with his gaze. "But you got to know your friends from your enemies, girl. Jack isn't controlled by this...thing. I am. You trust him over me for now, you hear me? Until *he* says otherwise, not me. If he tells you I'm safe, then I'm safe. If *I* tell you I'm safe, you run."

"But, Daddy..." Tears rolled down Sabrina's cheeks.

"Honey, I'm not trying to scare you, but you got to know. I trust Jack with my life, and have since you were a tiny little girl. More than that, I trust him with yours and Davy's lives. And your momma's. Now I don't want to hear you talking to him like that again."

The girl bit her bottom lip and wiped the tears from her cheeks as she nodded.

"Apologize, Sabrina."

She lifted dark sad eyes that about broke Jack's heart. "I'm sorry, Uncle Jack."

He leaned forward and put his hand on her arm. "You've always been the daughter of my heart, Sabrina. I'd hate to lose that, sprite."

She looked down at the floor between them, her mouth

twisting this way and that. Finally she met his gaze. "I don't want to lose it, either, Uncle Jack."

He grinned at her. "Good."

She gave him a tremulous smile, then turned in her seat, away from him.

When he glanced up, he caught Larsen's wink in the rearview mirror. He felt her approval and it warmed him to his toes. How was he ever going to live without her? The only saving grace was, he'd soon be so lost in the mess of his mind, he wouldn't even know she was missing.

They drove in silence for several miles until his phone rang. Jack snapped it open and lifted it to his ear.

"Hallihan."

"Jack, it's Harrison Rand. I'm back in D.C. What's your estimated time of arrival?"

"About half an hour, give or take. Depends on the traffic. How's your daughter?"

The brief silence that met his question wasn't reassuring. "The same," Harrison said tightly. "She hasn't said a word since the Kennedy Center. She barely responds to anything." Anger vibrated through his voice. Anger and helplessness.

"I'm sorry. We're going to catch him, Rand. We're going to get him."

"Yes. We are."

"Do you have time to get something for me before we get there?"

"Sure. I'm still in the car."

"I need a rug." Silence met Jack's request.

"A *rug?*"

"A nine-by-twelve should do the trick, or whatever comes close."

"O-kay," Harrison said. "Anything else?"

"Look for a holly bush we can prune."

"A rug and a holly bush." His tone was almost amused. "Is that it?"

"That should do it. Holly dampens the effects of the enchantment."

"Enchantment?"

"We've got a lot to fill you in on. Were you able to get in touch with your brother?"

"No. I left a message for Charlie yesterday, but it's unlikely I'll hear from him. He's a busy man. I'll see what I can do about your holly bush and rug."

"Can you meet us in the parking garage in half an hour? We'll need the rug to transfer our guinea pig."

"I don't even want to know," Harrison said dryly. "See you in thirty."

Jack hung up and looked out the window at the passing cars.

Damn, but he hated this. *All* of it. He'd gone into this business to catch the crooks, to clean up the streets. To make up for the mess his dad had made of his own life and career, and to restore the Hallihan name within the M.P.D.

Now he found himself fighting a villain he couldn't beat, with the entire police force trying to kill him, and suffering from the same madness that had pulled his dad under. He squeezed his eyes closed against the searing pain that felt twice the size of his head. Time was running out and he didn't have a clue how to beat the white bastard. He had twelve hours to find a cure for this damned enchantment. Twelve hours to catch the Esri and steal back that amulet.

Twelve hours to save the world.

* * *

"The kids can walk from here, Larsen."

Jack pulled out his phone as David and Sabrina unfastened their seat belts. They were back in D.C., the sun finally starting to break through the dreary clouds.

Sabrina met his gaze with sad eyes. "'Bye, Uncle Jack," then she threw her arms around Henry's neck and gave her dad a kiss.

"Be careful, little girl," Henry told his daughter.

David gave them each a quick wave. "'Bye, Dad! 'Bye, Uncle Jack, Miss Vale! Bye, Aunt Myrtle!" Then he hopped out of the van after his sister.

Jack called Mei.

"Jack! Oh, my God, Jack. What's happened? You have to tell me what's happened."

"Look out your front window, Mei."

A moment later he had to pull the phone from his ear at the squeal of happiness.

"Is he really all right?"

Jack chuckled. "He's fine."

"I love you, Jack Hallihan! You brought my babies back to me."

"'Bye, Mei."

Henry raised a brow. "You didn't tell her about me?"

Jack grinned. "She wouldn't have heard me through all her screaming."

Henry smiled, but his smile quickly dimmed. "She thought he was going to die. I wasn't there for her, Jack. My son was dying and I barely noticed."

"It wasn't your fault, Hank. You and I both know that. Mei will understand once she knows what's going on." He glanced at his watch. "Considering how fast those kids of yours can talk, I'd guess she'll be fully apprised within about five minutes."

A short time later Larsen pulled into the parking garage of Charlie's apartment building in Adams Morgan, then watched with Myrtle as Harrison and Jack rolled up their guinea pig and hoisted him onto their shoulders. No one saw them.

Jack tossed her the apartment key and Larsen went ahead to open the door. The apartment was dark, the drapes still closed. But as she started toward the window, intending to open the drapes and let in a little light, a hard arm hooked around her neck, slamming her backward into a rock-hard chest.

The press of cold steel bit into her temple.

Terror tore through her lungs, filling her brain. *They'd found them. The cops had found them.*

Her fingers clawed at the arm at her throat. She was getting seriously tired of being choked to death! Larsen kicked off her flip-flop and slammed her bare heel up and into her assailant's kneecap as hard as she could.

She was rewarded by his grunt of pain, but immediately punished by the tightening of his arm at her throat. *She couldn't breathe.* Again and again she kicked at his knee until he jerked her up and off her feet, strangling her with his arm.

"Put her down." Jack's voice, cold and deadly, came at a distance through the roaring in her ears.

And suddenly she felt the carpet beneath her feet. The pressure at her throat disappeared as the arm shifted to the top of her chest.

Sweet air tore into her lungs and her vision cleared until she could see Jack standing in the doorway, his gun held in both hands in front of him.

Still, the barrel of her assailant's gun pressed hard against her temple. "Drop your gun or she dies," the man at her back growled.

Harrison stepped in behind Jack, a look of disgust on his face. "Put the guns down, both of you."

Harrison pushed past Jack to step in between the men. "Jack, this is my brother, Charlie. Charlie, meet Detective Jack Hallihan and Attorney Larsen Vale."

The pressure at Larsen's throat released immediately. Coughing, she lurched out of the man's reach and turned to face him, backing away.

Charlie Rand resembled his brother only in the broadest sense. They both had the same grayish-green eyes and the same lean physique, but Charlie had a couple extra inches and far greater muscle definition than his brother. A lean, deadly warrior's build.

"You okay?" Charlie asked her, his expressive face registering concern and regret.

Larsen tried to speak, but the coughing that she'd just gotten under control started up again and she had to settle for nodding her head. She felt Jack's arm go around her shoulders.

"You need to sit down," he said.

"I'm...okay." She managed to get the words out between coughs, drinking in the feel of Jack's solid arm around her. It felt so natural...until she remembered why he'd touched her so often. Because she'd quieted the voices in his head. Not because he cared. As much as she needed a moment's comfort after the scare Charlie had given her, Larsen pulled away.

Harrison opened the drapes, flooding the living room with light. Charlie sank onto the upholstered chair, his expression collapsing into a mask of pain, the breath hissing out of him. "God-*dam*-mit, woman, you've got a mean kick."

Larsen's hand went to her throat as the adrenaline surging through her found an outlet in anger. "You nearly broke my neck!"

He rubbed his knee, sliding his kneecap back and forth. When he met her gaze, his eyes were grave over the pinched line of his mouth. "I'm sorry if I hurt you. I just got in a couple of hours ago after days with no sleep. When I heard someone coming in the door, my instincts kicked in."

His gaze went to his brother. "Maybe someone can explain why my apartment has suddenly turned into Grand Central Station."

"I guess you didn't get my message." Charlie shook his head and Harrison continued. "It's a long story." He glanced at Jack and her. "And I think I only have half of it. But before we sit around the campfire and tell our tales, let's get that rug inside before it hops in on its own."

Ten minutes later Jack paced the living room as he waited for everyone to get out of the bathroom or to get their glass of water, and get situated. The adrenaline pumping through his veins made stillness an impossibility even as every step lanced through his head like a blade. The riot had turned into a full battle inside his head, complete with swords and battle-axes. If only Larsen had cured him. Or left him the hell alone. If this kept up, he wouldn't last another week. If they failed tonight, it wouldn't matter.

But the thought of getting lost in the madness terrified him. Trapped in that hell, falling into that maelstrom for eternity…. He couldn't. He wouldn't. He'd kill himself first.

"Your head bothering you again, man?" Henry asked. He was tied to the sofa as he had been the car seat.

Jack met his friend's concerned gaze. Always before, he'd denied any problem, but there didn't seem to be any point. His sanity was in a spiraling free fall, complete with smoke and flames. Henry was bound to notice when Jack turned into a raving lunatic.

"I've got a devil of a headache," he admitted. Without meaning to, he looked at Larsen where she sat perched on one of the bar stools, sipping a glass of water.

She met his gaze, her eyes awash with regret and apology.

She hadn't meant to hurt him. Everything inside him knew that, but it no longer mattered. The damage was done.

"You got those headaches of yours checked, yet?" Henry asked.

"Haven't had much time for doctor's visits lately, Hank."

Henry gave him a rueful look. "I guess not."

Finally the others joined them. Charlie sprawled on the sofa beside Henry, as Jack motioned Myrtle onto the one upholstered chair.

Harrison remained standing, his arms crossed over his chest like a sentinel. "Tell us what you've learned, Jack. It sounds like you know more than the last time we spoke."

Jack nodded, then grimaced, regretting the movement as the pain rolled through his head. "We have reason to believe the murderer isn't human."

Harrison stared at him, his expression never changing, never giving anything away.

Charlie smirked. "Are you trying to say he's an alien?"

"We're not sure what he is, but he's a lot more dangerous than we'd believed. We're fighting magic. And if we don't win, if he gets back where he came from with the key he's stolen, the entire human race is in trouble."

Charlie scoffed. "Sounds like something out of a video game."

"Yeah," Jack said. "It does. Larsen can tell you, I wasn't any happier about believing it than you are. But your brother's seen him, seen what he can do." Myrtle made a snuffling sound and began to snore softly.

Harrison grunted. "I can believe just about anything at this point. I've turned that day over and over in my mind a thousand times and haven't come up with a single explanation for what he was able to do. I still don't know what he did to Stephie. Inhuman makes as much sense as anything. Any guess what he is?"

"Yeah," Jack said. "They call themselves the Esri. The best I can figure, they share this planet with us in an alternate universe kind of way."

"The two worlds used to open in a dozen places," Larsen added. "But now apparently there's only one."

Charlie laughed. "You're talking high fantasy. Crazy high fantasy."

Harrison ignored his brother. "Do you know where that place is?"

"No. We're going to have to stake out the police station and follow him. He's apparently enchanted the entire D.C. police force and turned them against us just as he did the audience at the Kennedy Center."

"Is there a way to break his control?"

Jack shrugged. "That's the million-dollar question."

"You can't really believe this crap," Charlie said.

"You up for a demonstration, Hank?" Jack met his friend's gaze. "If I can't get you back under control…"

"Just knock me out, man. You might as well know now."

Jack leaned over to untie the rope at Henry's ankle that held the holly sprig, but the movement set off a rocket explosion in his skull. He gripped his head to keep it from splintering into a dozen fragments.

"Jack?" Harrison said sharply.

"I'm okay. Fine." When the worst of the pain had passed, Jack completed the task. His other knots had better hold. The last thing he wanted was to have to shoot the man who was closer to him than family.

"Watch his eyes," he told the others as he lifted the stick of holly.

Even as he said the words, Henry's tired eyes sharpened to keen points, his gaze jumping from one to the next. He began to struggle against the ropes.

"Who are you?" Jack asked him.

"Henry Jefferson."

"What is your mission?"

The man stilled, looked Jack in the eye. "To kill you." Henry's words were without inflection, yet hard. Utterly truthful.

"And how do you feel about that?"

His face contorted with effort as he pulled against his bonds. "I serve Baleris," he said through clenched teeth.

Jack leaned forward to press the holly branch against his partner's arm and got clocked by the man's shoulder as he tried to barrel into him. Spears sliced through his brain, tearing a yell from his throat.

"Dammit, Hank." He felt the holly being pulled from his fingers.

"Let go, Jack," Larsen said, and shoved the holly against Henry's neck.

His friend stilled, then released a shuddering breath as his eyes turned calm. "Did you do it?"

Jack slowly lowered his hands, wishing someone would saw his head off and end his misery once and for all. "You don't remember?"

"No."

Charlie propped his feet on the coffee table and clapped. "Proves nothing except the man can act."

"It's not an act," Jack swore. He eased himself down onto Myrtle's footstool.

"I've seen it, little brother," Harrison said with quiet steel. "I've seen him in action. The entire audience rose up against us like a scene from some horror flick."

"You really believe this crap?"

"Yes. I do."

Charlie's expression slowly changed from rigid skeptic to determined warrior. He pulled his feet off the table and stood. "All right, then. I'll take care of him."

Jack scoffed. "All he has to do is open his mouth and you'll be controlled."

"Then we'll wear ear plugs."

"We?" Jack asked.

Charlie shrugged. "My colleagues and I have a little experience with terrorists here and there."

"Special ops," Larsen said, voicing Jack's own thought. She'd crossed one leg over the other, and now swung her foot back and forth as she cut Charlie a look that defied him to deny it.

When he neither denied nor confirmed her suspicions, she

went on. "This is no garden-variety terrorist. If he turns you, you'll be a heck of a lot more dangerous to us than the cops."

"We won't be turned."

"You can't know that," Jack said, pressing his fingers into his scalp. "You don't understand what's he's capable of, Rand. You can't possibly understand until you've seen him in action. And for your sake, I hope that never happens."

"Well, *you're* sure as hell in no shape to run this operation."

"*Charlie,*" Harrison warned, then turned to Jack. "I think we should let Charlie and his team give it a try. With earplugs and holly, it might be enough. If they can get past the enchantment, they'll get the job done. They're the best, Jack."

"And if they fail?"

"Then it's up to us."

And God help them if they not only had the entire M.P.D., but a crack terrorist special ops team gunning for them.

They wouldn't stand a chance.

"Do it, Jack," Henry said. "Get it over with."

Jack had spent all afternoon testing one thing after another on their human-size guinea pig—all to no avail. So far the only thing that worked was holly.

Nothing was going right. Harrison and Larsen had spent the afternoon staking out the police station in a last-ditch effort to catch the Esri and head off the night's events. But the guy never showed his face. The only activity at the station today seemed to be the round-up and arrest of dozens of young women. If and when this nightmare ever came to an end, the M.P.D. was going to face a public relations nightmare...or worse. If they didn't succeed in stopping the white bastard, those girls were going to disappear tonight and never return.

Jack clenched his jaw until his teeth ached. They had to stop him. He picked up the last knife, this one made of pure gold. "You ready, buddy?"

Henry nodded wearily, drops of sweat rolling down his temples. "Do it."

Jack nodded at Larsen who was back from the stake-out and now helping him. She untied the small cord that held the holly twig at Henry's wrist. They'd earlier discovered the twig itself worked rather than the leaves, so they'd stripped off the prickly appendages, much to Henry's relief.

With the holly gone, Henry's eyes slowly lost their humanity. Within seconds he was struggling with the ropes that bound him, hand and foot, to the sofa.

"Release me, Jack."

"No can do, buddy." He stood and moved behind Henry, taking a deep breath, hating what he had to do. He lifted the knife and pressed the tip into Henry's shoulder, just far enough to draw blood.

Henry roared.

Jack looked at Larsen who was standing in front of the big cop, watching his eyes. "Any change?"

"No. None."

Jack felt defeat pull him down like a drowning sailor. He pressed the holly to his friend's neck. Immediately, Henry quieted.

"Are you through stabbing me?"

"Yeah." Jack sighed. "That's it. That's the last idea. If there's any other way to break the hold he has on you, I don't know what it is."

They'd tried everything they could think of. They'd plied him with a variety of foods and dusted his skin with everything from the kitchen and medicine cabinets. They'd pressed every metal they could find against his skin and then, when that didn't work, *into* his skin until they drew blood.

Nothing but the holly had worked. Jack's hope of finding a cure for the enchantment was gone.

Larsen looked at him as she applied a Band-Aid to Henry's latest wound, her dark eyes shadowed. "What now?"

"Beats me."

"Dinner!" Myrtle called from the kitchen. "Jack, dear, can you help me serve it up?"

Larsen got to her feet. "I'll help, Myrtle."

Harrison was in the bedroom on the phone. The man was still trying to keep a computer business running through all this. Charlie was out making arrangements for tonight.

"I'll get you some food, Hank," Jack told his friend. But as he started for the kitchen, he heard a plate crash to the floor.

"Larsen!" Myrtle cried.

Jack's heart lurched. He ran into the small kitchen to find Larsen crouched on the floor in the middle of the broken plate, her arms over her head.

He knelt beside her and grabbed her by the shoulders. She was shaking. "Larsen, what's the matter?"

But she didn't answer. Didn't even seem to hear him.

He suddenly remembered the other times—that night in his house when he'd found her on the floor of his bedroom shaking and crying, the two times she'd frozen as he'd tried to make love to her. What kind of demons haunted her?

He pulled her against him. "Nothing's going to hurt you, angel. I won't let anything hurt you."

He prayed he found a way to keep that promise before it was too late for all of them.

Chapter 16

No. Larsen vomited over and over again, clinging to the cold toilet bowl. *No.*

Jack was going to die. They were all going to die.

Sweat broke out on her brow and ran between her breasts as the sour smell of bile filled her nostrils and poisoned her mouth.

Another of her death visions, the worst she'd ever had. She'd seen it all: the cops lining the street around Dupont Circle, the hordes of college-age girls clustered under the streetlights. For once she hadn't seen the Esri, but she'd known he was there, somewhere, orchestrating it all.

They'd failed. The attempted capture had gone terribly, horribly wrong.

So much blood. *Jack's blood.*

Tears slid down her cheeks and she began to cry in deep, wracking sobs. Oh, God. She couldn't lose him.

She loved him.

"Larsen?"

She felt the press of Jack's broad hand on her shoulder and whirled into his embrace, wrapping her arms around his neck and holding on tight. She wouldn't lose him. She *couldn't*.

"Sweetheart, what's the matter?" His arms tightened around her even as cold rippled over her skin, sinking beneath the surface to ride the rapid pounding of her pulse through her veins. She couldn't tell him. She couldn't tell anyone. Ever. If they knew…

She had to tell him.

"Are you okay?"

"No." Oh, God, what was she going to do? She didn't have a choice. No choice.

How could she tell? How could she tell?

She'd never told.

Terror, without bounds, without logic, pressed against her on every side until she thought her eyes would bug from her head. How could anyone love her? How could anyone *stand* her if they knew about the evil that invaded her head?

She was eight again. Her mother and brother dead. *Her fault.* She'd seen them die and they'd died. *Her fault.* She was bad. If her father knew, he'd send her away and then she'd have no one. *No one.*

Her tears turned to sobs.

"Larsen, easy. Deep breaths. That's it. In and out. You're going to be okay."

"Jack…"

His hands cupped her shoulders and squeezed gently. "Easy, angel. Take it easy. It's going to be okay."

"It's not," she said between sobs. "It can't ever be. You won't understand. You'll hate me."

His warm hand dug into her hair and pressed her head against his shoulder. "I'm not going to hate you. Believe me, I've tried. It's not going to happen."

She buried her face in his neck and hung on as the storm raged through her.

"It's all right, sweetheart. I promise. Whatever it is, we can handle it. Together, we can handle it."

He held her as she cried, as all the years of fear knotted inside her, turning and tightening until she couldn't breathe. She clung to him, to these last vestiges of comfort. After knowing the warmth of his arms, the aching loneliness would kill her.

And she would be alone…once she told him.

She drank in his warm, familiar scent as she struggled for the strength to strip herself bare and reveal the terrible deformity she'd lived with all her life—not a deformity of the body, but of her soul.

Please, God, let this be enough. Let them find a way to avert this disaster. Please don't let this vision come true.

Larsen shuddered violently and pulled out of his arms knowing she had to tell him. She backed away, putting distance between them, until she leaned against the closed bathroom door.

The words. Where was she to find the words? No matter what he thought, he was going to hate her.

Unable to hold his gaze, she closed her eyes. Hands behind her, between her hips and the door, pulse pounding in her ears, she took a deep breath and plunged in.

"I'm not normal, Jack." She swallowed hard, the words sticking in her throat. Words she'd never before spoken out loud. "I've been cursed with an ability—a terrible ability— to foresee death."

The words caught in her throat as remembered images flew at her like wraiths in the night. The spray of blood when her mother's head hit the windshield, her grandfather's convulsions as he succumbed to a massive heart attack after falling down the stairs. The scraps of her apple-green dress clinging to the wreckage of her own body.

Violent shudders tore through her.

"What do you mean?" Jack asked, his voice hard, without inflection.

She opened her eyes and met his eyes. Cop eyes. Cold. Probing.

"I see death before it happens. Premonitions. I think they're premonitions." But she wasn't sure. She'd never been sure she wasn't somehow to blame.

Jack stared at her, his thoughts hidden except for the clenching and unclenching of his jaw. "You saw the murder at the wedding."

His words brought it all rushing back. Watching her body slam to the ground, then disappear beneath an onslaught of pounding heels, leaving her bleeding and broken.

Her fist covered her mouth as she began to tremble, her lower lip quivering against the weight of unshed tears. "I died," she whispered. "I watched myself die."

Through a blur of tears, she saw him sink onto the side of the tub. "That's why your eyes looked so wild when I found you. You ran."

"I shouldn't have. I should have tried to save the others, but I didn't know I could stop it. I know that sounds stupid, but I hadn't had a premonition since I was a kid. When I was young, all I knew was that I dreamed someone would die and they died."

"You thought you killed them."

"Yes." The tears were flowing freely now. "My mom." She began to cry outright, unable to hold back the flood she'd damned up for more than twenty years.

"How old were you?"

"Eight."

"Oh, sweetheart. Didn't your dad tell you it wasn't your fault?"

"He didn't know. I never told him about the dream. I've never told anyone." She hiccupped, struggling against the tears. "I thought I was evil. If I told my dad, he wouldn't have loved me anymore. I wouldn't have had *anyone*."

"Larsen…" He sighed heavily. "You know better now, right? They're just premonitions."

She wiped the tears from her cheeks. "But that's just it. They're not. At the wedding… Baleris sees me watching. If they were just premonitions he wouldn't be able to see me, would he?"

Jack rose stiffly. "I don't know. He's magic. He can do a lot of things he shouldn't be able to do." His brows pulled together. "A lot of things are making sense now. The note in my paper about the Tony Jingles attack. Your just happening to be at the Kennedy Center. And now…you just saw another one, didn't you?"

The horror of that vision tore through her all over again. "Yes."

"Whose death did you see this time?"

She blinked back the last of the moisture and stared into those blue eyes she'd come to love.

"I can't…I can't do it twice. All of you must hear it. All of you need to know."

His gaze searched her face. "All right. But we need to tell them right away."

Larsen raked her swollen lip between her teeth and nodded, then turned to retrace her steps to the dining room feeling like a prisoner facing the gallows. Jack hadn't condemned her outright, but she'd noted the guarded look in his eyes and the way he'd kept his distance. With a last desperate attempt to shore up her heart, she told herself it didn't matter. She didn't need him. Didn't need anyone. But the lies were too little, too late. And her heart tensed against the pain to come.

Harrison and Myrtle were seated at the kitchen table, eating the casserole Myrtle had prepared. Charlie, who'd just walked in, was dishing himself a plateful. All looked up as she approached.

"Are you all right, dear?" Myrtle asked.

No. She never had been and never would be. "I'm fine. But I need to tell you something. All of you."

Jack held out a chair for her at the table, but she shook her head. She was too agitated to sit still. Besides, there was something about sitting at the table with them that was too close. Too confined. On her feet she could run.

No. No more running. She had to tell them the truth. All of it. She owed them that.

She owed Jack that.

Jack took the seat beside the one he'd held for her as Charlie slid onto the chair at the opposite end of the table and began to scoop the food into his mouth. All eyes were on her.

Larsen paced, once more unsure how to begin. The words strangled in her throat.

"Can I tell them the gist of what you told me?" Jack asked.

Her gaze met his, the pulse pounding in her throat. She nodded.

"Larsen's psychic…" he began.

"Oh, lovely," Myrtle exclaimed.

"She has premonitions of death," Jack continued. "The latest concerns us all."

She stared at him, listening to the simplicity of his explanation, feeling its discordant twang against her own self-perception. *Psychic,* he said. Not evil. If only she could believe it.

"Larsen?" Jack prompted.

Crossing her arms over her chest, she stopped her pacing and faced them, meeting their gazes one by one. Myrtle was beaming at her, Harrison's expression was closed and unreadable, and Charlie looked distinctly antagonistic, his mouth pinched, his eyes almost angry. They'd thrown too much at him in one day. Magic. Elves. Now this.

She took a deep breath, fisting her hands beneath her elbows. "The good news is that I know where the gate is—right in the heart of Dupont Circle." She felt like the accused standing in front of a hostile jury. "The bad news is the plan tonight is going to fail. Completely."

The men's eyes narrowed.

"How completely?" Jack asked. She saw the understanding in his eyes, the memory that her premonitions always centered around death. "We're all going to die, aren't we?"

She nodded slowly. "Yes."

Charlie scoffed. "What's she been smoking?"

"Charlie…" Harrison warned.

She met the more volatile Rand's hostile gaze as he shoveled another bite into his mouth. "I saw you and your team pile out of a red-and-black armored truck."

His mouth froze, mid-chew, his eyes widening.

"There were five of you dressed in black, your faces blackened. You were carrying rifles, or some kind of assault weapons. And knives. Seconds after your feet hit the pavement, your team turned on you. Two knives went through either side of your neck. A third through your eye socket. The fourth member of your team never reached you before your body slid to the ground."

Charlie swallowed his food whole as he stared at her, his gray eyes glowing dangerously. "My team wouldn't turn on me."

Harrison turned to face him. "Were you planning to use an armored truck?"

Charlie surged to his feet. "They wouldn't turn on me!"

Larsen's stomach clenched and she took a step back.

Jack rose, moving toward her, as if to protect her if the need arose. But he didn't touch her.

"You haven't heard a thing we've been telling you," Jack said, his tone sharp and angry. "The creature is *powerful,* Charlie. You're clinging to the belief that you and your team are stronger, quicker, smarter than anyone else. Well, you're not. He is. And if you don't accept that soon, you're going to die."

Charlie glared at him, his mouth curled brutally. "Sounds like I'm going to die anyway. At least that's what *she* says."

"We might be able to stop it. It doesn't have to go down the way Larsen sees it. She saw herself die almost a week ago, but it didn't happen. This doesn't have to, either. But we've got to come up with another plan."

"Tell us the rest, Larsen," Harrison said, his voice too calm, like a smoothly flowing river hiding a torrent beneath.

She swallowed and nodded. "Harrison ran for the Esri, drawing the cops' attention...and fire." She met the man's gaze.

"You gave Jack the chance he needed, but it wasn't enough. I'm sorry."

Pain lanced her heart as her gaze swiveled to Jack. "You tackled the Esri and grabbed the amulet. It should have worked. He didn't see you coming. All his men were firing at Harrison."

Jack watched her, his brows low over eyes sharp with turmoil. "Why didn't it work?"

"The amulet wouldn't come off. You yanked on the stone and tried to pull the chain over his head, but it wouldn't lift. It wouldn't budge." Grief clawed at her insides. "He turned the cops on you. Three cops shot you in the head."

Her pulse pounded in her throat as she waited for their reaction. They stared at her, then at one another, then at nothing, the air in the room thick enough to spread on toast. The silence suffocated.

Larsen wanted nothing so much as to turn tail and run, but she'd done too much running. Too much hiding. If they threw her out, so be it. She'd told them what she had to. The ball was in their court now.

Harrison's gaze zeroed in on her. "You see people before they die. Before these attacks."

"Sometimes."

"That's why you were at the Kennedy Center, isn't it? In your scarf, yelling about a bomb in the building. You knew we were going to be attacked."

"Yes." Larsen's heart shriveled.

"I saw you in the lobby. I caught you staring at us. Yet you never tried to stop us. You let me take my kids into that theater knowing—*knowing*—someone was going to try to kill them." With each word, his voice rose in volume and anger. "He *hurt* her. He stole the laughter from her eyes. *And you could have stopped it.*"

Larsen began to shake beneath his righteous anger, the guilt of twenty years raking her from within.

"Hold on just a damn minute," Jack said. "Do you really think she could have stopped you? *Think,* Rand. What would you have done if a strange woman had come up to you in the Kennedy Center and told you that you and your kids were going to die if you took them to see *The Lion King?* Give me a break. You'd have thought she was nuts. You'd have ignored her. Scorned her."

Harrison made a sound of denial.

"You know you would have. That's why she couldn't tell you. She knew what you'd think of her." He turned to look at her. "It's the reason you never told me what you were seeing, isn't it? The reason you've hidden your gift all these years."

"It's no gift," Larsen said vehemently.

"Of course it's a gift. You've just potentially saved all our lives. Our plan isn't going to work. Now we know."

Larsen met his gaze, watching him with wonder, feeling the passion of his defense like a strange, unexpected and wonderful present. *He understood.*

Harrison sat still as stone, his expression brittle, but controlled. "You're right. I wouldn't have listened." His gaze moved to encompass the others. "We need to come up with another plan." He sent his brother a pointed look. "One that doesn't involve your team. It's clear you're one of us, Charlie—one of the ones who can't be enchanted, otherwise he wouldn't have turned your men on you. Welcome to *our* team, brother."

With a grimace of resignation, Charlie turned his chair

backward and straddled it, leaning his arms along the back. "All right, then. Back to square one."

Harrison glanced at her. "Have a seat, Larsen. You're going to have to keep us on track, based on what you've seen. How many cops were there?"

Charlie jumped up in a single fluid motion. "I'll get some paper. We'll need to understand their positioning. Larsen, I want you to draw us a map."

Myrtle leaned over and patted her arm, beaming at her. A fragile warmth bloomed inside her, thawing the cold knot of fear and self-loathing she'd lived with most of her life. *They believed her.* She remained cautious. Wary. But the emotions stirred and stretched within her on this first tide of acceptance.

She sought out Jack and found him watching her with enigmatic eyes. He nodded his approval, a single, brief tilt of his head, and she knew she'd done the right thing by telling them.

They needed the information she could provide.

But as her gaze fell from Jack's eyes to the arms he'd crossed on the table in front of him, she knew true acceptance might be nothing but a dream.

The hair on his arms was standing on end.

Chapter 17

The sun hung low in the western sky, painting the clouds with a palette of pinks and golds. Jack paced the small apartment, tense and wired, full of a frantic energy he could barely contain. After Larsen's revelation, they'd spent more than an hour coming up with another plan.

But changing the plan in no way guaranteed they'd change the outcome. They were probably still going to die.

Jack turned from the window to find Larsen sitting on the overstuffed chair, watching him. Love for her swelled inside him until he thought it would burst from his chest. She was so beautiful. He never looked at her that her beauty didn't stroke something to life deep inside him. She filled him with wonder, and a deep, aching fear that he wouldn't be able to keep her safe.

"We need to talk," he told her.

Henry snored softly from the sofa where he remained

tied. Myrtle had long since gone to bed. Harrison and Charlie were out rounding up the supplies they'd need for the midnight offensive.

Jack crossed to the coffee table and sat on the sturdy piece, facing Larsen.

She eyed him warily. "About what?"

He reached for her hands, then clenched his in fists and pressed them to his knees. She was *psychic.* He'd said he was glad, and he was, but the knowledge unsettled him on a primal level. His skin tingled every time he thought about it.

Her gift had been the missing piece of the puzzle. Once she'd confessed, the rest had fallen into place. Her lies and subterfuge made a perfect kind of sense now that he understood what had driven her.

His gut had told him to trust her. Rightly so.

He gazed into those brown eyes and saw the future. A future he longed for with an intensity that took his breath away. A future he might well have no part in.

"Larsen, if we fail, it's up to you. You'll be the only one left to stop him."

Her mouth tightened. "I know. I'll do whatever I have to."

"You'll foresee more deaths. You'll have to stop them, recruit the unenchantables to help you in this fight."

"I've thought about it, too, Jack. It's all I've thought about since that vision." Emotion overflowed her eyes. "What am I going to do if I lose you?" she whispered.

His heart clenched. *"Larsen..."* He rose and reached for her hands, pulling her into his arms.

"I thought you were afraid to touch me."

"I always want to touch you," he said as his lips covered hers. She melted against him, all the invitation he needed. His fingers slid into her hair, his mouth slanted over hers. Fire flared between them, rising like a geyser, freeing passion denied through secrets and misunderstandings. Passion he didn't think he could douse again.

"I want you," he said against her lips.

"Still?"

"Always."

He swept her into his arms and carried her to the empty bedroom. They might not have a future, but they had tonight and he intended to spend every second he could touching her, making love to her. With frantic, desperate movements, they shed one another's clothes and fell onto the bed in a tangle of limbs and flesh and kisses.

"Jack…I want you."

Love and desire wrapped around him, pulling him from the mire of their impossible reality, depositing him in a place where there was only sensation, heat, joy. His lips found her bare shoulder where barely a scar remained from her arrow wound of just days ago. *Magic.*

He wanted to memorize every scar, every otherwise perfect inch of her. Memorize every taste. His mouth skimmed lower, closing over her breast until he could suck the soft flesh into his mouth, sending heat driving through his body on a sharp lance of need.

She arched against him, fire beneath his touch. The looming showdown lent a desperation to their love-making. They both knew tonight might be their last. Her hips began to rock against him, a moan forming deep in her throat, sending his need for her shooting skyward.

With a last slow twirl of his tongue, he released her breast and moved down her body. His lips grazed her taut stomach as he slid his hands between her thighs and pushed his finger deep inside her.

"Jack…" She writhed against his hand, her fingers raked through his hair, sending a sharp, unbearable pain knifing through his head. Jack reared back, gripping his skull.

Larsen rose on her elbows, realization sweeping through her eyes. "Your head. Oh, Jack."

"It's okay." But the tiny spears continued to tear through his brain.

She pressed her knees together and scooted to a sitting position, wrapping her arms around her updrawn legs. "This is all my fault," she said miserably. "I never should have tried the ritual without telling you."

"What ritual?" He gripped his head, then a shiver slid down his spine as he remembered her startling revelation. *She was psychic.* He lowered his hands slowly, the pain remaining in the level of mere sledgehammer instead of shooting fire, and met her gaze.

"Larsen, what really happened this morning? I know you get premonitions of death, but that was different." An unsettling thought hit him. "Were you able to see into my mind?"

Her mouth twisted into a sad smile. "No. I'm not a mind reader. Not exactly."

Now that his head was no longer in danger of exploding, he found his attention sucked back to the beautiful, very naked woman sitting in front of him.

"What are you…exactly?" He reached for her, lightly gripping her wrists and pulling them outward to free her knees.

She lifted a brow, but didn't fight him. "Psychic is as good a word as any, I guess. A heck of a lot better than the *evil* I've always used."

"You're not evil." With her hands out of the way, he parted her knees, pushing them open like the petals of a flower, revealing a perfect, nectar-filled center. Blood rushed to his groin, his breaths becoming labored. "What were we talking about?"

"What happened this morning." She sounded like she'd just run a two-mile race. "It's a little hard to explain."

"Try." The word left his lips, but at the moment he wasn't sure he cared. He was finding it harder and harder to pay attention to anything but the treasure in front of him. He grasped her crossed ankles and moved them out, spreading her open until her damp, heated sex was all he could see.

"Do you remember…Myrtle…telling us about her great-great grandmother who claimed to be able to talk to her a-ancestors?" Her words stumbled as his fingers started a slow, deliberate ascent from her ankles. "Jack…I can't think."

"Talk, sweetheart. Tell me everything." He leaned forward, his mouth following his fingers' path until his tongue dipped to the soft flesh behind her knee.

Larsen gasped. "They locked her up for it."

"I remember," he murmured, licking and nipping. Rising toward her center. "Keep talking."

"I think it was…real, Jack. I think…she—" he kissed her inner thigh and the slender crevice at the top of her leg "—she could talk to her ancestors through her mind. And I think you have the same gift."

His mouth covered her sex at the exact moment her words tore through his mind, but the sweet taste of her drove out all thought but one. *Larsen.* He drank of her, teased her with his lips and tongue until she was quivering and shaking with the need for completion.

"Jack…*please.*"

He needed one of the condoms he'd bought when he was out that morning, but he rose from the bed too fast, sending a barrage of agony through his head. He gripped the bedside table until the worst of it passed. Then he carefully removed one foil wrapper from the box and turned to find Larsen sitting up, watching him with worried eyes. She took the condom from him and patted the pillow.

"Lie down. Let me do the moving…unless you want a rain check."

He reached for her, running a single finger around one taut breast. "No rain check. I'm okay." But he was beginning to wonder how he was ever going to be any help to anyone tonight.

Carefully, he lay on his back on the bed. Larsen scooted beside him, then slid her hand ever so lightly over his erection, watching his face.

He scowled. "You're not going to hurt me."

"Good." Watching him, never taking her gaze from his, she slowly lowered her head and placed a kiss along his rigid length. The brush of a butterfly's wings, yet seeing her lips on him like that sent blood surging through him, hardening him almost beyond bearing.

"Larsen…"

With a sexy, challenging grin, she rose and straddled his hips, her sex poised over him, drenching him with heat. She met his gaze, her eyes filled with lust and devilish joy and he'd never anticipated anything more than those slender hips starting their downward slide.

Her fingers rested lightly on his abdomen as she dipped to touch him, brushing the tip of him against the very door to heaven.

"Baby…you're killing me."

"Wimp." She gave him a siren's smile and with a sexy little wiggle of her hips, took him inside. Her smile turned to ferocious joy. An exact mirror of his own as her tight sheath welcomed him. "Do you…want me to keep talking?"

"No," he said, even though he'd heard clearly the note of teasing. He grabbed her hips and shoved up into her at the exact moment she fell on him again. *Heaven.* His groan was echoed by her sharp cry of pleasure. Over and over they drove their bodies together, joining deeper with every thrust.

She closed her eyes and threw her head back, like a mermaid breaking water, sounds coming from deep in her throat that nearly drove him insane. She was so beautiful. So perfect. His angel.

He gripped her hands and felt them tighten in his as she gasped, her hips rising and falling at a frantic pace. Her gasps turned to low moans, the pressure building in his own loins until he was about to explode.

Suddenly her sheath tightened around him, squeezing him in hard, loving spasms as she cried out and flew, taking him with her. As she settled back to earth, she met his gaze through unshed tears, and smiled.

Love for her filled him beyond bearing. He wanted a future with her. He wanted…something. Anything. *Everything.* And he suddenly understood his father's marrying despite his affliction. The right love was worth all risks. Impossible to ignore.

He pulled her down to lay against him. As he stroked her back, his mind returned to the conversation that had been hijacked by lust.

"Did you really tell me you think the voices in my head are those of my ancestors?"

"Mmm-hmm." She rubbed her cheek lazily on his shoulder.

He'd had to accept some weird stuff the past couple of days, but this one…no way. "They're just noise, sweetheart. Noise that sounds like voices. I've been hearing them all my life."

"They've been communicating with me."

The hand stroking her back stilled midstroke. "What do you mean by 'communicating'?" How many more secrets did the woman have?

"They've been showing me things. Through my visions. Other visions—not the ones that foresee death."

He stared at the top of her head. "Just how many visions have you been having?"

She lifted her head and met his gaze. "Too many." She rolled off him, then stood and reached for her clothes. As she dressed, she continued. "I think your ancestors were able to communicate with me through whatever sixth sense I possess that gives me my death visions, or premonitions, or whatever you want to call them. I think that may be why the voices in your head quieted whenever you touched me. Your ancestors were trying to communicate with me. They were trying to tell me how to help you. They taught me the words that should have let you understand the things they were trying to tell you, but it didn't work."

Jack sat up, then grabbed his head. *Damn.* The pain was getting worse by the hour. At this rate he was going to be completely immobilized—pathetically useless—by the time midnight rolled around.

He forced his mind back to her words. "The ritual. That's what you called the thing you did to me by the creek."

"Yes." Standing in a wash of light from the setting sun, her skin took on a golden glow even as regret shadowed her eyes. "I never meant to hurt you."

He sighed. "I know." Her words slowly pierced the walls of his brain. "You really think they're my ancestors?"

"I really do."

"It's insane."

"So is foreseeing death. We're a pair, aren't we?"

Beneath the press of her revelation, his understanding of his madness shattered, forming and reforming, sliding into a new and wholly foreign shape. Mind whirling, he reached for her and pulled her down beside him on the bed.

"Why didn't the ritual work?"

"I'm not sure." She squeezed his hand. "You may be too old. Or I might have screwed it up." She wrinkled her nose and met his gaze with wry apology. "I think I was supposed to warn you not to fight it. Instead of letting you finish, I called you back."

"I was sinking." Just the memory of his fall into that black hole threatened to cut off his air.

"I know. I couldn't leave you like that."

"If you hadn't…if it had worked…? What then? The voices would have started speaking English?"

She pulled one leg onto the bed and turned to face him, taking his hand in both of hers, her gaze on his fingers. "All I know is that if the ritual had worked, you should have been able to understand them. They're supposed to be able to help you—guide you or give you advice or something."

"There are dozens of them in here. I wouldn't be able to hear one for the others no matter what language he spoke."

"That's just it, Jack." Her dark gaze rose to his face. "I think they'd all be silent unless you called them."

He blinked, afraid to hope. Afraid to believe. *"Silent?"*

She nodded slowly. "Silent. I don't think they were ever

meant to torment you. I think they were meant to be a gift, not a curse. But you were supposed to have gone through the ritual as a boy. It may be too late now."

"I could get stuck in that black death forever."

"Yes."

The breath of possibility rippled his skin into gooseflesh. "But if it worked, it could cure me."

"Maybe…but, Jack…"

He eased himself off the bed and reached slowly for his clothes. "I have to try, Larsen. I'm useless like this. Worse than useless. Maybe, if nothing else, finishing the ritual will get rid of the pain."

"Jack, there's something else. Something I forgot to tell you." As he met her gaze, she continued. "In one of the visions, the woman mentioned the Esri. She said her daughter might have the visions if she was Esri-touched."

Jack frowned. "What does that mean? Cursed?"

"Probably. But have you ever heard anyone else use the term before?"

"No." The relevance wasn't lost on him. "My ancestors knew about them."

"It would seem so. Yes."

"Then what are we waiting for?" He pulled on his clothes, jarring his head as little as possible. "Do you remember how to do it?"

"I think so." Larsen looked at him with dark, luminous eyes. "Jack, are you sure about this? I almost lost you last time."

"Believe me, I remember. But what if I could gain something that might help us win tonight? What if I could just get rid of this pain so I can function?"

She sighed deeply. "Okay."

"Where do you want me?"

"I suppose the bed. Lie on your back so I can reach your temples."

Jack snapped his jeans and was about to crawl back onto the bed when he heard Henry call for him.

Jack met Larsen's gaze. "Let's do this in the living room."

"In front of Henry?"

He smiled ruefully. "After all I've put him through, he deserves to see me in a little pain."

"A *little?*"

But he'd made up his mind and went to his friend, Larsen close behind.

"I need some water, man," Henry said, eyes still closed.

"I'll get it." Larsen started for the kitchen.

Jack went to sit beside his friend. "How you doing, buddy?"

"Tired, man. I'm tired."

"I hear you loud and clear. But if you're up for a little entertainment, I'm about to give you quite a show. Payback for all I've put you through."

"Don't need a show, just that Baleris's neck between my squeezing fingers."

"I hear you." Never had Jack wanted to get his hands on anyone like he wanted the Esri.

Larsen brought Henry a glass of water, then looked at Jack, the trepidation he was feeling written all over her face. "Ready?"

"Let's do it." His heart started a slow, heavy thudding as he remembered the last time. *The falling. The agony.* Sweat broke out on his brow as he lowered himself gingerly to the floor. He could do this. He *had* to do this. It might be their only chance.

She sank to her knees at his head, looking down at him. Even upside down, he could see the worry in her eyes.

"Do it," he whispered, fisting his hands against the tearing pain he knew would come.

Her soft fingers slid over his temples, feather-light. "Remember, don't fight it this time. Ride it."

"Easy for you to say." He closed his eyes, fighting the sickening dread that bound his chest like a vise, and tried to concentrate on the gentle touch of her fingers as she began to chant.

"Eslius turatus a quari er siedi," she whispered, her voice trembling. *"Eslius turatus a quari er siedi."*

Jack tried to brace himself for the onslaught, but the agony hit him like a round of bullets, searing his eyeballs to blindness and ripping his feet out from under him as he tumbled into the abyss.

Chapter 18

"Jack, quit fighting it! Fall through. You have to fall all the way through."

He was thrashing on the ground, his head whipping back and forth between her knees as if he were in the throes of a monster nightmare. She clamped her knees against the sides of his head, trying to keep him still so she could press her thumbs to his temples and get him through this. But she wasn't strong enough to hold him. Her thumbs kept slipping into his eyes and his hair.

"Jack, stop. You have to lie still."

But if he heard her, he couldn't respond. Or couldn't stop.

"Quit fighting it, Jack!"

Terrible yells erupted from his throat. It wasn't working. She was going to lose him.

"Jack, you can do this."

"What's going on?" Henry demanded.

Larsen scrambled around on her knees and tried to climb onto Jack's chest. She had to find a way to pin him down.

"I'm trying to help him, but I'm losing him. He won't lie still!"

As she tried to straddle him, Jack's fist flailed outward, slamming into her jaw and knocking her backward in an aching explosion of dancing lights.

She lay on the floor, half on him, half off, her head spinning, her sight bending and turning like a changing, colorful kaleidoscope while beneath her Jack bucked and twisted trying to escape the hell she'd sent him to.

"Free me, Larsen," Henry said from somewhere far out of her sight. "Let me help. I can hold him."

Larsen glanced toward the voice as the colors dancing in front of her eyes began to merge back into shapes. Two blurry shapes that slowly merged into one. Henry.

"Larsen, I can hold him. I have the holly. I'm protected. You've got to let me help him."

Jack howled like a wounded animal, the sound tearing at her heart like sharp blades, drawing blood.

She had to do something. She had to finish the chanting. If she could just finish it, maybe she could help pull him through to the other side. But she couldn't do it with him thrashing. In every vision, it had taken two people to bring one of the kids into their voices. One to hold him down, the other to do the chanting.

Jack's body turned suddenly rigid, jerking and vibrating like a man electrocuted.

She was going to lose him.

Larsen pushed herself to her feet and stumbled toward the sofa and Henry. She dug at the too tight knots until her fingernails were broken and bleeding, finally freeing him.

Henry rose stiffly, pulling the ropes off his wrists and ankles and followed her to where Jack lay thrashing like a wild animal caught in a trap.

"Hold him still," Larsen said as she knelt at Jack's head.

The cop sank to his knees at Jack's side. As his big hands pinned Jack's shoulders to the ground, Larsen dug her thumbs into his temples, closed her eyes and resumed the chant.

"Eslius turatus a quari er siedi. Eslius turatus a quari er siedi." Over and over and over.

Slowly Jack stopped fighting. "That's it, Jack. Let it happen. It's the only way."

"Eslius turatus a quari er siedi. Eslius turatus a quari er siedi."

He was finally calm, finally still. Praying it was over, Larsen opened her eyes…and froze.

Henry's hands were no longer pinning Jack's shoulders. They were closed around his neck. Jack's face was blue.

"No!" Larsen grabbed the big cop's hands and tried to pry them loose, but they didn't budge.

The holly. It was no longer around his wrist! When he'd freed himself from the ropes, the holly must have gone, too. She looked up into eyes that had turned cold and lifeless. Eyes that had taken on the inhuman fervor of the enchanted.

"Henry, stop!"

But Henry's mind was beyond reach, caught in the Esri's snare. *And he was killing Jack.*

Larsen lunged for the big cop, going straight for his eyes, digging her thumbs into the soft sockets. Henry roared and reared back, covering his eyes with his hands. But Jack didn't move. He didn't cough or gasp…or breathe.

Desperate, Larsen tipped his forehead back with quaking

hands, opened his airway and gave him a quick rescue breath. "Breathe for me, Jack. Don't you dare die on me."

Out of the corner of her eye, she saw Henry's hands drop and knew she was out of time. She had to stop him from killing them both. With a furious surge of adrenaline, she lunged to her feet and grabbed the nearest table lamp, swinging it hard at the man's face. But he deflected the blow and knocked the ceramic lamp out of her hands where it crashed to the floor inches from Jack's motionless head.

Larsen's frantic gaze scanned for something else to use as a weapon when she remembered the knife behind the sofa. But she never got there. Before she could take a step toward it, Henry grabbed her from behind and slung her over his shoulder.

"Put me down!"

"Mr. Baleris wants you. I must take you to him."

"Myrtle!" She pounded on Henry's back as he carried her to the door. "Myrtle! Help Jack. He needs your help!"

But the woman never responded and Larsen was terrified it no longer mattered. Grief and terror rushed with the blood to her head. Jack was gone. And soon she would be in the hands of a monster.

Baleris stared at her with eyes that glowed yellow-green out of a face as white as toothpaste. Fear thudded through her even as grief threatened to choke her.

Jack was dead.

Henry shoved her into the police interrogation room and closed the door behind her, leaving her alone with the monster in his strange lair. Pillows and cushions lined the floor, a hodgepodge of the fancy and the mundane. Musty-smelling sofa and chair cushions lay beside silks, satins and velvets. Bedspreads and beach towels draped the table and chairs.

In the center stood the man—the *creature*—who threatened them all. Her nightmare come to life.

Terror danced along her spine.

Dressed as she'd always seen him, looking more like a Medieval minstrel than the inhuman murderer and rapist she knew him to be, he watched her with cruel interest.

Her heart pounded a dull rhythm as Larsen lifted her chin and stared at her enemy through a haze of anger and despair.

Jack was dead and this devil was to blame.

A fine trembling ignited her limbs, but not from fear. From fury, savage and overpowering.

He was going to kill her. She already knew that. But instead of terrifying her, the knowledge freed her and she fed the rage. The girls he'd raped. The murders he'd committed and tried to commit. *Jack.*

The Esri smiled, teeth as unnaturally white as the rest of him, flinging chills across her flesh. Slowly, he started toward her, moving through the pillows with an uncanny grace as he circled around her, studying her from every angle with a gaze that slithered over her skin.

"How is it I see inside your mind?" His words were accented, his tone eerily conversational. "I see you watching me. Your ability intrigues me, Sitheen. 'Twill intrigue my king."

Larsen moved with him, keeping him in front of her, a trickle of fear lancing her hatred. "What do you want with me?"

"I will take you with me, of course. If the Esri are to conquer your world, we must find a way to break through the barriers your mind erects against us."

"Because you can't enchant me."

"Aye. But you are human. Weak." The eerily white man chuckled. "Three score virgins, the Lost Stone and you, Sitheen. My king will be most pleased. He'll reward me well." But something flickered in his eyes that told her he wasn't quite as sure as he wanted her to believe.

He masked his doubt with a sneer. "All is in readiness. We shall leave soon. But there is time to test my growing power. This time against you, Sitheen.

"I smell your hatred and taste your fear. But still your mind resists me." He stepped closer and Larsen backed up until she was pressed against the wall. "Your fear grows, Sitheen."

"Bastard." She struggled for the anger that had raged through her moments before. The image of Jack's lifeless body rose in her mind, igniting a whirling, reckless anger that straightened her spine and tensed her muscles.

Larsen Vale wasn't going down without a fight.

She braced herself, hands raised in front of her, palms out. As he reached for her, she drove the heel of her hand up and under his chin, driving his head back hard. Taking advantage of her moment's upper hand, she grabbed his left shoulder, pulling him against her as she slammed her knee into his groin.

He roared with pain and doubled over. Larsen grabbed his head, shoving it downward as she rammed her knee up into his face.

It should have worked. He should have gone down, unconscious, or at least been so stunned, she'd have had a few minutes to get away. Instead, he rose, rage flaming in his eyes.

"I may not be able to control your actions, Sitheen. Nor your mind." With lightning speed, he snagged her hand. Searing shards of pain sliced into her flesh and up her arm. "But I *can* hurt you, human. I can control your suffering."

Larsen struggled to free herself, struggled to escape his fiery touch, but his grip was too tight. Tears swam in her eyes as the pain grew beyond bearing, tearing a raw scream from her throat.

Baleris beamed at her with malicious victory. "You will thwart me no more."

Jack opened his eyes. Harrison and Charlie were standing over him, looking at once concerned and relieved.

"You made it," Harrison said. "We thought we'd lost you."

"What…happened?" His throat was on fire, the words coming out as little more than croaks. He struggled to sit up, but every muscle, every tendon, ached like a bastard. Charlie and Harrison grabbed him under the arms and hauled him into the chair.

Harrison sat on the coffee table, facing him, his forearms on his knees, his eyes grave with concern. "Jack, we need to know what happened. Do you remember?"

"Larsen." Jack shook his head, trying to clear the fuzz encasing his brain. "Where is she?"

"We don't know. We just got back. Myrtle says you were injured and she healed you, but she doesn't remember anything but hearing Larsen call her."

"Your aunt is staying with my neighbor, now," Charlie added. "We thought it better not to leave her here since Henry knows where to find us."

"Where's Henry?"

"Gone. They're both gone. We found the holly branch on the sofa."

Jack's gaze slid from one brother to the other as the implications tore through his brain, shredding his heart. Henry…

"I've got to find them. Larsen's in danger." He tried to rise, but Charlie pressed him back in his seat.

"Hold on a minute. We need to know what happened."

Jack told them what he could, but he remembered almost nothing after Larsen sent him into that free fall through hell in a last-ditch effort to bring him into his voices.

The voices...

He stilled, his hands gripping the arms of the chair. The pain was gone. His head...was silent. Except for the sound of his own racing thoughts, his head was empty.

It had worked.

But no rush of joy filled his chest at the thought. Nothing but fear for Larsen. Jack lurched to his feet, shrugging off Charlie's hand. "We've got to find her."

"There isn't time," Harrison said, rising, blocking his path. "You don't know how long you were out."

Jack stilled. "What time is it?"

"Forty-five minutes until midnight."

Despair swept over him, sending him reeling. *Larsen.* She'd been gone for hours. "He'll kill her."

"Perhaps," Harrison said. "But then, why bother to have Henry take her, if he's just going to kill her anyway?"

The question sickened him with dread. "I don't want to know the answer to that." God knew what the Esri wanted with her. He pinned the other men with his gaze. "Tell me you've worked out a new plan."

Charlie nodded. "It took us a while to get what we needed." He grinned suddenly. "But we're all set."

Harrison clapped his hands. "Let's move. If the legend is right, if that gate really opens at midnight, we don't have much time."

As he started for the door, Jack's head suddenly flooded with sound. Despair nearly swept his feet out from under him until he realized…he could understand them. *They were speaking English.*

One by one, the voices inside his head dropped away until only one remained. A deep male voice he recognized as clearly as his own. *"Hello, son."*

Chapter 19

The police van rumbled through the city streets, Larsen and a crowd of young women packed into the dark van like cattle. Streetlights flashed through the front windshield, illuminating the expressionless faces of the captives as they sat unnaturally silent, unaware of what was going on, unaware of the fate that awaited them on the other side.

Tight ropes bit into Larsen's wrists. Her body felt battered and bruised, her head aching, her skin stinging as if real fire had shot through his fingers and scorched her.

And all he'd done was touch her.

She concentrated on the pain, so much easier to deal with than the grief and despair.

Jack was gone. And her fate seemed destined to lie in another world, as a guinea pig of a different kind. Torture as they sought a way to break into her mind. Unimaginable pain.

Her breath caught in her throat as crushing fear lanced her chest.

The police van hit a pothole, slamming her head against the metal wall at her back, jarring her out of the spiraling terror. The girls jostled one another, their mindless expressions never changing.

If only she were like them. Not immune. Not a Sitheen. Blissfully unaware the world was about to be overrun by the most evil creatures ever to walk the earth.

Anger bubbled up inside her. She couldn't give in to fear, to the despair. She *wouldn't*. There had to be a way to beat them. All she had to do was find it. For once in her life, she longed for one of her hated death visions. For a clue, *anything,* that might tell her how to stop this from happening.

The van came to a sudden halt, sending Larsen and the girls tumbling into one another. The back doors opened, and a dozen policemen ordered the girls out. One by one, they obeyed.

Larsen dug in her heels, fighting against the tide of unnaturally silent young women, but they pushed her forward until someone grabbed her arm and pulled her out, a man she didn't know. Larsen stumbled into him, then righted herself as he jerked her along.

As she'd seen in her vision, police cars and vans clogged the roadway that was Dupont Circle. Police officers stood in a perfect circle around the cars, guns pointing outward against possible attack. A bit of overkill considering the only ones who could possibly attack were Harrison and Charlie. If anyone else came near, they'd simply be sucked into the Esri's enchantment and stand docilely by while the creature stole scores of young women from the nearby community. And her.

The cop pulled her toward the small grassy park within the traffic circle, in the middle of which stood the high marble fountain like a sacrificial altar, along the path to where Baleris's white hair shone in the moonlight. He had an air of excitement about him, like a conqueror returning with the spoils of war.

Wild terror shot through her limbs at the sight of him, as her mind scrambled from the memory of the molten pain he'd subjected her to. She forced air into her lungs, struggled to calm down.

Beside Baleris stood his two bald minions, Tarrys, looking distinctly unhappy, and the man, Yuillin, who'd elfshot David. No longer were the pair dressed in jeans and T-shirts, but clothing of an ancient design—long shapeless gowns of a grayish color, tied at the waist with a glittering purple sash. Each had a bow slung over one shoulder and a quiver of arrows strapped to their backs. Ready for battle.

Baleris turned as Larsen approached, a gleam of brutal satisfaction in his eyes. He flicked his hand toward Yuillin and the little man made a quick bow and took off toward the fountain in an easy jog.

Larsen's police guard pulled her to a stop several yards from the white murderer, well out of his reach. Relief shivered through her, though she knew her situation could change with a single thought from that inhuman head.

The grassy park slowly filled as two more police vans pulled up, each filled with girls. *Three score virgins,* he'd boasted. Without exaggeration, apparently.

Yuillin returned, holding his quiver steady as he ran. "'Tis time, m'lord. The gate is open."

Baleris smiled with wicked satisfaction and reached for

her. Larsen jerked back like a terrified animal, drawing a laugh from the Esri.

"I've broken you so quickly, have I?"

Not broken. She wouldn't accept that. As the Esri's white hand clamped hard around her upper arm, panic bubbled up inside her, blocking out everything but a single silent scream.

But she felt only the cool pad of his flesh. No searing pain. Nothing.

She stared at him in confusion.

"It only hurts if I wish it." He chuckled with sadistic delight. "And I always wish it."

His touch turned to flame. The scream escaped her throat. And then the fire was gone once more and he jerked her forward and held her fast, leaving Larsen to sag against her jailer, tears of pain burning her eyes, terror clawing at her lungs. This was only a taste of what awaited her. How long would she last? How much would she be forced to endure before she died?

Baleris lifted his free hand and the stolen girls began to line up behind Larsen, ready to follow the Pied Piper into hell.

Pain exploded in her head. What new torture had he devised for her now? But then her vision went black and she knew. Her devil's sight this time, not the devil himself. She was thrown into another premonition, witnessing another death she feared would be her own.

Her vantage point suddenly flipped as she watched from above, the scene almost exactly as she'd left it except the procession of enchanted young women was no longer forming, but moving. Baleris, at the head of the line, had almost reached the fountain. Police officers circled the group like soldiers frozen in place.

Then one of the cops moved his hands. A slight movement.

The small blade glinted in the moonlight as Larsen watched him slice open his palm. Blood welled against the pale flesh. His knife dropped to the ground and he launched himself forward, straight at Baleris in a running gait she instantly recognized.

Jack.

Shock vibrated through her body. *Jack was alive!* Here. Now. As she watched with tense joy, he lunged at the Esri and grabbed the amulet with his bloodied hand. The chain melted from the Esri's neck as if severed by an invisible knife. *The amulet wanted blood!* How did they know? Around the circle, the enchanted cops and girls collapsed, unconscious. Only two cops remained standing and Larsen quickly recognized them. Harrison and Charlie. The Rand brothers grabbed the two small minions, thwarting their attempt to aid their master, while Jack set the Esri on fire.

Engulfed in flame, his white hair flying around him, Baleris lifted terror-filled eyes to the sky above him and met her psychic gaze.

The vision ended as quickly as it began. Larsen was back in her body, trembling and disoriented, and filled with the purest joy. *Jack was alive!* And the plan was going to work. *The Esri was all but dead.*

But as her gaze refocused, she looked up to find Baleris staring at her. Not with the sadistic pleasure of moments ago, but with the same terror that had shone from his eyes as their gazes met in her vision. And suddenly she understood.

He'd seen her watching him in the vision. He must have seen what she had, or at least enough to know what was going to happen…that he was about to die.

As he stared at her now, his hair shining like silver beneath the full moon, the terror in his eyes evaporated in a burst of fury. She knew, in that moment, the battle wouldn't happen the way she'd seen.

They'd lost the element of surprise.

"He knows!" she screamed, her voice echoing through the unnatural quiet. "I had a…" The Esri's grip on her arm turned to fire, sending molten flame shooting through her body, wrenching a scream from her throat. "I had…a premonition. Of his death. He knows what you plan to do!"

Even as her words rang out over the streets of the nation's capital, the enchanted fell to one knee in perfect synchronicity, leaving three cops standing—three fake cops who'd infiltrated the ranks of the controlled: Jack, Harrison and Charlie.

A heartbeat later, in the same eerily perfect move, the enchanted bounded upward and attacked the three Sitheen.

"No!" He'd kill them in the same horrible way she'd watched herself die at the wedding reception a week ago…a lifetime ago.

In a single, desperate move, she lifted her free hand to her mouth and bit down hard, letting the pain rip through her jaws to draw the needed blood. Then she whirled her body toward the Esri and snatched the amulet from his neck.

The pain grew a thousand times worse as the white devil fought to retake the prize from her. Beyond the haze of pain, she saw bodies fall to the ground. The enchanted were out.

But so, too, were Jack and the others. As her gaze strafed the area, she saw no movement but that of two small archers, their arrows aimed at her heart.

Jack moaned and tried to roll over. Every bone in his body felt crushed to dust. Son of a *bitch*. He'd never taken such a beating in his life.

Larsen. The bastard had Larsen.

Fear surged through him, propelling him through the pain and onto his feet. His rattled head took a split second to take in the scene, and what he saw turned his blood to ice—Larsen held fast in the Esri's grip, two arrows flying directly toward her from two different angles.

No!

But at that moment, no more than a yard from their fatal destination, the arrows converged. The one shot from Tarrys's bow collided with the first, knocking it harmlessly into the grass.

Even as relief surged through him, he saw the small male archer pluck another arrow and aim. Jack pulled his gun and fired, hitting him square in the chest and sending the minion sprawling to the ground.

He took off at a painful, limping run toward where Larsen struggled with the Esri, the amulet's chain dangling from her hand. *She'd done it!*

Larsen's scream rent the air and Jack launched his battered body at her attacker…and into the fires of hell. Invisible flames licked at his skin the moment he touched the white devil. But Larsen was free. And he knew what to do. The voices had finally started talking to him in an odd, disconnected kind of way. But he had the information he needed and that was all that mattered.

As he pinned the struggling Esri beneath him, he saw movement to his side.

"Stop me!"

Tarrys. She had another arrow tight in her bow…aimed at Larsen's head. The Esri was controlling her.

"Stop me!"

Jack didn't think. His heart propelled him forward, directly between her and Larsen even as a shape rose out of the dark behind the small minion. Charlie grabbed the girl around the waist with one hand while he wrenched the bow out of her hands with the other.

"Jack," Larsen cried. "He's getting away!"

But as Jack turned, he saw Harrison tackle the Esri at the base of the fountain and start pounding him into the ground. A father's revenge.

Jack turned to Larsen who was weaving unsteadily toward him.

"I thought you were dead," she said, throwing herself into his arms.

Jack winced, his body aching in places he didn't know existed, and gathered her tight against him, burying his face in her hair. "Are you all right? Did he…"

"He didn't rape me or anything like that. But he has one mean touch."

"I felt it." The fear for her that had been riding him since he'd discovered her gone shuddered out of him. "Thank God you're all right."

As one, they pulled away. He took her hand. "Come on. We've got a job to do."

She eyed him curiously, but joined him as he made his way to the fountain and the two men—*males*—locked in a bizarre combat. Harrison was the only one throwing punches, but the Esri was far from the only one feeling pain.

"Drag him away from the fountain, Harrison," Jack said. "I have some business with him that needs tending to."

"Can I set you down?" Charlie said to his small captive.

Jack glanced back to see the pair had followed them. Tarrys was slung over Charlie's shoulder, her small wrists gripped in one of the man's hands.

"Nay," the girl said. "He controls me. He bids me to kill you. All of you. If I am freed, I will try."

Harrison stood and jerked the Esri off his feet, hauling him into the grass. "This far enough?" The man's words were tight with pain, but he never loosened his grip on the Esri.

"Perfect." Jack pulled out his lighter and flicked it to create a single flame.

"Nay!" the Esri cried, staring at the flame. "Nay!"

"Go to hell, you bastard," Jack murmured, then began to chant the odd collection of syllables one of his oldest ancestors had shared with him on the ride over here. The same ancestor who told him the stone could be called with blood. Who would have thought the voices in his head would turn out to be such a valuable source of information?

Chanting, Jack thrust the small flame against the bare flesh of Baleris's arm. Instantly the fire rose in a perfect circle around the Esri, engulfing him.

Harrison leaped back.

Larsen's soft hand slid into his as she stepped up beside him and picked up on the words of his chant, adding her voice to his. Jack squeezed her hand, clinging to her, feeling the power that flowed between them. A power less of magic than of something far more basic. Emotion. Caring.

Love.

Through the fire, the Esri began to sparkle with colored lights, as David had done. The lights gathered, moving like a million iridescent lightning bugs. They rose from his body to hover for a single perfect moment above him. Then in a rainbow burst, like the best fireworks display, they erupted.

The Esri's body fell to the ground and disintegrated into a pile of ash. The fire evaporated as if it had never been.

As one, they stared at the ash, then one another.

"Is it really over?" Larsen breathed.

Jack looked around them at the unconscious bodies littering the small park. "How are we ever going to explain all this?"

"We don't have to explain it, if no one knows we were here," Harrison said. "Let's get gone."

Charlie grunted and pulled the small archer off his shoulder and set her on the ground in front of him, holding her pinned against his hip. "What are we going to do with this one?"

Tarrys's frightened gaze moved from one to the other, like a doe caught in a hunter's trap.

"We can't let her go back," Jack said. "We can't let them know this gate is here."

The girl watched him with an odd mixture of fear and hope.

"I would stay. I would serve the humans instead of the Esri."

"Serve? Hell, yeah." Charlie laughed, drawing the girl's gaze. "You can start by teaching me to shoot like that. You're bloody well amazing!"

The girl smiled, a shy, uncertain bending of the mouth. But when she turned her gaze forward again, she froze.

"Yuillin!"

Jack saw the movement out of the corner of his eye and whirled around, but he was too far—and too late—to do anything more than watch as the small archer leaped onto the fountain's edge and disappeared.

"What in the hell?" Jack said. "I shot him!"

Tarrys began to struggle in Charlie's hold. "You must release me. I must go after him. I must stop him or he'll bring others!"

Charlie's helpless gaze locked on Jack's, but Jack didn't know what to do any more than he did. His gut said trust her. So he did.

"Let her go."

Charlie released her and the small woman took off, flying barefoot across the grass and the paved walk to leap onto the fountain's ledge…and into the water.

Tarrys turned slowly, the soaked hem of her gown clinging to her legs, her gaze startled and dismayed.

"The gate has closed."

"Now what do we do?" Larsen asked.

Jack sighed. "What we were going to have to do anyway. Guard this place every full moon."

Charlie chuckled without humor. "With a blowtorch."

Chapter 20

"Who wants champagne?" Charlie called as they piled into his apartment a short while later.

Larsen's head spun. The Esri was dead. All the pain and suffering he'd caused, all the terror, were gone. Over.

She sat on one of the bar stools as Charlie pulled the bottle out of the grocery bag.

Knowing she'd soon be able to walk the streets again, the courtroom, the marina, without fear of being gunned down was a heady thing. But the greater miracle was that Jack and the others knew of her curse and didn't seem to care. Her *gift*. Without the warning from her visions, they all would have died.

It was Jack who had helped her understand that. Jack who had helped lift the weight of that terrible secret, of the dark shadow that had trailed her all her life. How was she ever going to live without him?

A deep sadness spread through her chest. He'd needed her before, to quiet the voices that were ripping apart his mind. But his voices were silent now, unless he asked for them. He didn't need her anymore. The larger-than-life events that had drawn them together were over. Their relationship was done.

Except she'd somehow gone and fallen in love with the man.

She'd never tell him that. It wouldn't be fair. He deserved to be happy, truly happy, with a woman he could love as much as she loved him.

And she was afraid she wasn't that woman.

Charlie popped the cork on the champagne, liquid spilling out as Jack walked in the door. He'd stayed behind at the park to watch over things until the cops and the girls started to wake up.

Larsen drank in the sight of him, relief flowing warmly through her that he'd made it back safely. "Did everything go okay?"

"Henry's going to handle things. He doesn't remember trying to strangle me, or anything later, but he remembers Baleris well enough to piece together all that's happened this week. We'll have to explain it to the captain, then let him decide how to spin it. The M.P.D. has been on a rampage the past few days. It's going to be tricky as hell. But, ultimately, it's all politics. We'll handle it."

"Let's see that stone," Charlie said. "I want to see what all the fuss was about." Jack pulled the blue amulet out of his pocket and handed it to him.

"What's this engraved on it?" Charlie asked.

"A seven-pointed star," Larsen told him, remembering the news report she'd pulled up online.

"A seven-pointed star," Myrtle exclaimed from the living room behind her. They'd checked on her at the neighbors' when they got back and found her awake and waiting for them. She'd followed them back to Charlie's and was now lounging in the upholstered chair. "Why, that's an elf star!"

Charlie tossed it back to Jack. "What do we do with it now?"

"Hide it," Jack murmured, slipping it back into his pocket. "In a locked vault where no Esri can ever get his hands on it again."

"It must remain with the Sitheen." Tarrys's soft voice carried from where she sat on the floor, leaning against the wall, a sharp reminder to Larsen that everything had not returned to normal. Tarrys was of that world, yet here she sat in Charlie's apartment. "Only the Sitheen can protect it. Only to their Esri blood will it answer."

An odd silence descended over the group.

"What do you mean, our Esri blood?" Jack demanded, voicing Larsen's thoughts. He turned to lean against the counter beside her, his warm, beloved scent wrapping around her, filling her with a longing that tore at her heart. He wasn't hers.

"Why, Jack, dear," Myrtle said, fluttering a single hand as she tilted her champagne glass to her lips with the other. "I did tell you we had an elven ancestor."

Jack stared at his aunt, his jaw working silently.

"'Tis what the Sitheen are," Tarrys added quietly. "What all of you are. The descendants of a long-ago union between an Esri and a human."

"Like hell," Harrison swore.

Larsen's eyes widened with disbelief…and wonder.

"'Tis what makes you immune to the Esri's tricks and makes you a danger to them. 'Tis why you have gifts. Sitheen oft possess at least one of the gifts of their Esri ancestor."

Jack's gaze swung to Larsen, the weight of a thousand questions heavy in his eyes.

"So that's why the elf was so determined to kill anyone he couldn't enchant," Charlie murmured.

"Aye. Only you could stop him." She smiled, her cheeks tinting pink as she gazed at Charlie. "And you did."

"Damn," Charlie said, delight rippling through his voice. "I've got elf blood."

Harrison glowered at his brother, a sound of disgust rumbling in his throat.

"I'm not sure why you didn't believe me, nephew," Myrtle said, then giggled and lifted her empty champagne glass.

Jack gave Larsen a bemused look and turned to his aunt. "Didn't you also say something about witches and Gypsies?"

Myrtle waved her hand. "Oh, I may have exaggerated a *little*." She burst into a fit of giggles, drawing laughter from all but Harrison.

The full realization hit Larsen in a blinding moment of understanding. "My visions," she breathed. "They were always of relatives or people the elf couldn't enchant. They were all people with Ersi blood."

Jack laid his hand on her shoulder as she met his gaze in a shower of wonder and relief. "And the voices in my head. Never the curses we believed, just true faerie gifts."

"Anyone for more champagne?" Charlie called.

Jack slid his hand off her shoulder and held it out to her, palm up. "Come with me?"

His eyes burned with an intensity she'd come to know. He wanted sex. Something contracted painfully inside her. And she wanted so much more.

"No, Jack. I…"

"We need to talk."

"Just talk?"

"I promise."

Larsen's heart sank. Suddenly she wished he *had* been looking for a quick roll in the sheets because a talk could only mean one thing. He wanted a clean break. And he wanted it now.

With a sigh, she nodded and hopped off the stool.

"We'll be back in a little while," Jack told the others, then ushered her out the front door.

"Where are we going?" Larsen asked as they walked down the empty corridor.

"The roof."

They took the elevator to the top floor, then climbed the single flight of stairs to the door that led to the night sky. Together they walked to the railing that rimmed the building and looked out over the nation's capital, the lights of the city shining in a bright display.

Jack didn't touch her as they stood there, which was unlike him. With a heaviness, she remembered that his touch had never been the result of natural affection. He'd only ever touched her for the relief she provided him.

Jack rested his forearms on the rail, his face turned to the D.C. skyline. "What are you going to do now?" he asked her.

The last flicker of hope that she'd meant more to him than a cure to his voices sputtered and died in her chest. "I need to get back to work. And to try to get my houseboat repaired so I can live there again."

"I want you to lay low for a couple more days until that APB on us is canceled." He looked up at the stars, then tilted his face toward her. "I was wondering if…do you think…?"

Oddly, he sounded nervous.

"What, Jack?"

"I'd like to see you again. Maybe we could go out on an actual date." His tone was almost...*hopeful*.

Her pulse kicked up and she turned to him. "Why?"

He dipped his head, for a moment looking like a man with the weight of the world resting on his shoulders. Slowly he raised his face and met her gaze. "I'm not going to push you, Larsen. If you'd rather end it here, we'll do that. But I'd like to spend more time with you." His mouth kicked up in a regretful smile. "I owe you. I used you."

A pity date.

"Jack...don't. I understand why you used me. If I'd had that riot in my head, I'd have touched you every chance I got, too." She'd have touched him anyway, but that was because her feelings for him had sparked and grown and turned to love. "I get it that you never really had feelings for me. It's okay. But I don't..."

His hands gripped her shoulders and he turned her to face him in the moonlit dark. "I never said I didn't have feelings for you."

"You're offering me a pity date."

"A pity..." He made a strangled sound that was half laughter, half groan. "Larsen...it's not a pity date. It's a desperate attempt to try to charm you, to try to win your affection. To try to get you to care for me even a fraction of the way I care for you."

Larsen gaped at him. "What are you saying?"

His expression turned pained, then softened into the most beautiful sight she'd ever seen.

"I love you, Larsen Vale. I know that probably scares the hell out of you, which is why I was trying to take it slowly, but dammit, I need you." He squeezed her shoulders, telegraphing the emotion that had him suddenly as tense as a bow string. "Give me a chance. *Please*."

Larsen stared into his worried eyes as joy flooded her heart and tears blurred her vision. She reached for him, cupping his strong, prickly jaw with her hands. "You don't need any chances with me. I already love you, Jack Hallihan."

He didn't move. Only the steadily increasing pressure on her shoulders told her he'd heard her at all.

"Are you sure?"

A tear-filled laugh escaped her throat. "I've never been more sure of anything in my life."

"Marry me?"

"Oh, Jack. If *you're* sure, then yes. A thousand times yes." Then he pulled her hard against him and kissed her with so much passion, so much love, the tears rolled down her cheeks.

He knew everything about her. *Everything*. And he loved her anyway.

At last, her heart and spirit soared free.

Set in darkness beyond the ordinary world.
Passionate tales of life and death.
With characters' lives ruled by laws the everyday world
can't begin to imagine.

n●cturne

It's time to discover the Raintree trilogy...

New York Times bestselling author
LINDA HOWARD
brings you the dramatic first book
RAINTREE: INFERNO

The Ansara Wizards are rising and the Raintree clan
must rejoin the battle against their foes, testing
their powers, relationships and forcing upon them
lives they never could have imagined before...

Turn the page for a sneak preview
of the captivating first book
in the Raintree trilogy,
RAINTREE: INFERNO by LINDA HOWARD
On sale April 25.

Dante Raintree stood with his arms crossed as he watched the woman on the monitor. The image was in black and white to better show details; color distracted the brain. He focused on her hands, watching every move she made, but what struck him most was how uncommonly *still* she was. She didn't fidget or play with her chips, or look around at the other players. She peeked once at her down card, then didn't touch it again, signaling for another hit by tapping a fingernail on the table. Just because she didn't seem to be paying attention to the other players, though, didn't mean she was as unaware as she seemed.

"What's her name?" Dante asked.

"Lorna Clay," replied his chief of security, Al Rayburn.

"At first I thought she was counting, but she doesn't pay enough attention."

"She's paying attention, all right," Dante murmured. "You just don't see her doing it." A card counter had to remember every card played. Supposedly counting cards was impossible with the number of decks used by the casinos, but there were those rare individuals who could calculate the odds even with multiple decks.

"I thought that, too," said Al. "But look at this piece of tape coming up. Someone she knows comes up to her and speaks, she looks around and starts chatting, completely misses the play of the people to her left—and doesn't look around even when the deal comes back to her, just taps that finger. And damn if she didn't win. Again."

Dante watched the tape, rewound it, watched it again. Then he watched it a third time. There had to be something he was missing, because he couldn't pick out a single giveaway.

"If she's cheating," Al said with something like respect, "she's the best I've ever seen."

"What does your gut say?"

Al scratched the side of his jaw, considering. Finally, he said, "If she isn't cheating, she's the luckiest person walking. She wins. Week in, week out, she wins. Never a huge amount, but I ran the numbers and she's into us for about five grand a week. Hell, boss, on her way out of the casino she'll stop by a slot machine, feed a dollar in and walk away with at least fifty. It's never the same machine, either. I've had her watched, I've had her followed, I've even looked for the same faces in the casino every time she's in here, and I can't find a common denominator."

"Is she here now?"

"She came in about half an hour ago. She's playing black-jack, as usual."

"Bring her to my office," Dante said, making a swift decision. "Don't make a scene."

"Got it," said Al, turning on his heel and leaving the security center.

Dante left, too, going up to his office. His face was calm. Normally he would leave it to Al to deal with a cheater, but he was curious. How was she doing it? There were a lot of bad cheaters, a few good ones, and every so often one would come along who was the stuff of which legends were made: the cheater who didn't get caught, even when people were alert and the camera was on him—or, in this case, her.

It was possible to simply be lucky, as most people understood luck. Chance could turn a habitual loser into a big-time winner. Casinos, in fact, thrived on that hope. But luck itself wasn't habitual, and he knew that what passed for luck was often something else: cheating. And there was the other kind of luck, the kind he himself possessed, but it depended not on chance but on who and what he was. He knew it was an innate power and not Dame Fortune's erratic smile. Since power like his was rare, the odds made it likely the woman he'd been watching was merely a very clever cheat.

Her skill could provide her with a very good living, he thought, doing some swift calculations in his head. Five grand a week equaled $260,000 a year, and that was just from his casino. She probably hit them all, careful to keep the numbers relatively low so she stayed under the radar.

He wondered how long she'd been taking him, how long she'd been winning a little here, a little there, before Al noticed.

The curtains were open on the wall-to-wall window in his office, giving the impression, when one first opened the door, of stepping out onto a covered balcony. The glazed window faced west, so he could catch the sunsets. The sun was low now, the sky painted in purple and gold. At his home in the mountains, most of the windows faced east, affording him views of the sunrise. Something in him needed both the greeting and the goodbye of the sun. He'd always been drawn to sunlight, maybe because fire was his element to call, to control.

He checked his internal time: four minutes until sundown. Without checking the sunrise tables every day, he knew exactly when the sun would slide behind the mountains. He didn't own an alarm clock. He didn't need one. He was so acutely attuned to the sun's position that he had only to check within himself to know the time. As for waking at a particular time, he was one of those people who could tell himself to wake at a certain time, and he did. That talent had nothing to do with being a Raintree, so he didn't have to hide it; a lot of perfectly ordinary people had the same ability.

He had other talents and abilities, however, that did require careful shielding. The long days of summer instilled in him an almost sexual high, when he could feel contained power buzzing just beneath his skin. He had to be doubly careful not to cause candles to leap into flame just by his presence, or to start wildfires with a glance in the dry-as-tinder brush. He loved Reno; he didn't want to burn it down. He just felt so damn *alive* with all the sunshine pouring down that he wanted to let the energy pour through him instead of holding it inside.

This must be how his brother Gideon felt while pulling lightning, all that hot power searing through his muscles, his veins. They had this in common, the connection with raw power. All the members of the far-flung Raintree clan had some power, some heightened ability, but only members of the royal family could channel and control the earth's natural energies.

Dante wasn't just of the royal family, he was the Dranir, the leader of the entire clan. "Dranir" was synonymous with king, but the position he held wasn't ceremonial, it was one of sheer power. He was the oldest son of the previous Dranir, but he would have been passed over for the position if he hadn't also inherited the power to hold it.

Behind him came Al's distinctive knock on the door. The outer office was empty, Dante's secretary having gone home hours before. "Come in," he called, not turning from his view of the sunset.

The door opened, and Al said, "Mr. Raintree, this is Lorna Clay."

Dante turned and looked at the woman, all his senses on alert. The first thing he noticed was the vibrant color of her hair, a rich, dark red that encompassed a multitude of shades from copper to burgundy. The warm amber light danced along the iridescent strands, and he felt a hard tug of sheer lust in his gut. Looking at her hair was almost like looking at fire, and he had the same reaction.

The second thing he noticed was that she was spitting mad.

nocturne™

IT'S TIME TO DISCOVER
THE RAINTREE TRILOGY...

There have always been those among us
who are more than human...

Don't miss the dramatic first book by

New York Times bestselling author

LINDA
HOWARD

RAINTREE:
Inferno

On sale May.

Raintree: Haunted by Linda Winstead Jones
Available June.

Raintree: Sanctuary by Beverly Barton
Available July.

SNLHIBC

REQUEST YOUR FREE BOOKS!

2 FREE NOVELS PLUS 2 FREE GIFTS!

Silhouette®

nocturne™

Dramatic and Sensual Tales of Paranormal Romance.

YES! Please send me 2 FREE Silhouette® Nocturne™ novels and my 2 FREE gifts. After receiving them, if I don't wish to receive any more books, I can return the shipping statement marked "cancel." If I don't cancel, I will receive 4 brand-new novels every other month and be billed just $4.47 per book in the U.S. or $4.99 per book in Canada, plus 25¢ shipping and handling per book plus applicable taxes, if any*. That's a savings of about 15% off the cover price! I understand that accepting the 2 free books and gifts places me under no obligation to buy anything. I can always return a shipment and cancel at any time. Even if I never buy another book from Silhouette, the two free books and gifts are mine to keep forever.

238 SDN ELS4 338 SDN ELXG

Name _____ (PLEASE PRINT) _____

Address _____ Apt. # _____

City _____ State/Prov. _____ Zip/Postal Code _____

Signature (if under 18, a parent or guardian must sign)

Mail to the **Silhouette Reader Service™:**

IN U.S.A.: P.O. Box 1867, Buffalo, NY 14240-1867
IN CANADA: P.O. Box 609, Fort Erie, Ontario L2A 5X3

Not valid to current Silhouette Nocturne subscribers.

Want to try two free books from another line?
Call 1-800-873-8635 or visit www.morefreebooks.com.

* Terms and prices subject to change without notice. NY residents add applicable sales tax. Canadian residents will be charged applicable provincial taxes and GST. This offer is limited to one order per household. All orders subject to approval. Credit or debit balances in a customer's account(s) may be offset by any other outstanding balance owed by or to the customer. Please allow 4 to 6 weeks for delivery.

Your Privacy: Silhouette is committed to protecting your privacy. Our Privacy Policy is available online at www.eHarlequin.com or upon request from the Reader Service. From time to time we make our lists of customers available to reputable firms who may have a product or service of interest to you. If you would prefer we not share your name and address, please check here. ☐

Silhouette

nocturne™

COMING NEXT MONTH

#15 RAINTREE: INFERNO • Linda Howard
The Raintree Trilogy

An extraordinary people live among us, and for the
first time their leader, Dante Raintree, is falling in
love. But when an old enemy returns, the Raintree
clan will need their king's strength—and he, the love
of an equally astonishing woman.

#16 LOVE CALLS • Caridad Piñeiro
The Calling

Diego Esperanza vowed never to give his heart to a
human, but after five hundred years, temptation is
too much. Ramona Escobar is dying of a rare blood
disease, and only a vampire can help her. But when
the feeding begins, only one heartbeat separates
death from eternal love.

SNCNM0407